Brigit

The sequel to Elizabeth's Diaries

Sue Towler

Sue Towler

ISBN 978-0-473-35703-0

Cover Design by Sue Towler using Book Brush

Contents

Title Page

Copyright

Epigraph

Introduction

Prologue

Chapter One — 1

Chapter Two — 10

Chapter Three — 19

Chapter Four — 41

Chapter Five — 48

Chapter Six — 81

Chapter Seven — 105

Chapter Eight — 134

Chapter Nine — 174

Chapter Ten — 187

Chapter Eleven — 210

Chapter Twelve 220

Chapter Thirteen 227

Chapter Fourteen 236

Chapter Fifteen 248

Chapter Sixteen 253

Chapter Seventeen 260

Chapter Eighteen 264

Chapter Nineteen 269

Chapter Twenty 283

Chapter Twenty One 290

Chapter Twenty Two 301

Chapter Twenty Three 310

Introduction

Brigit is the daughter and only child of Ellen and Luke Williams of Duffield Station in New Zealand. At the end of the first book, *Elizabeth's Diaries*, Brigit was a precocious four year old child. Now in her 20's she is married to Jax, the son of Outback Station owners Sid and Janet Jamieson who farm beef stock on a large property in the challenging Northern Territory of Australia. Brigit's strengths and tenacity help her to survive the harsh realities of life in the outback and the life changing traumatic event which brings her back to her home in New Zealand to heal.

The dirty, scruffy old man stood in the doorway of the roughly built wooden shack, his shadow falling across the foot of the bed touching the leather thonging that bound Brigit to the dirty, rusting wire wove. She could hear his ragged breathing, smell his distinctive sweaty stinking body odour. Bile rose in her throat like burning acid. Her body trembled with fear and loathing. She waited, breath held, for his next onslaught.

'Hello my lovely, did ya miss me?' He took a step into the room, and came up close to the bed. 'Ready for a little more playtime are we?'

Brigit's heart hammered like rapid gunfire. She looked up at his toothless leering grin her mind racing.

When will this nightmare ever end? How will it end? Why me? How the hell did I get here? Just where the bloody hell am I. Will anyone be able to find me?

Tears welled up in her bloodshot eyes and rolled down the sides of her cheeks leaving a track in the dirty layer of dust covering her pale, pretty face.

Chapter One

7 Years earlier

Brigit's scream ripped through the fabric of the quiet dawn bringing her husband barrelling down the wide, white walled hallway to the bathroom, heart pounding with sudden exertion.

'Brigit?'

'Hmmph.'

'You Okay Hon?' Jax tentatively pushed open the bathroom door. Brigit was standing in front of the toilet bowl with her back to him, arms wrapped around her body, shivering with revulsion. He crept up behind her gently putting his arms around her waist and looked over her shoulder.

'Ahh, the little green frogs again huh?'

'God I hate those things,' her voice quivered. I'm sorry Jax but they really freak me out.'

'It's okay darlin,' you'll get used to them. Look, just pick up the dunny brush and run it around the rim, with any luck they will let go and fall back into the bowl. Then all you do is flush the little suckers back down the drain from whence they came.'

Brigit could feel the warmth of his body and drew strength from it. He hugged her tight and started nipping at the soft, delicious skin below her ear. She giggled and relaxed, leaning back into his chest.

'Wait till you see the cane toads honey, ya gonna love those babies,' he laughed.

'Oh you are so gonna regret teasing me lover boy,' she said as she spun around to face him.

'Really? Come on then show me what ya got,' he taunted beckoning her with a lustful wink.

Brigit chased her playful husband back up the hallway to their bedroom, two sets of bare feet slapping on the cool polished floor boards, green frogs forgotten for the time being.

The rest of the day started like any other with Brigit cooking bacon and eggs for Jax and toast and coffee for herself. But this morning she stood by the old white stove mindlessly poking at the bacon spitting in the pan, seemingly miles away.

'What's up honey, you're lookin' a bit down this morning. You okay? Not still worried about them little green frogs are ya?' The cheeky glint in his gorgeous blue eyes melted her heart as a tear trickled down her cheek.

'Hey hey hey, what is it?' He leapt out of

his chair and, spinning her around, drew her into his chest in a comforting cuddle. 'What is it Hon?'

'Oh it's nothing really,' she said, her voice muffled as she buried herself in his warm chest. 'I'm just a bit homesick, I really miss the greenery. Isn't that silly.'

'Greenery? We got green frogs,' he teased.

'Ouch, that hurt,' he said as she stomped on his foot. 'Oh you mean trees and flowers and grass and stuff.'

She nodded, 'Yeah, here it's just so….'

'Barren?'

'But it's not really barren is it. Don't get me wrong, I really love the outback but it's just…'

'It's just not home babe. So why don't you go call your Dad. You've been here three months and hardly spoken to your family since you arrived. You know you can call home anytime you want to eh. We're not exactly paupers.'

Brigit's face lit up. 'Have I got time before we head out?'

Jax laughed, 'We'll make time honey, just go make the call.'

'Hi Dad, it's me. Yeah, no, I'm fine, just missing you guys that's all. Absolutely. No, no problems at all. I was just a bit homesick so Jax said to phone you so here I am. So what's happening there, have you started shearing yet? early. So you've started mustering then? Oh good. Was it just the five of you or did Lucy go too?' Brigit giggled. 'Sorry Dad but she is a bit of a diva don't you think? Not sure what you see in her but as long as she makes you happy that's okay by me. She'll never make it as a shepherdess though. Has she even learned to ride a horse yet?'

Brigit could hear her Dad trying to suppress his laughter as he responded to her questions.

'Hey your parcel with the wedding photo album and video arrived a couple of weeks ago,' said Brigit. 'Sorry I haven't written back to thank you. The photographer did a fabulous job on them eh! Yes, Stoneridge Estate was perfect, pretty hard to get a bad photo there. Please call DaVella, Wayne and Suzanne and thank them again for us. It was an amazing day, one I will remember forever. Yes the house is lovely Dad, a lot different to ours but I love the big wide open verandas. We spend most of our time out there when we're home. We eat out there and stay there untill bed time just reading or chatting with whoever's around. Nah, no time to be lonely Dad,' she laughed. 'No time for TV either. Yeah very different to home eh. So how are things panning out with the farm work now that I'm out of the picture?'

'Rees has stepped in. Really? I knew Stella wasn't interested in the farm but Rees never really showed an interest before either. That's great. Selwyn and Sandy must be stoked that their son is finally doing something other than studying. Listen Dad I'm about to head out to work with Jax, so can I have a quick word with Rees? Ta. No I think we are fencing today. I will. Say hi to Sandy and Sel for me too okay. Love you heaps Dad, I miss you too.'

There was a pause as Brigit waited for Rees to come to the phone. He and his twin sister Stella had grown up on the farm together, their father had been the farm manager for as long as Brigit could remember. The three of them were like siblings.

'Yo ugly, what's the haps,' she laughed as Rees picked up the phone and said hello.

By the time Brigit returned to the kitchen, Jax had finished his breakfast and was nowhere to be seen. Brigit walked out onto the large veranda surrounding the house and leaned out over the balcony. 'Oh there you are,' she said as she spotted him standing around the side of the house.

'Yep all saddled up and ready to go. Finish your breakfast and we'll be off, we need to get a good start before it gets too hot.'

Brigit filled the saddle bags with food and water and carried them out to Jax to attach to the saddles. The heat hit her as soon as she walked out into the yard. She quickly applied sun-block to her exposed skin which she noticed was becoming pleasingly tanned. She pulled on her leather ankle-high riding boots, threw on her leather Akubra slouch hat and wraparound sunglasses that stopped the flies from crawling over her eyes then mounted her horse, 'Shy'. She loved the smell of sweat stained leather and horses, it reminded her of home. She reached down and patted Shy on the neck.

'Good morning girl, ready for another day's work?' The mare lifted her head, shook it and gave a soft whinny in response. 'Are we fencing in the west block again today?' She turned in her saddle to watch Jax.

'Not this morning,' he said, adjusting the straps on his mount. 'I thought we'd better check the stock over in the channel block first to make sure they still have plenty to eat and drink, then we can carry on with the fencing.'

They made their way past the stockmen's quarters and met up with the group of employees detailed to work with them for the day. Brigit felt a little out of place. She was the boss's wife and while they had all welcomed her warmly when she arrived, she still felt out of her depth. This outback life was all very new to her.

The work group included Jax's three uncles, Fred, Jasper and Nick. Jax's father was the owner of the property and he'd offered his three brothers whatever positions they wanted to take up as they were not in the least bit interested in owning any of the land, they all preferred the freedom of being labourers. 'All care and no responsibility,' the men had told their brother when, being the eldest son, had inherited the Station from his father. 'So long as we get paid each month we're happy just working on the property,' they'd said. When Jax and Brigit got married, Sid gave Jax the southern block to manage and had asked his brothers if they would be happy to work alongside him. Nick was a bit reluctant at first as he loved living on the main homestead compound but when Fred and Jasper said they would love to go help their nephew out, Nick decided to join them. He knew he would miss the jackasses if he didn't go with them. There were twelve men and three women working for Jax now, including Brigit. Five of the men were married. Two of the wives helped out with the round ups and crop harvesting while the other three women looked after the food and accommodation side of things at the homestead compound. Brigit loved living in the main house with Jax and was grateful they had it all to themselves but she felt a bit uncomfortable about having a couple of the workers wives doing the cooking and cleaning for them. Back home in New Zealand it had been just her and her Dad and dear old Gracie living in the homestead. Grace did most of the cooking and cleaning. Brigit loved to get in and help out when she wasn't out working with her father but she preferred to be outdoors. Grace had made a promise to Brigit's mother on her death bed that she would do everything she could to give Brigit a loving stable home. And she had done just that. Luke was immensely proud of his daughter; she was the light of his life. She had been spoilt for the first few years after her mother died, but once she got to the age of four Grace decided that she was becoming too precocious and suggested to her father that they might tighten up on the discipline a bit. Luke hated the idea but he certainly didn't want Brigit growing up to be a spoilt brat. Brigit fought back for all she was worth, eventually succumbing, but she never let go of her fiery passion for the things she loved and believed in. She was tom-boyish and loved to rough and tumble with anyone who would take her on. She was never one to shy away from a challenge. She'd taken the odd tumble off her horse over the years and had come second best in a tussle with a stroppy old ram. While it was highly amusing, it had left Luke shaken and concerned. It was all he could do not to interfere or try to molly-coddle her. He'd learned that lesson very early on in the piece.

Jax was initially smitten by Brigit's beauty and was pleasantly surprised that she also had a good head on her shoulders. When he found out she was a farmer he decided he had to get to know her better. During their long-distance courtship where they spent time travelling between each others homes across the Tasman, he got to see and admire Brigit's strengths and tenacity. It wasn't long before he proposed; she was definitely the woman for him.

Brigit was a little hesitant with Jax at first. He was an Australian and she'd always imagined she would marry a Kiwi. The fact that he came from a large sheep station in Australia's Northern Territory was daunting too. It was so vastly different from her beloved high country that she wasn't sure she would ever be able to make the transition. They did discuss Jax coming to live with her in New Zealand but in her heart of hearts she knew that would never happen. In the end, her love for Jax took over and she followed her heart, all the way to the Australian Outback.

Chapter Two

On the job

Brigit and Jax rode along in silence for a while both lost in their own thoughts, until a couple of the herd appeared from behind some bushes. Jax sat back quietly on his horse and checked them over. Sweat was making rivulets down Brigit's back; she didn't mind the heat so much as it was a dry heat, a bit like mid-summer back home in New Zealand. What she loathed more than anything were the flies. She hated them getting up her nose and in her mouth and crawling all over her skin. She wasn't sure it was something she would ever get used to.

'Don't these fucking flies ever bother you?' she asked Jax.

'I guess because I've grown up with them I've gotten used to them. Are they getting at ya a bit?' he laughed. Her colourful use of language told him she was getting angry.

'Yeah, they really piss me off.'

'No kidding?' Jax was trying not to let her see him laughing. 'You did pack your Aeroguard didn't you?'

'Yeah I did but it only lasts for a little while,' she grumped waving her hands in front of her face angrily and slapping her neck at the annoying pests.

Jax had to ride ahead of her for a while until he could control the laughter bubbling away just below the surface. They rode on for a couple of hours checking the water courses and the amount of food available and then checked the stock over to make sure they were healthy and uninjured. Brigit became entranced with her surroundings as they rode in silence and with the help of another dosing of Aeroguard spray, was able to put her fly problem behind her for a while.

'It is sooo quiet out here,' she whispered.

'Is it? I hadn't noticed,' Jax whispered back.

Brigit poked her tongue at him and rode on. Despite the ground resembling a giant dust bowl, there was a surprising amount of vegetation. She led the horse up close to one of the bushes and reached down to break a piece off so she could study it and smell it. She heard a rustling noise and gave a little shriek as a large cattle beast appeared from behind the bush.

Jax laughed at her, 'it's okay honey, he won't bite.'

'He just gave me a fright that's all,' pouted Brigit defensively. She studied the bull for a few moments and watched him walking around beside her.

'I like these Brahman cattle Jax, they seem so docile and friendly. Is it in their nature or is it just too darned hot for them to get rattled?' Brigit urged her horse up so she was riding alongside Jax.

'They're not always this docile,' he laughed. 'Some of them can get pretty stroppy but most of the time they are quiet. Makes handling them in the yards a lot easier that's for sure. Not like those crazy sheep you've got back home.'

Brigit laughed. 'God, remember that first muster you did with us when you came to stay. I think the sheep must have put on a show just for you.

'What a bloody performance,' he laughed, 'how could I forget.' He threw her a broad grin. 'That was one of the funniest experiences I've ever had, man they were an unruly mob. It was fun though.'

Once the stock were checked and Jax was satisfied that all was okay they headed back over to the eastern side of the property to carry on with the fencing. They stopped beside a stream where they dismounted, tied the horses reins to the saddle pommels and let them roam and forage for whatever sustenance they could find. The workers had all gathered at the same spot and once Jax and Brigit were ready they piled into two jeeps and a truck waiting for them under the trees. The truck carried the fencing gear. They headed across to continue the seemingly endless miles and miles of fencing that needed to be repaired. It was hard work in the relentless heat with the sun beating down unmercifully, but no-one seemed to notice, except Brigit.

'I need a break Jax,' she said after a couple of hours. 'I just need to get out of the sun for a bit, I'm feeling a bit light headed.' Brigit had been trying to keep pace with the others trying not to lag behind.

'You been drinking your water? Here let me see.'

Brigit held out her water bottle for him to check.

'Not nearly enough Brigit, you have to drink, a lot. It's really important.'

She nodded, tears welling up in her eyes. 'Sorry Jax, I didn't think about it. I'm really finding it hard getting used to this heat.'

I know Hon, I'm sorry but I just really need to get through to you how important it is to keep drinking water otherwise you will get seriously dehydrated.'

Jax heard the crackle of his walkie talkie radio and tuned in.

'Lunch time everyone,' he called down the fence line.

They jumped into their vehicles and made their way back to the river. Lunch had been set up by one of the women staff members who had stayed behind to keep an eye on the horses and prepare lunch. The first thing the workers did was strip off to their underwear and jump into the welcoming cool clear waters of the gently trickling stream.

'No crocs here then?' Brigit already knew the answer but was curious as to why.

'Not since I had a quick look last year,' Jax laughed and flicked a towel at her. 'Nah you're all good Hon, crocs don't come this far up.'

'Besides, if they do, we'll just shoot em and cook em on the barbie,' quipped Jax's Uncle Jasper. He made a leering gesture at Brigit with his gap-toothed grin.

Brigit was not amused. She was terrified of the huge reptiles. Jax wanted to distract her so he signalled to Jasper and the two men picked Brigit up and dumped her unceremoniously into the water. After the initial shock and a few expletives she relaxed and enjoyed her fully clothed swim, all the time keeping a watchful eye out for crocodiles, just in case.

After the swim they all sat under the sparsely leafed trees in whatever shade they could find and enjoyed a hearty lunch of meat and salad sandwiches, homemade fruit cake, apples, fruit juice and tea and coffee. There was always a bit of light banter and leg pulling during the lunch break and Brigit found herself the brunt of most of it this day. It tugged at her inner tenacity and she was beginning to get wise to their antics so she decided to join in the fun and give back as good as she got.

'So how are you enjoying life in the outback Brigit?' asked Nick.

Nick was the youngest of Sid's brothers and married with two young children.

'It's hugely different, obviously, but actually I'm beginning to quite enjoy it. The more I learn and the more I see I can understand what it is that you all love about the outback. Struggling a bit with the heat though.'

'Well, you're doin good so far Brig, you're a gutsy wee thing and you sure need that strength to survive out here. And to survive bein married to Jaxxy boy too,' he laughed.

'Gee thanks Nick, I love you too,' laughed Jax.

Brigit could feel her cheeks redden, it was heartening to hear this accolade from one of Jax's family and it made her feel more confident.

'You're married to Elizabeth right?'

'Yep, Lizzie. We got two little girls, Emma and Fliss, short for Felicity.'

'What about Jasper and Fred? I haven't really caught up with who's married to who yet.'

'Fred, he's the second one, he's not married. I think he loves horses more than wimmen, eh Fred,'

'What's that?'

'You love horses more than wimmen eh,' repeated Nick.

'Bloody oath mate, wimmen have too many moving parts.'

Brigit dissolved into fits of giggles. 'Okay, so what about the crazy one over there?' She pointed to Jasper.

'Oh, him. Well what can I say. Number three. Dropped on his head as a baby that one, gone a bit funny in the head,' he whispered to Brigit twirling his finger beside his head to indicate crazy.

'Oi, I heard that little brother.' Jasper came over and with Jax's help was picked up and tossed back into the stream.

'Don't listen to a word he says,' laughed Jasper, and turning to Nick as he waded out of the river, 'he's full of shit.'

'Okay you guys, let's get back to work,' called Jax.

'Ooop, the boss man has spoken, hop to it.' Jasper grabbed Jax around the shoulders and grappled him to the ground in a playful tussle to put him in his place.

'Sweetheart, why don't you stay here with Emily for a while. Take some more time out in the shade,' Jax offered, after he'd got to his feet and dusted himself down.

Brigit smiled gratefully. 'Thanks Hon, you sure you don't mind? I should be helping.'

'You're the boss's wife, comes with privileges,' he winked meaningfully at her.

She blushed again and gave him a kiss.

'Thanks hon.'

'Come on you love birds, give it a rest or find a room.'

'We gotta find that man a woman to tame him down. He's always been too cocky for his own good,' Jax responded.

'Aint neva gonna happen Jaxxy boy, aint neva gonna happen.'

'Why, you prefer the boys do ya Jasper?' Fred couldn't help himself. In response to a hand gesture from Jasper he continued, 'well, ya left yerself wide open for that.'

The team worked on till late afternoon before stopping for the day. As they gathered up the horses, Jax walked his horse over beside his Uncle Fred who was loading up the truck with the fencing gear.

'What time are you and Uncle Jasper heading off to the homestead on Saturday?'

'Thought we might head off around six before it gets too hot. You guys coming with us?'

'Nah, we might stay on with Mum and Dad for a couple of days afterwards. You guys can cope without us for a day or two can't ya?'

'Cheeky little sod, we were workin this land when you were still in nappies. If any of us were married we'd be kickin you out of that big old house and movin back in ourselves.'

'Does it bother you that Brigit and I are in there on our own? It's big enough for all of us.'

'To be honest with you Jaxxy boy it's

actually rather nice having a cabin to myself after years of sharing and I think Jasper feels the same. Nick and Lisa have their own place with their two little girls and they are very happy with what they've got. If we wanna spend some time together we do but otherwise we have our own private spaces. I like it and, as I say, I suspect Jasper does too so don't you worry about it.'

He ruffled Jax's hair as Jax playfully punched his uncle in the ribs. He was relieved as he'd never been quite sure how his uncles felt about him moving into the main homestead after he and Brigit got married.

Chapter Three

Bullock Creek Station

Brigit and Jax drove the 50kms down red dusty roads to get to the main homestead on Bullock Creek Station. The size of the property and the area immediately surrounding the homestead had never ceased to amaze Brigit. Sid had taken her up in his fixed wing plane on her very first visit when she and Jax were courting, so she could see the farm from the air. She noticed that along the banks of the streams and around the homesteads, willows and ghost gums grew more readily than anywhere else on the property, playing host to a variety of colourful birdlife.

'Your homestead looks like a small town. How many acres have you got all up?' she'd asked Sid through the microphone on the plane's headset.

'Bout 130,000 acres give or take.'

'Good thing you are able to see it by air whenever you want then,' she smiled at her soon to be father in law.

'Yes it is, makes life a helluva lot easier

that's for sure.' His voice was muffled through her headphones.

Brigit had stared out the windows transfixed, marvelling at the incredible diversity between the lush green mountainous terrain of her beloved New Zealand High Country, and the raw intoxicating beauty of this vast, mainly flat isolated desert outback. The variety of the outback terrain surprised her with its occasional deeply gouged gorges, high rocky outcrops and vast expanses of dry and seemingly endless barren land. The gorges fascinated her the most.

'Looks pretty down there,' she commented.

'It is. The walls of the gorge are pink would you believe. Jax will take you down there sometime to have a closer look, they're really quite something. Quite a few crocs down there though, but they are only freshies.'

'Freshies?'

'Yeah, only little fellas and if you keep out of their way they'll keep out of yours, not like the big crocs in the bigger rivers.'

Jax and Brigit pulled up outside the homestead just as Janet and Sid came out on to the veranda. They came down the stairs together to greet their son and his lovely wife.

'So good to see you my darlings,' gushed Janet. 'How are you settling in Brigit?'

'Good. Great. Yes everything's going well,'

she spluttered not having really given the question much thought. Sid grabbed her up in a bear hug.

'How's my favourite daughter-in-law then?'

'Thought I was your only daughter-in-law,' she laughed and kissed him on the cheek.

They unpacked and sat down for a cold drink to unwind. Nick, Emma, Jasper and Fred were well settled and on their third round of cold beers, enjoying a bit of banter when Jax and Brigit joined them.

'Where's Trey?' asked Jax of his only sibling.

'Oh he's gone to Darwin. It's orientation day at the University today. Willem flew him up yesterday, they should be back tomorrow though,' explained Janet.

'Can't believe little brother is off to Uni. Has he got his courses all sorted?'

'We'll find out tomorrow. He's hoping to get into animal husbandry, cropping and pest control if he can,' his father explained.

'Good, that will give us an expert in most fields,' said Jax. 'Pity you guys aren't experts in anything,' he threw at his uncles.

They all looked at each other. 'Cheeky little shit. Who wants to be a snotty nosed little expert anyway,' said one.

'Yeah, besides an ex-spurt is just a drip under pressure,' said another. The three men laughed heartily putting young Jaxon in his place.

After lunch Brigit excused herself and went for a walk while Jax and his father talked business and Janet and her staff organised dinner. Apart from the large rambling homestead, Brigit counted sixteen smaller dwellings of various sizes and about eight large purpose built sheds in a range of shapes and materials, mostly corrugated iron. The main house had a low fence around three sides as if to set a boundary from the rest of the compound. Some of the dwellings were just one room cabins all joined together in a row with shared facilities, a lot of them empty at this time of the year. Then there were more substantial houses for the staff, some with flower gardens, some with nothing but an old chair and a beer crate or wobbly old wooden table outside on the shady side of the house. She assumed that the houses with nice tidy curtains and pretty gardens belonged to female staff or couples and that the plainer ones were occupied by single men.

As she walked around the compound she tuned into the sounds of generators, the swish and clunk of the wooden windmill and then, surprisingly, the sound of children's voices. She made her way towards the sound and came across a large wooden building with a dark interior. She stepped inside the door and immediately felt the coolness of the rattling old air conditioner. A dozen or so heads turned around to look at her.

'Sorry,' she said shyly, 'I didn't mean to interrupt.'

'That's okay,' said the young woman at the front of the group. 'Come in. You're Jax's wife aren't you?'

'Yes.'

'I'm Lisa, Bobby's wife. Sorry we couldn't get to your wedding. Unfortunately one of the kids had the chicken pox didn't you sweetie?' A pretty little pink faced child with a pony tail and yellow ribbon nodded shyly.

'Everyone; meet the new Mrs Jamieson.'

'Good morning Mrs Jamieson,' they chorused, giggling.

'Please, call me Brigit.' She smiled at the delighted faces of the children. 'Do you do correspondence?' she asked the teacher.

'Yes, and we also have the School of the Air which is great for keeping the kids up with the rest of the children in their age group so that when they leave home and go to Tafe or College, they are not behind in their studies.

'I did correspondence when I was your age,' Brigit told the children, but I hated it.' The children all giggled and glanced around at each other nodding. 'I just wanted to be outdoors playing with the animals and riding my horse,' she explained.

'Doesn't take much to distract this lot

from their studies,' confessed Lisa.

Brigit spent a good half hour with them swapping stories and experiences before she left them to get on with their school work. Heading back towards the homestead she was impressed at how successfully Janet had managed to grow plants and flowers around their two storied wooden structure. The house was a grand design for a homestead, and not as high up off the ground as hers and Jax's one was. It had a wide veranda that went right around three sides of the house and was furnished here and there with a variety of stylish but comfortable lounge chairs and tables in white cane and sun bleached wood. There were wooden stairs leading down towards the compound from one side of the veranda and eight wide curved concrete steps that led up from the driveway to the front door. When she got back inside she sought Janet out and found her still in the kitchen.

'Sit down Brigit dear, would you like a coffee?'

'Love one thank you.'

'So, did you have a good look around?'

'Yes, it's great, a lot bigger than I thought. I've seen it from the air of course but it looks different from down on the ground, bigger. I spent some time with the children too. Aren't they lovely.'

Janet smiled at her and placed two cups of steaming coffee on the kitchen table. 'Hmm some of them maybe but there's some little tearaways amongst that lot believe me,' she laughed.

It was dark and cool in the kitchen; they hadn't started cooking the roasts yet. Brigit had seen a couple of Aboriginal children in the classroom.

'So you must have Aborigines working here then, I saw some children in the classroom.'

'Yes we have three working for us now. Two of them are married and that's their children you would have seen. They are great trackers and stock handlers and they know the land better than anyone, after all, they lived on this land for 40,000 years before we came here, they are a real asset. We had a lovely Aboriginal man named Monti working for us too but he was killed a few years ago.'

'How? Was it an accident?'

'No, he was murdered.'

'What?' She wasn't expecting that.

'Yes,' she sighed, 'one of the older men we had working for us got drunk one night and started beating up on one of the women. Monti stepped in to protect her but the bugger ran a knife through him and killed him. We are still looking for him and God help him when we find him. Monti was a lovely gentle man and one of our hardest workers.'

'Couldn't the Police help you find him? Didn't they want to charge him with murder?'

'Yes, they still do but there are too many places for someone to hide out here if you know the terrain, and unfortunately Braithwaite knows it only too well,' she sighed. 'He grew up on the land the hard way. Big family, not much money, carted from pillar to post while his Dad laboured on cattle stations. He's a survivor that one, but we'll get him one day, he's gotta come up for air at some stage and we'll be waiting.'

Brigit was surprised at the harshness in Janet's normally soft voice. This had obviously hit her hard. It was a pretty awful story and it had surprised and unnerved Brigit a little knowing that a murder had taken place right here on this property and that the killer was still running around loose.

Janet continued. 'You might as well know the full story. You'll hear about it one day anyway. Braithwaite found a bit of gold on the property and wanted to prospect for it but we wouldn't allow it.'

'I have seen a bit of quartz around,' commented Brigit, 'and I wondered if there was gold on the property. So why didn't you let him?'

'If we let him do that and he found a decent amount of gold we would have had every man and his dog in here wanting to prospect, and the gold mining companies would want to bring their drilling machines in to see whether it would be worth setting up a gold mining operation here. We were worried about the consequences of all that so we decided to just not go down that track. Oh believe me we discussed it at great length but in the end pretty much the whole family agreed to stick with what we knew best. Farming has been in the Jamieson family blood for many decades, we all love it and we don't want to lose what we've got. We are not hard up, we don't need the money and the Jamieson's are not greedy people.'

Brigit was thoughtful for a moment. 'So was Braithwaite okay with that?'

'Hell no,' Janet shuddered, 'he was furious. He's not a nice man Brigit and certainly not one you want to cross. He became quite belligerent after that and when he murdered poor old Monti that was the last straw. It was just as well he took off when he did because I swear Sid and his brothers would have strung him up if they had caught him, they were so angry.'

'Why did you keep him on if he was such a horrible man?'

'He was a good stockman and had a lot of experience. It was really only in the last year or so that he started getting cranky. Not sure whether it was just old age or whether he was unwell or what it was. Guess we'll never know now will we.' She stood up and collected the coffee cups. The conversation was over.

The following morning Sid took the opportunity to discuss the upcoming roundup with everyone while they were all together.

Brigit noticed that it was set for a particular date. It wasn't weather dependent like so much of the kiwi farming life she was used to. Stock trucks were coming in on a certain date and the cattle needed to be rounded up, sorted, and ready to go. The only hold up would be if it rained and the roads became bogged.

'Long range forecast looks good,' said Sid. 'Let's pray we don't have a repeat of last season eh.'

'Why? What happened last season?' asked Brigit, leaning against the door frame.

Sid swung around.

'Oh Brigit, thought you'd gone off with Janet.'

'Sorry, am I not supposed to be here?'

'You're welcome to stay Sweetheart, most of the women find all this stuff boring that's all.'

'Well I don't, so what happened last season?' She moved further into the room and sat on the arm rest of Jax's chair.

'One of the trucks got bogged. It wasn't so much the cost of the exercise,' explained Sid, 'but the truck was needed elsewhere so that put some other poor farmer a day or two behind and the stock weren't exactly impressed about being yarded up for so long either.'

Sid turned back to the others and carried on with the planning and discussions about the muster. Brigit would love to have stayed and listen to more but Janet beckoned to her from the doorway.

'I'm just going through some old linen and stuff I've hauled out of the attic,' she said, 'and I'd like to pass some of it on to you and Jax.'

Brigit would have preferred to stay and listen in with the men, but she didn't want to hurt Janet's feelings. After all, she was Janet's daughter-in-law and Janet didn't have any daughters of her own to fuss over so Brigit decided to relax and enjoy the attention.

'Where did you live when you were growing up?' Brigit enquired as Janet stopped to look at an old photo album which had been tucked away amongst the linen in an old trunk. They were both kneeling in front of the trunk gently unpacking long forgotten treasures.

'I was born in Perth and lived there until I went to teachers training college.' Janet paused to cast her mind back.

'My Mum came from Perth too,' Brigit said casually. 'Isn't that a coincidence, my mother and my mother-in-law both grew up in Perth. What are the odds of that happening,' she laughed.

'What was your mother's maiden name?'

'McKewen.'

'Not Ellen McKewen?'

'Yes' said Brigit, 'did you know her?'

'I went to college with an Ellen McKewen, we were great mates. We lost touch when I went off to training college and she went off to be an air hostess if I remember rightly.'

'Oh my God,' laughed Brigit excitedly. 'Yes, my Mum did become an air hostess, that's how she met Dad. Oh my God, this is unreal.' She was bouncing up and down on her knees clapping her hands like a little girl.

Janet started to flick back through the pages of her old photo album.

'Look, here, my old college photos.' She quickly scanned the line-up of faces until her finger stopped over one photo. A pretty girl with blonde curly hair.

'Oh my Brigit, except for your hair, you really do look a lot like her you know, look.'

Brigit peered intently at the photo. A tear trickled down her cheek but she said nothing. Janet looked up.

'Oh my dear girl, I didn't mean to make you cry.'

'No, it's okay,' Brigit was quick to reassure her mother-in-law. 'I love this photo. I have the very same one in my Mum's diary. I have all her old photos. So which one is you? No, let me guess.'

Brigit ran her finger along the line of faces.

'There, that one. That's you isn't it.'

Janet laughed. 'Well spotted.'

'Did you and Mum ever go to a coffee bar called *Alfred's* on Marchant Street?'

'Yes, we did, quite often in fact. Why do

you ask?'

'I've got a photo of you and Mum sitting at a table with a couple of men in uniform. Do you remember that?'

Janet was thoughtful for a moment. 'Oh, yes, I do remember. A navy ship had called into port and your Mum and I were in the coffee bar after the movies and some of the sailors were there. My goodness this does bring back memories. I say Brigit, this is rather delicious isn't it, both of us connected to Ellen in some way.'

'I never knew her unfortunately, only what the family told me. And they talked about her – a lot,' she laughed. 'When I was thirteen Dad gave me Mum's diary, the one she wrote when she was dying. Dad said she would sit up in her bed and watch me sleeping in my bassinet and would write to me in her diary. I used to take the diary up the hill to my special place and as I read it I could almost hear her talking to me. I'm so glad she did that. You knew that my wedding dress was Mum's eh.'

'Yes I did and it fitted you perfectly. You looked a real picture in it sweetheart.'

'Maybe you could tell me some stories about your Mum sometime, I would love to hear what she did with her short life. How sad that we never got to meet again.' She was silent for a moment then she lifted her head with a sniff and said, 'but at least I get to spend time with her precious daughter. Let's forget about the linen and stuff for now. I'll get the photo books out and see what else we can find shall we. I'm bound to have heaps of photos, we were camera mad back then, and each photo will have a story to it.'

'Are you girls still at it?' Sid poked his head round the corner of the door scaring the living daylights out of them. We're about to have lunch.'

'Lunch? Good heavens is that the time.' Janet checked her watch.

'Don't worry Abigail has it all sorted. She saw how engrossed you two were and decided to leave you to it. What's with the photo albums, I thought you were going through the linen trunks?'

'Oh Sid, you'll never guess.'

'Guess what?' chipped in Jax poking his head over his father's shoulder.

'You're not going to believe this but Brigit's mother and I went to college together.'

'You're kidding me,' laughed Sid, 'really?'

'Yes. She was off being an air hostess by the time you came along so you wouldn't have met her.'

'That's a shame,' pondered Sid, smiling at Brigit, 'I would like to have met your mother.'

They were all seated around the table, everyone talking at once, when a woman appeared in the doorway. The chatter stopped for a moment.

'Ruth, you look wonderful, how was the trip?'

'Did you meet any blokes?'

'Come, sit down and tell us all about it.' Everyone was talking at once again.

'You haven't met our Brigit yet.' Janet and Brigit stood up to face the woman. 'Brigit this is our much-loved Station Nurse, Ruth.'

Ruth held out her hand. 'Nice to finally meet you Brigit, I've heard so much about you.'

'Hi,' said Brigit, 'I wish I could say the same. I didn't realise the Station had its very own nurse. That's awesome.'

Ruth smiled. 'Well aren't you the sweetest thing. Can I get a hug?'

Brigit laughed and gladly hugged her new acquaintance. She liked Ruth immediately.

'I hope we get to spend some time together before we go home,' said Brigit as the two sat side by side at the lunch table.

'Me too, that would be great.'

Ruth was encouraged to fill everyone in on her trip to visit family in England so she and Brigit didn't get to chat by themselves until later in the day. Ruth was in her early 40's, spirited, attractive and full of life. She had never married. She was engaged to a young man in England but he was killed in a car accident which left her devastated. She had buried herself in her nursing studies and for the past ten years had hidden herself away on Bullock Creek Station. She was well loved on the station, and she loved the life. It was busy and distracting and gave her a chance to heal. As well as nursing, she also helped with the children's education and among other things had taught them all first aid and survival skills.

'Jax why don't you and Brigit stay on for a few days,' pleaded Janet after they'd all had a sumptuous ploughman's lunch of leftover cold meat and salad sandwiches. She thought it might be nice for Ruth and Brigit to spend some more time together.

'Sure Mum, we can stay a few more days.'

Janet was delighted. 'Good, oh and how much room have you got in the back of your wagon?' she winked at Brigit.

'Oh no, you're not giving us all that attic stuff are ya Mum?'

'Don't worry yourself about it my boy,' she said reaching out and giving Brigit's hand a conspiratorial squeeze, 'this is women's stuff, isn't it Brigit.'

Brigit smiled apologetically at Jax but he just laughed and said, 'we can only take a small cabin trunk, otherwise we will have to borrow the truck and trailer.'

Brigit and Jax both thoroughly enjoyed their extended stay with Sid and Janet. The men talked a lot about their future plans and dreams for the farm while Janet and Ruth spent as much time as they could with Brigit. One afternoon Janet joined Ruth and Brigit out on the veranda. The subject had turned to children.

'We do plan to have kids, said Brigit, but it's too early yet. We thought we'd give ourselves a year or three to get really settled in then see how it goes from there. We both love the freedom of working together.'

'Just don't make me wait too long for my grandchildren dear, I'd like to be able to play with them and run around with them before I get too old.' She leaned across and patted Brigit on the knee.

Well that gives me heaps of time then' laughed Brigit, 'because I can't see you getting old for a very long time. You and Sid are the same age as Dad and I still see him as a young man with a lifetime ahead of him yet.'

'So what do you really think about having kids?' Jax broached the subject with Brigit on their drive home.

'I would love to have kids but not just yet. There's no hurry is there?'

'None at all, I was just curious that's all.'

Jax popped their favourite CD into the player and they sang and hummed their way home. Brigit allowed her mind to drift off and imagine her life in her new home filled with kids and noise and laughter.

There were several houses and large sheds

surrounding their house which, like Janet and Sid's, was also set apart at a respectable distance. The house was built up off the ground to allow the air to flow underneath and come up through gaps in the floorboards to help keep the interior cool. Brigit loved the wide verandas most of all. They surrounded the entire house allowing them plenty of options to get out of the weather. She and Jax spent most of their time out there eating their meals, reading or just relaxing. Sometimes when the nights were really hot and sticky they would sleep out on one of the veranda day beds. The interior doors were open most of the time which allowed for any breezes to blow through the house. In contrast to the big picture windows which let in the light and sunshine that Brigit was used to, her outback home was cool and dark inside with a distinct lack of big windows in order to keep out the sun.

When Brigit had stepped into her new home for the first time she'd noticed that the interior walls were plain and painted a greyish white as opposed to the bright cheerful wallpaper she was used to. There were various pieces of artwork hanging on the walls but little else in the form of decoration. The furniture was sparse, plain and serviceable but it seemed to fit the basic style of the house. The outdoor furniture was a collection of old wooden beds with overstuffed mattresses, fraying cane chairs and time worn wooden tables but it didn't look out of place on the old veranda.

'Can't get over how there's no gardens here, just red dirt everywhere, nothing but red dirt,' Brigit had remarked to Jax one night.

'Bit different to green grass everywhere nothing but green grass,' Jax had quipped back. 'But hey, you're welcome to try your hand at gardening if you like. Can't promise you'll have much success, it took Mum years of patience and hard work to achieve what she's done.'

Not to be put off Brigit replied with, 'now there's a challenge. I don't expect to have gardens like Grace had back home but we must be able to do something to break the monotony of the dirt yard.'

'Good, then make a list of what you want and we'll put in an order for the next trip to the city.'

'Must be just about our turn to go again is it?'

'The uncles have got this month covered but I think it's us next month,' said Jax trying to remember the schedule that had been set up for supply runs.

Once a month on a Sunday night everyone on the compound would get together to go over the previous week's events and make plans for the coming weeks.

Brigit would help the women make salads while the men gathered around the barbecue talking, beer in hand, pushing beef steaks and sausages around the hot plates.

Why do you call these 'shrimp on the barbie' nights'? Brigit asked Alison, one of the men's wives.

'Dunno love,' she looked across at Rose, another of the wives. Rose shrugged.

'Just always been called that. I suppose it's because we often do cook shrimps on the barbecue,' decided Alison.

Jax and his uncles put the beer and wine on the tables which, along with the food, was paid for by the Jamiesons as a show of appreciation to their employees. Work on the station was hard and the conditions unforgiving at times and those strong enough to tough it out year after year were much appreciated.

Brigit, being the 'newbie', enjoyed sitting back at these get-togethers and listening to them talking. She loved to hear all the banter and leg pulling that went on but most of all she loved learning new things about her new life as a stockman's wife.

'I was thinking of taking you on a road trip through the outback sometime next year? Think you'd like that?' asked Jax as they ambled back arm in arm to the house after the meeting.

'Outback? Isn't this the outback?'

'Nah, you ain't seen nothin yet,' Jax said proudly. 'I wanna take you to places like Marree and Birdsville and Innamincka.'

'I've heard of Birdsville, isn't that where they have camel races or something weird like that?'

'Sure is. Actually Dad and the uncles try and get to the camel races every year if they can. We could tag along next time if you like.'

'That'd be great, sounds like a lot of fun.'

'It is. They usually take the fixed wing plane and land right beside the Birdsville Pub. My uncles like to sleep out in the open under the wings of the plane, but Dad always stays at the pub when Mum goes with them. Takes a couple of plane trips to get us all out there but it takes too long for us to go by road.'

'So do you take the camp trailer when you go outback?'

'Some of the family take it away on their holidays but if we do this trip we'll stay in motels. They're all nice and modern now, not like the old wooden hotels we stayed in when we were kids.

'Wouldn't mind a trip with the trailer sometime too. I've never seen anything quite like it the way it folds out from a small trailer to a bloody great house,' she laughed.

'I'm sure we will make good use of it, especially when we have kids.'

'Speaking of kids, big kids I mean, I'd love to get Stella and Rees over here sometime, they've never been to Australia. Next time I'm talking to them I'll get them to start saving up to come over and the four of us could do a road trip together. I've only ever been to Darwin once when I went with you to that wedding.'

'Don't forget you've been to Canberra too my darling, how could you forget that.'

'Of course, the stock conference where we first met. How could I forget that.' She slapped at her forehead in mock despair.

'Yeah, and you thought my name had been misspelt on my name badge.'

Brigit blushed.

'And, as if I didn't know, you kindly pointed it out to me,' he laughed.

'Well, at least it got us talking. And how was I to know your father named you after an American school friend.'

Chapter Four

The Muster

Jax folded up the topographical map which had been spread out over the old wooden kitchen table. The table had seen several decades of kitchen use, meals and happy family gatherings, and because of its convenient size it often served as an office desk and meeting table.

'Nick and Jasper are going to be taking a team each,' Jax was explaining to Brigit. 'Fred and I are going to be tied up down at the stock yards so I thought you might like to ride along with the Jillaroos.'

'The what?'

'The Jillaroos. That's what we call the female version of a Jackaroo.'

'You're kidding me right? Jackaroo and Jillaroo, like Jack and Jill went up the hill?' She was laughing now.

'No babe, I'm not kidding,' Jax couldn't help but smile at her amusement. 'That's what they are called.'

'You Aussies are so weird, you know that. All these funny sayings you have.'

'What funny sayings, like what?'

'Like what? Well, let me see, we call a barbeque a barbeque but you call it a barbie. We have chilly bins and you have Esky's. We have jandals and you have thongs, we have togs and you have swimmers. Then there's that ee thing you guys do.'

'What ee thing?' Jax was beginning to get a little miffed.

'Well, if we call someone Bruce, you would do the ee thing and call him Brucee and if we…..

'Okay, okay little miss prim and proper English. You Kiwis sound so English and you speak so damned fast some times we don't even know what you're saying.'

'Yeah that's because you guys draaaawwl,' said Brigit exaggeratedly.

'At least Jackaroo and Jillaroo haven't got eeee's on the end of them,' he responded defensively.

'No but they sound like some kind of constipated kangaroo.'

By this time Brigit's giggling was getting a little out of control. Tears of laughter started down her face. Jax gave up on being affronted and leapt out of his chair, pulled her up into his arms and they started play-fighting. As it started to become more erotic and suggestive, clothes were torn off and tossed aside and Brigit eventually found herself sitting astride Jax riding out his excited erection. She reached a climax and was just about to bring Jax to the same conclusion when there was a loud knock at the door. They stopped, shocked at the intrusion, and tried desperately to stifle their giggles.

'Who is it? Called Jax hoarsely.

'It's Adam, Jax. We just want to go over some more details for the muster.'

'Be right with you Adam, I'll meet you down at the lunchroom shortly okay?'

'Right you are.'

Brigit rolled off Jax letting out her held in mirth and they rolled around on the floor laughing.

'You owe me one,' said Jax playfully. 'I would like you to make good on that tonight, okay.'

'Aye aye cap'n,' saluted Brigit as she gathered up her strewn clothing.

Once they had re-dressed and calmed down, they ventured hand in hand down to meet the others, trying to keep a straight face. They walked into the cool interior of the corrugated shed which was framed with large round poles and wooden cross beams. The dirt floor had packed down over the years. Around the walls was a variety of old lounge chairs, some with stuffing escaping from torn seams. Old wooden tables sat awkwardly on uneven legs, bookcases strewn with magazines and scruffy dog-eared paperbacks leaned haphazardly against the walls. In the centre of the shed was a large trestle table surrounded by at least a dozen straight backed wooden chairs. Off to one side was a small lean-to which served as a staff kitchen. It had a plain sink bench, an old chipped enamel oven and a refrigerator. On the curtained off shelves underneath the bench was a variety of mis-matched crockery, a tray of cutlery, a selection of old pots and pans and packaged and tinned food. Then there was the constant hum of generators and refrigerators which was only really acknowledged if the hum stopped and there was a sudden silence.

Jax took Brigit over and introduced her to one of the Jillaroos sitting on the edge of a chair in the corner of the room. Kirsty was from Gisborne in New Zealand. She'd come over to visit an aunt in Darwin, saw the ad in the paper one day seeking mustering staff and decided to try her luck. She'd had shepherding experience and Henry, the station employment manager at Bullock Creek, knew the people she had worked for back in New Zealand and had hired her after phoning them for a reference.

'This is my second muster here,' Kirsty said to Brigit as they sat down. 'I'm from Gisborne, I understand you are from New Zealand as well?'

'I am' said Brigit delightedly. It's nice to meet you. I grew up on a high-country sheep station in the South Island.

'Really?' Where abouts?'

'Skippers Canyon.'

'Oh wow, I have always wanted to go to Queenstown and visit Skippers and Macetown.'

'Whenever you want to go, let me know I can arrange a visit,' said Brigit enthusiastically.

'That would be fantastic, thank you. So where did you go to school?'

'I did correspondence until I was 16 then I went off to Otago University for a year to study Zoology.

'Zoology?'

'Yeah animal biology. Hated being away from the farm though and I really missed Dad so I only did a year, then went home.'

Kirsty laughed. 'Well, you must be homesick being here then.'

'I am a bit, but I do love living here and the family and staff are really awesome, they make me feel at home.'

'That's true, they have been really nice to me too. I didn't go to Uni I went straight from home to my farm job. I went to England and did some waitressing and had a look around at one stage for a year. My big OE. You been anywhere other than Australia?'

'Nope. Been a real homebody. Dad and I did take off on trips now and then though. We both loved doing weird stuff like bungy jumping and heli-skiing and of course we lived in a snow skiing paradise so we were right into that too.

My Aunty Sandy is an avid skier so we set up our own ski lane on the farm, it was awesome.'

Brigit turned to the other girl who appeared beside them.

'Hi, I'm Brigit, I'm…'

'Yeah, I know who you are,' the girl sneered sarcastically. 'Name's Sam. And who are you?' she enquired of Kirsty.

'I'm Kirsty, I'm from New Zealand too. So where are you…

'Hmmph another bloody Kiwi,' Sam huffed, and stalked off.

Brigit was stunned. 'Well, that was rude. Wonder what's eating her?"

Kirsty shrugged. 'Beats me, never met her before, she wasn't here last year.'

Adam, the overseer, joined Brigit and Kirsty to talk about what they would be doing during the muster and what would be expected of them. Brigit caught Jax's eye and he winked at her as he watched her and Kristy bonding. When he turned and caught sight of Sam leaning against the door frame, Brigit saw Jax stiffen and his demeanour changed completely. Sam was watching them both sulkily from beneath her wide brimmed hat.

'You girls wanna take a break from all that gas bagging and join us for a minute,' called Fred from the back of the room.

'Sure,' they chorused.

They joined the rest of the workers sitting

at the trestle table. Sam sauntered over and pulled up a chair close to Jax. Brigit noticed he looked decidedly uncomfortable and tried to move away without being too obvious. Once the details had been talked through and any issues ironed out, Jasper went over and opened the fridge.

'Okay, who's for a cold one?'

There was a resounding chorus of 'yes please' as he grabbed an armful of bottles and took them to the table. Tops were popped off, snacks were brought out from the kitchen and all talk of work was over for the time being. Brigit saw Jax take Nick aside and watched with interest as the two got into an animated discussion, occasionally looking across at Sam. Later that night Brigit asked Jax about it but he shrugged it off saying it was just staff issues and nothing for her to worry about.

Chapter Five

Samantha

The musterers sat in the cool, silent, pre-dawn gloom of the large dining area of the shed and ate their breakfast. Eventually the clattering of plates and cutlery signalled breakfast was over and the workday had begun. Brigit and Jax walked hand in hand from their house down to the shed just as the sun was breaching the horizon with a golden glow of the promise of another brilliant blue sky day. Sam was leaning on the door frame of her bunk room. She threw Jax such a cold glare that it made Brigit's heart skip a beat.

'What did you ever do to her for her to glare at you like that?'

'Like what?' he said defensively. Brigit looked up at his reddening face.

'Is there something between you two?'

'Not now Brig, I'll tell you later.' He turned his back on Sam and gave Brigit what he hoped was a reassuring kiss.

Brigit was not at all reassured but decided to let the matter drop for now, this wasn't the time. There was an increasing buzz of excited chatter as more and more people appeared, wiping the sleep out of their eyes.

'What time did you lot get to bed last night?' Jax asked the men as they sloped through the door.

'Wasn't too bad, was it mate?' said one looking at the other.

When the 'Jill's' came in, Brigit gave Jax a peck on the cheek and said, 'See ya at the yards later today then?'

'Should do, that's if you ladies don't get yourselves lost,' he laughed.

Brigit punched him on the arm and feigned annoyance as she sauntered off, swaying her little bum at him. Jax watched her for a moment and laughing turned back to Fred and Jasper ready to face the day.

Brigit, Kirsty and Sam checked their horses over to make sure they were sound, re-checked their saddle bags before attaching them to the saddles and tightened the saddle straps before putting their feet into the stirrups and throwing a leg over their mounts.

'My very first cattle muster,' said Brigit, 'how exciting.'

'Yeah ya never know how the day is gonna pan out,' sniped Sam as she swung her horse around and rode off.

'What is it with her?' asked Kirsty.

'Dunno but I think it has something to do

with Jax.'

'Really, what makes you say that?'

Before Kirsty could say any more they were called to get moving so they turned their horses around and caught up with the new girl. They headed out of the yard towards their designated area to look for cattle. It was going to be a long hot day. It took two hours of solid riding before they spotted the first of the herd. The cattle were surprisingly unfazed at the sight of three horsewomen approaching.

'I'm glad they are a quiet breed of cattle,' whispered Brigit.

'I've worked with other breeds before,' said Sam, 'some of them would scare the pants off ya, but I like these Brahmans. They're a relatively new breed. They were introduced because they don't suffer from the tics like most of the others do. Those tics can do a lot of damage and drive the poor things crazy, that's when you need to be on your game. When an animal is crazy with tics, you gotta be able to stay on ya horse and go like the clappers.' She laughed as she turned her horse around and rode off ahead of them.

Kirsty and Brigit looked at each other quizzically.

'I just don't get her?' whispered Kirsty, 'one minute she's a right bitch, next thing she's halfway human.'

Brigit agreed and they both spurred their

horses on to catch up with her. The girls discussed a plan to spread out and work their way out and around the herd, making sure they weren't leaving any behind. Sam took the lead.

'Kirsty you head out to the left and get in behind that mother and calf over there. Brigit you head out the other side and bring that lot slowly in towards me. I'll stay behind them and keep them moving forward. Keep watching for my signals okay.'

'Okay,' they chorused.

An hour into the ride all was going well so Sam signalled for the girls to stop for a break. They sat on the ground legs out-stretched in front of them to ease their stiff muscles and relax with their welcome cool drinks and biscuits.

'So when did you meet Jax?' Sam's blunt question broke the silence.

'About two years ago.'

'How long ya been married then?'

'Six months, why?' Brigit was starting to feel a little uncomfortable with Sam's questioning. It felt more like an inquisition.

'So how did he meet a sweet little Kiwi girl like you then. Have ya ever even been on a farm before?' she sneered.

'Actually we met at a stock conference in Canberra that my Dad and I came over to. And yes, I was born on a high-country sheep station in New Zealand. I've lived on a farm all my life and I've worked on the farm since I was old enough to sit on a horse with my father. I've done my fair share of sheep mustering,' she quipped defensively.

'Quite a catch is Jax. You broke some hearts when you married him you know.'

'Really? I didn't know that.'

'Was yours one of them?' asked Kirsty

Sam blushed and turned her head away saying nothing.

'Oh I'm sorry Samantha, I didn't know.'

'Yeah, whatever. Best we get back on the job eh.'

Brigit was a little taken aback.

'No wonder she's been so cool towards you,' Kirsty said to Brigit.

'Hope there's not going to be any ill feeling between us,' Brigit said, a little unnerved.

Samantha mounted her horse and started to round up the grazing stock and get them moving again. Brigit and Kirsty quickly drank some more water before joining her.

'She'll come around,' said Kirsty kindly, placing a comforting hand on Brigit's arm.

Sam called the homestead base on the satellite radio at regular intervals with an update. It was a vital safety check that everyone was required to do. The girls would be the first to reach the stock yards with their mob. Nick and Jasper's groups were further afield so they had a jeep each for back up and food supplies. Sid worked from the air. He had flown over the whole area in the fixed wing aircraft first thing that morning and had radioed stock locations back to Nick who was manning the radio. Nick then passed the information on to the men and women on the ground.

Sid had then flown back to the homestead and he and his foreman, Willem, had taken off in the two small helicopters to help with relocating staff and some of the stock round up. One of the helicopters was a four-seater which was used mainly for moving staff around and for emergencies. The more manoeuvrable two-seater was used for stock round up. It wasn't ideal as it stirred the cattle up, but it did save a lot of time. Once the cattle got close enough for the men on horseback to take over, the helicopters would back off and give the stock a chance to settle down before they reached the yards.

Sam, Kirsty and Brigit turned up with the first herd in good time. The stock were lead into the yards and left to settle while a couple of the men sat on the fence rails and studied them. Jax went over to help Brigit dismount.

'How'd it go?"

'Good. I really enjoyed it. So what happens now?'

'We'll be looking at the calves mainly, checking for males and females. The males will be separated from the group first. Any particularly good-looking bulls will be set aside, the rest will be penned up waiting to be loaded onto the trucks.'

By the time the last of the stock had been rounded up the place was alive with shouting workers, banging gates, bleating and crying stock and great clouds of red dust. Once all the male calves had been separated, the young females were put into another pen where they were checked for any diseases or deformities and then branded for identification.

'I thought you'd use ear tags,' said Brigit.

'We do that too for our own identification purposes but we have to brand all our stock in case they get into a neighbouring property. Makes it easier to identify them.'

The smell of burning hair wasn't pleasant and neither was seeing the animals jerk in pain as the hot iron was applied.

'They have strong hides and it only stings for a minute or two,' explained Jax defensively when he saw Brigit's face.

'How do you know that?' she winced as the young calf cried out.

'Come on Brig, you were born and raised on a farm, you know how it goes.'

'Yeah, I know. I absolutely hated docking time at home, and ear clipping, but I just had to accept it. Still hate seeing an animal in pain though,' she sighed heavily.

While the calves were being branded the adult female cattle were being sent down a chute where they were clamped into a device to keep them still while a man with a long rubber glove up to his arm pit tested them to see if they were in calf.

Brigit giggled at the sight.

'The herd tester. That is one job I never wanted to do,' she laughed.

'Gyno, meet Brigit,' said Jax.

'Gyno? Seriously? I love it,' Brigit was laughing fit to burst. 'Is your real title 'herd tester' like it is in NZ then?'

'Among other things, yeah.'

Brigit looked back across to the pens where the bull calves were.

'They are so darned cute aren't they,' she commented to Jax.

'Yeah, love the little buggars. Just a shame they have to go though. We will keep as many heifers as we can but too many bulls is too many bulls?'

The hot, tired, and thirsty round-up crews had straggled into the food tent as they arrived, and when the stockyard workers got a break from what they were doing, they headed to the tents too and made short work of the delicious food laid out on the trestle tables.

'Coming over for something to eat Brig?' Jax asked as they sat on one of the fence railings.

'Nah, I grabbed something earlier before all those hungry blokes tucked in. You go though, I'll wait here.'

'What about a coffee?'

'Sure, a coffee would be great thanks.'

Brigit watched him walk away towards the tent and was just about to turn her attention back to the yards when she spotted Sam pull herself off the pole she was leaning against and started walking towards him. Jax tried to ignore her but she grabbed his arm and pulled him round to make him look at her. Jax looked back over his shoulder to see if Brigit was watching but she quickly looked away. She couldn't resist looking back and she saw Jax grab Sam roughly by the arm and march her around the back of the food tent. At that point, Kirsty wandered over to the fence.

'How's it going Brig, enjoying your first muster?'

'Yes it's been a fantastic day, how about you?'

'I always love working out here in the outback, there's nothing quite like it,' she said as she climbed up to sit beside Brigit. 'Say, are you okay? Looks like something's bothering you. Where's Jax, is he looking after you?'

'He went off to get me some coffee but he got hijacked by Sam. I just saw them disappear round behind the tent.' Brigit tried to hide her concern.

'Want me to go and check on them for ya?' winked Kirsty conspiratorially. 'I'm sure it's nothing but perhaps they have some unfinished business. I heard a couple of the men talking before and from what I hear Sam used to work here a couple a years ago but she and Jax had a major falling out. Apparently, Samantha left and got another job hoping Jax would follow her, but he didn't.'

'Why would she want Jax to follow her? Were they that close?'

'Don't know, that's all I got, sorry.'

'It's okay Kirsty, thanks for telling me. Looks like she still has feelings for him doesn't it.'

'Hey Brig, he married you didn't he. He's in love with you, anyone can see that. I'll go do a bit of eavesdropping if you like.'

When Brigit didn't answer she said, 'I'll be back shortly, and with coffee.'

Brigit chewed on her thumb nail as she waited for Kirsty to come back. Was she being paranoid? Did Jax and Sam just need to clear the air or was there more to it?

Kirsty came back a short time later with coffee as promised.

'Well?' enquired Brigit eagerly.

'They were arguing. I couldn't really tell what it was about but it sounded as though they were planning to meet up later tonight. Maybe they just need to iron things out. Brig, please don't let this upset you, I'm sure it's all in the past, maybe they just need to get some closure or something.'

'Yes you are probably right, I'm sure there's nothing to worry about.' But that wasn't really how she felt as she watched Kirsty heading back to the tent.

Jax's voice broke through her thoughts sometime later.

'Sorry it took so long' he said handing her a steaming cup of coffee. 'Oh, you've already got one, good.'

'Yes, Kirsty brought me one. So what took you so long?'

'Oh just something I had to deal with. Just staff stuff, you know how it is.'

She wasn't sure she did, but now still wasn't the time to discuss it. Brigit watched the last of the double-decker, three trailered trucks pull out and turned her attention back to the cows and calves standing quietly in the yards waiting to be set free. The calves had been branded, the cows checked for fertility and all had been drenched and given the once over.

'Another muster over for another year,' Jax laughed as he came and sat with Brigit in the food tent. 'Look I've got some finishing up to do here. Dad's gonna fly you back home, there's no need for you to stick around here, not much for you to do anyway. I'll catch up with you later on tonight, okay.'

Brigit was relieved at not having to ride all the way back home but disappointed Jax wasn't coming with them. Then all of a sudden it got eerily dark and the air became electric.

'Damn,' exclaimed Sid as he dashed into

the tent. 'Thought we'd beat that storm out of here. Sorry Brig, we better stick around here till it passes over.'

A blinding flash of light filled the tent causing Brigit to jump. An almighty crash of thunder followed causing the ground to shudder beneath their feet. Brigit's heart was pounding.

'Is this normal?' she squeaked to no-one in particular.

'It's okay honey, these storms roll in sometimes, they're pretty wicked but they don't last long, it'll be over soon,' Jax pulled her onto his knee and cuddled her like a baby.

She giggled and snuggled into him allowing his manly sweaty smells to take her mind off the chaos going on around her. The rain was heavy and deafening. She glanced up and saw Sam glaring daggers at her and shuddered. Jax hugged her tighter.

'You okay honey?'

'Yep, all good,' she lied. 'This is like sitting under a giant waterfall,' she exclaimed peering out at the deep grey marauding clouds dumping their load unchecked on the dry earth. Then, almost as quickly as it started, the storm had passed over and the sun came out again. The clay was now sticky and wet but if there was no more rain it would be dry before long.

'Come on Brigit, we better get going,' said Sid.

He strapped Brigit into the chopper and as

they took off she could see Sam watching them. She waved to Brigit with a triumphant smirk on her face. Brigit's heart jumped, she was annoyed. Jealousy was beginning to rear its ugly head and she didn't like it. She had never had cause to be jealous of anyone in her life before so this was a new and unpleasant experience. She was distracted by Sid's voice in her headphone.

'Just going to check that the trucks made it out to the bitumen before the storm,' said Sid. 'Don't want them getting stuck and running behind on their schedules.'

They spotted one truck sitting idle on the side of the road, the rest seemed to have got through. Sid called the truckie up on his radio.

'You okay down there mate?' Yeah, all good Sid, just thought I'd double check me load, struck a bit of rough stuff coming through this last bit of track. Looks like everything is good to go. Thanks for checking though.'

'You're welcome Gazza, any time. If you guys run into any trouble be sure to give us a call, only too happy to help out if we can.'

'Thanks Sid, catch up again next year.'

'Sure thing,' said Sid signing off.

'I guess it's really important for people to keep in touch with each other in the outback,' Brigit said to Sid through her mouthpiece.

'Sure is, could mean life or death in some situations.'

'You ever been in any of those situations?'

'Unfortunately yes, once or twice. Remind me to tell you about it some time. There's home just up ahead. Tired?'

'Now that you ask, yes, I'm bloody exhausted,' she laughed, 'but happy. It's been an awesome experience.'

As soon as the helicopter touched ground she hopped out, turned and thanked Sid for bringing her home and walked slowly up to the house. She had a long refreshing shower, washed all the red dust out of her hair and put on fresh clean shorts and singlet top before going out to the kitchen and pouring herself a large cold crisp chardonnay.

She was sitting on the veranda enjoying her third glass of wine when Jax, Sam, Adam, Fred and Jasper turned up in the two jeeps. They had left the horses back at the yards to be brought back the next day. Nobody noticed Brigit on the veranda. They parked the jeeps and the men went into the community shed while Sam went off to her room. Brigit could see the men from where she was sitting. She watched as Jax sat down with his Uncles at the table and popped the tops off their bottles of beer. She decided not to interrupt them, she figured they probably wanted to talk about work anyway. She reached for her book and picked up where she left off. As she reached out for her wine glass a short time later her heart sank as she saw Sam appear, hair still wet from her shower and wearing very tight cut off shorts. She walked across to the shed and took a seat beside Jax pulling it up close. She put her hand along the back of his seat so she could play her fingers up an down his spine. He pulled forward away from her touch but Brigit hadn't missed it. It wasn't long after that that Jax excused himself and came up to the house. Brigit pretended she hadn't seen anything and Jax didn't say anything either.

That night after dinner Brigit headed to bed for an early night expecting Jax to follow. She sank gratefully into the soft pillows as Jax lay down beside her still fully clothed. He lay with his hands behind his head, deep in thought. Brigit started to drift off to sleep.

'You coming to bed hon?' she snuffled into her pillow.

Jax leaned over and kissed her on the forehead. 'No I'll leave you to sleep my darling, I've still got some paperwork to do.'

Brigit was disappointed but didn't say anything. Instead she just nodded and turned her head to the wall so he couldn't see the tears welling in her eyes. She lay awake for a while and was just drifting off back to sleep when she heard footsteps on the veranda stairs outside. She sat up on the side of the bed and looked out the window. It was dark now. She could see the accommodation block and the doors of the rooms facing into the courtyard, one of which was Sam's. A movement out the corner of her eye caught her attention. A figure was creeping around the shadows of the buildings, staying close to the walls almost as if they didn't want to be seen. She gasped when she saw it was Jax. He was heading for Samantha's room.

'Surely not,' she held her hand over her mouth as a bitter bile rose up in her throat.

He stopped outside Samantha's door looking over his shoulder to make sure he wasn't being watched. Brigit was sitting in the dark so he wouldn't have seen her watching him from the bedroom window. A shaft of light spilled out onto the doorstep as Sam opened the door for him to enter. Brigit was mortified. What was he up to? Surely they wouldn't sleep together. Maybe Kirsty was right, maybe they just needed to clear things up between them. But why would he creep around if that was the case. She got up and went out to the kitchen and made herself a coffee and sat at the kitchen table hoping Jax would soon reappear and tell her all about it. Sleep was now out of the question. After what seemed like an eternity, Brigit gave up waiting and decided to go down and see for herself what was going on. She made her way silently across the yard. The old ragged curtains on Samantha's bunkroom window didn't quite meet in the middle so Brigit was able to see inside. It was a small room, the same as the other single huts. It had two single beds a large dresser, two chairs and a table. She could see one bed, which was empty but as she angled herself around to see the other side of the room she had to stop herself from screaming. Samantha lay on her side with her naked back to the window. Her head was propped up on one arm. She was running her fingers up and down the abs of the naked man lying on his back beside her. Brigit couldn't see much of him but she knew it had to be Jax, she was devastated. Her knees went weak as she started to sink to the ground. She didn't want to get caught spying so she willed herself to move until she reached the homestead veranda and sank heavily down on the second step. She threw up over the railing and started to cry.

How could he? I can't believe it, this is unreal. She shook her head in disbelief and blindly made her way back into the house. It was another hour before Jax looked in on her. She feigned sleep so he quietly closed the door again and didn't return to their bed that night. At one point she heard him talking on the telephone.

Jax was gone when Brigit got up next morning. There was no note or anything to say where he was or how long he would be gone. She raced down to Samantha's bunkroom. It was empty.

'They must be off somewhere together,' she steamed.

She was so angry she grabbed some food and water without stopping for breakfast and headed out to the stables to go riding.

'I need to think,' she told herself.

Riding had always been her way of dealing with things when she was upset. About an hour later she stopped under some willows by a stream and had something to eat and drink. While she was paddling in the stream she felt as though someone was watching her but glancing around she couldn't see anybody so she put it down to her fragile emotional state playing tricks on her. She sat on the banks of the river for a while to think.

'What am I going to do about Jax and Sam?' she thought. Tears trickled down her cheeks. She was absolutely gutted at his betrayal and so soon after their wedding. She looked at her watch, it was almost lunchtime. She decided it was probably time she headed back. Perhaps Jax was home and they could talk, she thought hopefully.

She repacked the saddlebags and mounted her horse. Just as she was riding out from under the trees there was a loud 'thwack'. Her horse reared up and took off at an alarming pace in the opposite direction to the homestead. She hung on for dear life until the horse slowed down. When she tried to dismount her foot got caught up in the stirrup. She hopped on one leg cursing, trying to get her foot untangled. The horse was edgy and unsettled and kept moving around. Through gritted teeth Brigit snapped at the horse to stand still, realising too late that that was not the smartest thing to do to an already agitated horse. She lost her footing as the horse jumped and she was thrown to the ground with a thud. Her scream caused the horse to bolt once again, dragging Brigit along the ground over stones, through the bushes and the desert dust. Fortunately the extra weight of dragging Brigit slowed the horse down again and it eventually stopped. Brigit lay quiet for a moment, trying to gather her senses. Every inch of her body was screaming in pain. She talked quietly to the horse trying to soothe it and get it settled. She would need it to get her back home. Nobody knew she was out here. With tears of pain and frustration running down her face she kept talking to the horse until she felt it was calm enough for her to release her foot from the stirrup without startling it again. The adrenalin was pumping keeping her mind clear but the pain was excruciating. She bit down so hard on her lip to stop herself from screaming that she drew blood. Finally her foot came free and she lay back down on the ground exhausted, and took stock of where the worst pain was and what possible injuries she might have. The most painful of all was her ankle.

'Damn, must be broken,' she decided.

She gingerly rolled over onto her stomach and pushed herself up on her knees ignoring the flashes of fiery pain ripping through her. She reached up for Shy's reins and pulled herself up balancing on one leg. Giddiness threatened to overcome her but she leaned against her horse hanging on tightly to the saddle until it passed. It was a long and painful process but with the horse now calmed down and sensing Brigit needed it's help, she managed to drag herself up across the mares back and swing around into the saddle. She reached around and took the water bottle from the saddle bag and had a good long drink and waited for her head to clear. It was throbbing so much she wondered if she might have concussion. She tied the reins around her wrists and then to the pommel, lay herself along Shy's neck and whispered, 'home girl, take me home.' Then everything went black.

A sudden commotion brought her round.

'Brigit, thank God what's happened to you?'

It was Ruth, the station nurse.

'Ruth? What are you doing here?' she mumbled.

'Fred saw the state you were in when your horse arrived back in the yard and called me straight away. Sid's standing by with the plane to take you to Darwin.

'Where am I, where's Jax?' She tried to sit up but the pain brought her back down again.

'You're at home in your bed. Jax had to go to Darwin on urgent business early this morning, he'll meet us at the hospital.'

'Was Sam with him?'

'I don't know why?'

'No reason.' She lay back down and allowed herself to be carried out to the waiting aircraft. It was uncomfortable and extremely painful but Brigit was almost oblivious to the physical pain as she began to conjure up visions of her beloved Jax off somewhere with Sam.'

Sid and Ruth were sitting beside Brigit's hospital bed when Jax arrived later that afternoon. They left to get some coffee and to give Jax and Brigit some time alone.

'Brigit, bloody hell what's happened to you?'

'Something, or someone, spooked my horse. My ankle is broken, they are setting it in plaster as soon as the swelling goes down,' she sobbed.

As Jax reached down to give her a hug she cried out in pain.'

'What the hell?'

'She's covered in cuts and bruises and has a nasty bang on her head. She was dragged some considerable distance,' said the nurse who came running into the room when she heard Brigit scream.

'Dragged? You were dragged? Oh my darling I am so sorry.' He gently picked up her hand and kissed it. 'How bad is it? How soon can we get you home so I can look after you?'

'Do you really want me home Jax?' she

snuffled between sobs.

'Whatdya mean do I want you home? Of course I do. What a silly thing to say.'

The nurse quietly left the room.

'What is it honey, what's the matter?'

Tears were streaming down her face.

'I saw you Jax, I saw you and Samantha in bed together. Last night. I bloody saw you. How could you?'

'What? It wasn't me, how could you think I would sleep with Sam?'

'I saw you go to her room last night and you didn't come home so I know it was you.'

'Yeah explain that Jax?' Sam was standing in the doorway smiling smugly.

'What the hell are you doing here?' he demanded.

'Nice. What's got up your nose. You were happy enough to see me last night.'

'Get out!' he raged. 'Get the hell out of here, NOW.'

Samantha shrugged and sauntered off.

'What's she doing here Jax, did she come with you? Your Dad said you had to come here on urgent business.'

'I did sweets, there's a problem with some of the stock we loaded for Indonesia. I had to come and deal with it. I left a note for you on the kitchen table. And no Sam didn't come with me, I have no idea how she got here. Probably talked Willem into flying her, he was always pretty sweet on her. Look, I've got to get back to the port, but please Brigit, don't stress over this, I can explain everything okay. I love you so much, this is not going to come between us, I promise.'

'It already has Jax.'

'Please don't say that,' he groaned.

Sid came back into the room. 'Sorry to do this to you Brigit but Jax and I have to go. We've got a plane to catch to Indonesia.

Jax was disappointed. 'Be right with you Dad.' Turning back to Brigit, 'look hon, please don't believe anything that Sam says. I'll see you as soon as I can okay.' And he was gone.

Later that night Brigit stirred and became aware of someone standing at the foot of her bed. It was hard to make out who it was. She couldn't see their face because the room was dark and the light of the open door was behind them.

'Jax?'

'Sorry honey it's not your lovely husband, it's only me.'

'Samantha? What are you still doing here?'

'Just come to see how you're doin. How's the head? Enjoy the ride did we? I didn't expect you to get dragged, I only meant to scare you really. The dragging bit was a bonus. Puts you out of action while I work on Jax.'

'What do you mean work on him?'

'I'll get him back honey and there's nothing you can do about it. I have a hold over him that you can't even begin to compete with so you might as well give up now.'

'Why did you leave him in the first place and why wait all this time to come back. Why wait until he got married.'

'Well, you see, everyone thought I'd gone down south to another job but in fact I was serving time in prison. For Jax.'

'What!'

'Yep. Your sweet innocent man committed a crime that I took the rap for and now he owes me, big time.'

'I don't believe you. How come nobody knows about it.'

'Because I never told anyone. I went to the cops, made a full confession and took the rap on my own all because of my love for Jax. Had his baby while I was in prison too so honey you ain't got a shit show in hell of hangin on to him. Best walk away while you can still walk. Hang around here and there will be more little accidents, if you catch my drift.'

With that she picked up her jacket from the bed rail flung it over her shoulder and walked out. Brigit rang the bell for the night nurse.

'I'm going to be sick' she gasped. The nurse grabbed a bowl from the shelf beside the bed and held it out for Brigit, gently stroking her head.

'Do you have a headache?' she asked.

'Yes I have now.'

'Gosh you're trembling, what's happening, here let me check your vitals.'

'I'll be okay, I just had a visit from a really nasty lady, she just frightened the hell out of me that's all'

'Oh, you mean your sister?'

'My sister!' she spat

'That girl, Samantha who just left, said she was your sister. She's been hanging around most of the day. She said your husband was responsible for your accident and not to let him see you.'

'That girl is definitely not my sister,' she yelled, fury building up inside her. She clutched at her throbbing head. 'That girl is pure evil, I don't want her anywhere near me. She is the one who caused the accident, not my husband.'

'Oh dear, I will put the record straight with the staff. I'm sorry Brigit we should have checked with you first. She was very convincing you know.'

'Yes so I am beginning to find out.'

'Do you want me to get hold of your husband for you?'

'No it's late and I'm really not feeling up to it right now.'

'I'll get you something to help you sleep.'

As the nurse turned away from the bed her foot kicked a ball of paper lying on the floor.

'Oh, is this yours?'

She handed the crumpled ball to Brigit

and left the room.

Brigit opened it up and smoothed it out. She reached up to turn on the light above her bed, wincing at the pain. She gasped when she saw the handwriting, it was Jax's.

"Good morning sweetheart, you were sleeping so soundly when I came in last night I left you in peace. I had to head off to Mum and Dad's first thing, there's a problem with some of the stock we sent up to Darwin for the Indonesia export and Dad wants me to go up with him and sort it out. I might be gone a day or two but I will phone you as soon as I can. I love you. Jax"

The paper trembled in Brigit's hand. 'Oh my God, this must have fallen out of Samantha's pocket. Or maybe she left it here on purpose for me to find. How did she get it? Was she in the house with Jax last night? Our house?' A myriad of horrible images were coursing their way through Brigit's already overworked brain. The nurse reappeared with some sleeping tablets and pain killers which Brigit eagerly threw down and followed with a big gulp of water. She just wanted this nightmare to end.

Ruth appeared at her bedside shortly after Sam left.

'Are you okay honey, you look dreadful.'

'Samantha has just been here, she said some pretty disturbing things about her and Jax. I don't know whether to believe them or not.'

'I thought you knew about Samantha,'

said Ruth, a little alarmed, 'I thought Jax would have told you about her'

'Knew what about her? I only just met her yesterday and since then my life has turned upside down.'

'Tell me what she said,' demanded Ruth.

Brigit related almost word for word what Samantha had said, after all it had been burned into her soul like a hot iron.

'I honestly don't know the full story Brigit,' Ruth said kindly, all I know is that they had a big fight a few years ago and she left in a huff. Sid and Janet never liked her but she was a good worker. Anyway she suddenly up and left after the fight and apparently she got a job down south. I think she thought Jax might follow her but Sid and Janet put a stop to that and I doubt Jax would have gone anyway. Samantha never meant that much to him. As for the rest of the stuff about her covering up a crime for Jax and going to jail and having his baby, well my guess is that's all a load of bull dust. Wait and talk to Jax when he gets back, I'm sure he will put your mind at ease.'

Brigit shook her head. 'She threatened me Ruth, she's already admitted she spooked my horse and she said if I didn't get out of the way that more accidents would happen. She scares the shit out of me, she really does, there's something not right about her. Ruth, will you do something for me please?'

'Sure honey, what is it?'

'Can you get back to the house and pack a bag for me. I'm not going back there. I wanna go home to Dad as soon as I'm allowed out of here.'

'Brig..'

'Don't argue with me Ruth, please.'

'Don't let this girl get the better of you Brigit, you're better than that. Samantha has a way of manipulating people.'

'And she's very good at it.'

'Why don't you stay and get this sorted out. The family will protect you, I'm sure once they hear what she's done she will be kicked off the property.'

'See that's the thing. I reckon she will fight back, if she's capable of revelling in my being dragged along by a horse she has just spooked, what else is she capable of. Even if half of what she said is lies, it just shows where her head is at. I'm tired and sore Ruth, I just don't have any fight left in me at the moment.'

'No of course you don't honey, I'm sorry. Maybe some time at home with your Dad will do you good. Jax can sort things out with Samantha while you do some convalescing and get your strength back. Look, if Willem did bring Samantha to Darwin I'll see if he's still here and he can take me back tonight. I'll explain to Janet that you are homesick and that you just want to be with your Dad right now and she can explain that to Jax and Sid when they get back from

Indonesia.'

'Thanks Ruth, I don't know what I would do without you.'

'You're welcome sweetheart. Give me a list of what you want and where to find it and I'll pack what I can and see you in the morning.'

As Ruth was heading for the door folding the list to put in her handbag Brigit called to her.

'Ruth,'

'Yeah'

'Come with me.'

'What?'

'Come to New Zealand with me. You've never been there have you?'

'Umm, I went to Auckland once but that was only for a week on business.'

'Then what's stopping you. Tell Janet that I will need a nurse to accompany me on the plane or something.'

Ruth smiled. 'I don't think I need to come up with an excuse, I'm sure they will be only too happy to let me come with you.'

She came back to Brigit's bedside and leaned over and kissed her on the forehead.

'See you in the morning sweetheart. Try and get some sleep okay.'

The nurse appeared then and gave Brigit two sleeping tablets. 'Figured you could use a good night's sleep,' she said.

When Brigit woke up the next morning,

the sun was trying to break into her room through the thin pale yellow curtains. She lay back listening to the black crows cawing outside, trying to ignore the pain and the unnerving flashbacks of the previous day's events.

'About time you woke up sleepyhead.'

Brigit glanced towards the voice and saw Ruth sitting in the visitor's chair. 'Ruth, what time is it?'

'It's just gone ten o'clock. The Doctor has been and done his rounds and you've missed breakfast. It was yummy too,' she laughed.

Brigit smiled weakly. 'Did the Doctor say when I can leave?'

'He said your cast has set nicely but he didn't want to disturb you to check your back and head. He said he'd be back when he'd finished the rest of his rounds. I told him you wanted to fly home to New Zealand. He wasn't that keen on the idea but in the end, when he knew I would be going with you, he gave the okay on the condition that you travel first class. I've been on the phone to Sid this morning, he's insisted on paying for our airfares. Of course there's no first class on this trip so he's flying us business class, both ways.

'Both ways?'

'Yes, for when we come back.'

'I may not be coming back Ruth.'

Ruth's face dropped, her mouth hung open.

'What? Not coming back, why? Look Jax sends his love, he didn't want me to wake you but said he would fly over to see you as soon as he can.'

'I don't want him to Ruth. I don't want him to come over to see me.'

'Why on earth not? What's happened?'

'After that visit from Samantha last night I've decided she's too much for me to compete with. That girl is evil and I want to get as far away from her as possible. I have never met anyone like her in my life, she terrifies me.'

'Brigit, that girl is obviously unbalanced and delusional, don't let her scare you off, don't give her the satisfaction.'

'If I wasn't in so much pain and if Jax had warned me about her maybe I would stay and fight but if it's true that she has a baby with Jax then I won't get in his way. Honestly, right now, I feel so freakin rat-shit all I want to do is go home and lie around the pool in the sun with my family around me.' She managed a weak smile and said, 'I am so glad you're coming with me.'

'I'm looking forward to coming with you too Brigit. In fact I'm getting really excited about it. I have a good feeling about this trip, nothing I can put my finger on, but it feels right. I just wish we weren't going under such sad and difficult circumstances. I wish you could get this mess sorted out with Jax first.'

'Wish I could too. I wish I could get

excited about the trip, but right now I'm just too tired and homesick, I just want to go home and see my Daddy.' She burst into tears.

'I'm not surprised you are tired young lady,' smiled the Doctor as he walked brusquely into the room. 'Now come on dry those tears,' he said handing her a tissue from the box on her bedside table. Let's try and get you sitting up as gently as we can so we can have a look at those bruises and cuts on your back shall we.'

Holding on to the Doctor's strong arm, Brigit gingerly pulled herself forward, trying not to moan as the skin pulled tight across her wounds.

'Ah, that's looking better than I hoped. You will have some nasty bruises for a while but the cuts are healing over nicely, no sign of infection. Now, let's have a look at your head.' The Doctor felt around for lumps then shone his light into her eyes.

'Any dizziness or blurred vision?' She shook her head. 'Nurse said you had a headache last night, still got it?'

'No it's gone now and I had a good sleep.'

'Good. Well let's just keep you in here under observation for another night seeing as you are planning on leaving the country.'

'Thank you Doctor.'

He smiled. 'You're welcome, see you in the morning.'

Brigit smiled across at Ruth. 'Looks like

we can go tomorrow. Have you checked out the flights yet?'

'Sure have. We will get in to Melbourne around 7.30pm. We can stay the night close to the airport and catch the 9.30am flight to Queenstown next day. Pity we can't fly direct.'

'Yeah, it's a long way but I really don't mind the stop over. I'm sure the break will do me good.'

'I'll order wheelchairs at all the airports.' Ruth was scribbling on her note pad.

'Aahh nup, ain't goin in no wheelchair, sorry.'

'Aah well ain't goin on no airplane if ya don't.' Ruth shot a determined glance at Brigit over her glasses. 'I mean it Brigit, I think you will appreciate it when the time comes.'

Brigit stuck out her bottom lip in an effort to look pouty which only caused Ruth to laugh.

'Have you any idea how silly you look young lady. You do pouty very well.'

Brigit's face broke into a beaming smile. 'Okay Miss bossy boots, you win. Anyone would think you were my mother.'

'Would that be so bad - for now.'

'Actually it would be nice having a motherly figure telling me what to do for a change. I never really had that with Dad, he was always so indulgent. If it wasn't for dear old Gracie keeping a firm hand on me I might have turned into a real brat.'

Chapter Six

Time Out

'Would all passengers on Flight NZ7477 please make your way to Gate four, your flight will begin boarding in fifteen minutes.

'That's us,' Brigit said casting around as if looking for someone.

'Jax won't be here honey, he's stuck in Indonesia.'

'I know, I was just a bit nervous that Samantha might show up.'

'You really are spooked by her aren't you.'

'Well she's such a weirdo I don't know what to expect.'

Once settled comfortably in their seats Brigit stretched out with a sigh and was soon sound asleep with Ruth keeping one eye on her and one eye on the magazine she was hoping to read.

'Excuse me miss, it's time to get you set up for landing.'

'Oh, are we there already?' said Brigit gently stretching out her cramped limbs.

'Yes, you slept soundly all the way. Looks

like you've been in an accident.'

'Yes I fell off my horse and got dragged. Bit sore, but I'll survive, good Kiwi stock and all that. Where's Ruth?' Brigit looked around anxiously.

'It's okay, she's just gone to the loo.' Brigit let out her held in breath and smiled weakly at the hostess.

'Sorry, it's been a rough few days.'

'Oh you poor thing,' she soothed, 'Is there anything I can get you before we land?'

'No, I'm all good. Thanks.'

Ruth came back and settled into her seat. She reached across, grabbed Brigit's hand and gave it an excited squeeze.

'Can't believe we are really doing this,' she enthused.

'Me neither,' smiled Brigit, 'me neither.'

She turned and looked out the window taking in the lights of Melbourne as they came in to land. They spent the night at the luxury Parkroyal Hotel close to the airport and indulged in a sumptuous meal, fine wine and a private jacuzzi before falling into bed and welcome dreamless sleep. Both women were bright eyed and bushy tailed next morning as they ate breakfast in their rooms and waited for their car to arrive.

'I am so excited I can hardly wait,' gushed Brigit.

'I haven't seen you look this happy in days, this was a good idea of yours to come home. I'm sure it will do you the world of good. Oh and listen, all that stuff you told me about Samantha and your accident, can I tell Jax and Sid. I'm sure they'd want to know.'

Brigit hesitated. 'I think I'd rather tell Jax face to face myself. I'm not sure he'd believe me, I want to see the expression on his face when I tell him.'

Oh I'm sure he would believe you.'

'No' demanded Brigit, 'I'll tell him when I think the time is right. He's pretty distracted with the export stuff at the moment anyway.'

'You know what, let's not dwell anymore on Jax or Samantha. I'm going home and my bestest buddy is coming with me so let's just forget everything else and have some FUN.'

'Bestest buddy huh? I like that, cheers.' They clinked their coffee cups and finished off their breakfast.

Luke was at Queenstown airport to meet them. He broke down when he saw his battered, broken daughter.

'Oh my poor baby, what's happened to you,' he cried.

'Dad, shush, people are staring. I fell off my horse. I'll tell you all about it later, let's just get out of here. Oh and Dad, this is Ruth, my guardian angel.'

'Hi Ruth, guardian angel, smiled Luke. 'Welcome to New Zealand.' He glanced around, 'where's Jax?'

'He's on business in Indonesia, couldn't come.' Brigit quickly brushed over the question and changed the subject. 'Oh I had forgotten how gorgeous the Remarkables are, even without snow, and the air is so fresh.' She took a deep breath and let it out in a long satisfied sigh. 'God it's so good to be home,' she said as she limped her way out of the airport to the waiting car, not giving her father a chance to ask any more questions.

'I had no idea she was hurt,' Luke whispered to Ruth as he was putting the suitcases in the car. Brigit was off to one side looking up at the mountains.

'Sorry Luke, I thought she'd contacted you.'

'She did text me but all it said was *coming home, need a break, explain later, see you soon,*' he hissed. 'We'd better stop off and get some pillows and a blanket to try and make her as comfortable as we can, it's quite a haul up to the farm.'

They stopped at the shopping mall beside the airport.'

'Why didn't you tell me you were on crutches Brig, I could have arranged for a helicopter to pick you up or something. Luke was still annoyed that he hadn't been advised of Brigit's injuries.

'Dad please stop fussing, I'll be fine, I am just happy to be home.'

'Well I'm absolutely stoked you're here, but I'm gutted it has to be under these circumstances. Sorry Ruth, I don't mean to be such a grouch. I'm just shocked to see my girl like this.'

'I understand' she smiled warmly, 'but I can assure you she has been in good hands.'

Luke visibly relaxed and placed his hand on Ruth's arm. 'I'm sure she has and thank you, I really appreciate you coming all this way with her.' They were standing at the back of the car out of earshot.

'It's my pleasure Luke, I'm very fond of Brigit. She's become like a daughter to me over these past months.'

They both climbed into their front seats and buckled up. Luke looked over his shoulder at Brigit. 'You comfortable my darling?'

'Yes Dad,' she sighed, please stop fussing and take me home.'

'Yes *ma'am,*' he chuckled as he turned the key in the ignition.

Luke and Ruth talked nonstop all the way to the farm, which suited Brigit. She was free to stare longingly out the window at all the wonderful imposing mountains she had grown up with and loved with a passion. She'd missed them. She allowed silent tears to roll down her cheeks as nostalgia and the events of the previous few days took their toll. Unfortunately her mind kept going back to what Samantha had told her in the hospital.

Just how much of a hold did Samantha really have on Jax? After all he did sleep with her. And then there's the baby. Oh God I can't compete with a baby. He never said anything about a baby, I wonder if he even knows ? How long should I stay away? Will he even want me back?

She gazed out at the impressive walls of Skippers Canyon. She knew every bend on the winding narrow road, the shape of every hill and all the places where she could get a glimpse of the stream way down below in the rocky gorge. She'd spent much of her childhood roaming the Skippers Canyon on horseback, sometimes alone, but more often than not, with her father. They would camp down by the river or up on a hillside with just bedrolls, sleeping bags, a bit of food and a couple of thermoses of hot water for coffee. Sleeping under the stars was a passion they shared. No one else was ever invited to join them and they never told anyone where they were going. It was their little secret. Brigit giggled at the thought.

'Home, thank God I'm home,' she sighed.

'Maybe we could invite Ruth on one of our secret escapades sometime Dad. When I'm up to it.'

'I thought that was our secret Brig?' She could see him smiling at her in the rear-view mirror.

'Well, maybe we could make an exception,

just this once.'

'Okay by me,' he responded.

By the time they arrived at the farm Stella, Rees, Selwyn and Sandra were standing outside the homestead waiting for them. They'd seen the dust from the vehicle coming from miles away.

'Where's Lucy Dad?' asked Brigit scanning the welcome home committee.

'Umm, we had a bit of a parting of the ways.'

'Oh dear, how sad, not,' smiled Brigit. 'Glad she's gone, I really couldn't like her you know.'

'Yes Brigit I do know. I couldn't put up with her petty jealousies and insecurities anymore either. Who needs a self-centred diva when you have a farm to run eh.'

They came to a stop outside the house and as the welcoming committee gathered round Brigit's door Luke had to jump out and stand guard to make sure nobody caused his precious girl any more pain than she was already in.

'Guys, guys please. I know you are excited to see Brigit but her leg has just been put in plaster. She's just come out of hospital and needs to take it easy for a few days. Oh and this is her nurse, sorry, guardian angel, Ruth.'

'Hi Ruth.' they chorused.

'Hi guys.' Ruth smiled and greeted everyone finally putting a face to the names of the people she'd heard so much about.

Luke carried Brigit very gently into the lounge where Sandy had raced ahead and set up some pillows on the couch to rest Brigit's plastered leg.

'What happened honey?' asked Sandy.

'You don't have to fuss guys, PLEASE, and I don't really want to talk about it right now, okay,' pleaded Brigit.

'Sorry kiddo, you don't come home lookin like that and expect us not to go overboard and ask questions,' laughed Luke.

The others heartily agreed. Brigit just glared at her father in defiance.

'We're gonna bug the hell out of ya Sis,' laughed Rees as he leant over and gave her a kiss on the top of her head in a rare show of affection.

'Mwaaa,' said Stella, 'ain't you the softy Rees.' She got down on her knees beside Brigit. 'Can I give you a gentle hug? I have missed you so much and God you look awful.'

'Thanks little sister, I love you too.' She allowed Stella to hug her trying not to wince in pain.

Once the greetings were over and Sandy and Ruth had sorted out the bedrooms, everyone gathered in the lounge for a catch up over wine and snacks. They chatted away for a while, talking about what was happening on both Duffield Station and Bullock Creek Station in Australia. Ruth was prompted to tell her story too which she felt a little uncomfortable about.

She wasn't used to being quite as open as this family seemed to be. Finally the conversation got around to the elephant in the room, Brigit's injuries.

'Ruth looked across at Brigit, 'You okay to talk about it now hon, or would you like me to.'

'No, I'm all good, ta. There's nothing much to tell really. I went out for an early morning ride and...'

'What were you doing riding out there on your own,' demanded Luke.

'Oh Dad, don't fuss, it's okay I stayed within sight of the house.'

'Clearly it wasn't okay though was it. Do you often go off on your own?'

'No, not normally. There was no-one around that morning and I really wanted to go riding. I used to go off riding on my own all the time here, remember?'

'Yes I do remember and it used to worry the hell out of me. I never stopped worrying until I saw you tearing down the hill flat out on that poor old mare of yours.'

Everyone laughed and turned back to Brigit for more of her story.

'I was just a little out of sorts and needed to clear my head so I went riding, that's all. Anyway, I stopped down by a river for a little while and then when I remounted my horse I heard a 'thwack' sound and the horse took off.'

'A what sound?' laughed Rees.

'Oh shut up Rees.' Brigit threw a pillow at him then winced with the pain the sudden action caused.

'Yeah shut up Rees and let Brig get on with her story, it's almost time to dish up dinner,' scolded Stella.

'Smells like roast mutton, is it?' he asked wrinkling his nose to capture the delicious aromas emanating from the kitchen.

'Sure is. We knew Brigit would love a good old mutton roast, isn't that right,' smiled Sandy.

'Absolutely. My favourite, I've missed it actually. Ruth, you think you've tasted mutton in Aussie, but wait till you taste ours, it is sooo much better.'

'Can we pleeeese get back to the story,' pleaded Stella.

'Okay, well…,' just then the phone rang.

'Ruth, it's Sid for you,' called Sandy from the kitchen.

Brigit carried on with her story cutting out everything except the basic facts of her stay in hospital. When Ruth reappeared Brigit asked, 'everything alright?'

'Yes, that was Sid just making sure we arrived okay. Jax is still in Indonesia but otherwise everything is okay. I'm just going to give Sandy a hand with dinner.'

They decided to have dinner on their laps instead of at the large rimu dining room table. That way Brigit could join in instead of being left on her own in the lounge. Stella and Rees sat on the stoops either side of the schist rock fireplace while the others sat in the large comfortable arm chairs spread around in a sociable semi-circle facing the large TV cabinet which took up the whole corner of the room. They watched the news in silence apart from the odd comment on a particular news item.

When the sporting highlights came on, Brigit sat back and looked around the comfortable familiar room. Now though, she could see the ageing décor, the old dark brown curtains and the dated pale cream wallpaper with gold stripes that Brigit had grown up with. Before she had a chance to suggest that new wallpaper and curtains might be a good idea Stella caught her attention.

'So how's Jax, what's he think about you leaving him behind? Why didn't he come with you?' She was full of questions.

'Oh there's a bit of a crisis with the livestock export contract so Sid and Jax had to fly to Indonesia to sort it out,' she said quickly. 'He may follow on later, just depends how busy they are. They haven't got time to fuss over an invalid right now that's why I decided to come home for a while. Perfect opportunity for a catch up, right? And besides, it was a chance for me to do something nice for Ruth. She runs around looking after everyone else on the farm and she's been an absolute godsend to me so this is for her too,' she winked at Ruth.

'Thanks Brigit, Janet and Sid send their love by the way. I am so enjoying this trip already. The scenery I've seen so far is breathtaking.'

'Ah but wait, there's more,' laughed Luke.' Do you ride?'

'Of course, I was an outback brat before I became a nurse.'

'Good. How would you like to take a look around the property?'

'Love to.'

'Great. How long are you planning on staying? I'd like to spend some time with Brigit first so perhaps in a day or two?'

'You're on, thank you. We haven't actually set a time limit on this trip, our tickets are open ended. It's really up to Brigit and her recovery, we'll let her call the shots on this.'

Brigit mirrored Ruth's warm smile with gratitude.

Sandra caught Brigit's eye and gave her a secret thumbs up and got an ok sign in return at the prospect of Ruth and Luke hitting it off. Brigit went to bed that night with something else to think about. *How cool would it be if Dad and Ruth got together. They are well suited. Better than me and Jax.* The tears started up again and she cried herself to sleep.

When she awoke in the morning it took her a moment to get her bearings. The beautiful birdsong of the Thrush made her smile. It wasn't the usual morning greeting of the Australian black crows.

'Home, I'm back home,' she smiled and gingerly stretched before sitting up and gently placing her feet on the floor. The sheepskin rug beneath her feet felt so familiar and comforting as did the pale-yellow wallpaper with the same old bluebell pattern she had woken up to all her life.

'Oh Dad, you really must get this place re-wallpapered,' she sighed reaching for her dressing gown. She set herself up on her crutches and clumsily made her way out to the kitchen to be greeted with the delicious smell of bacon and eggs cooking on the green and cream enamel coal range. The old, blackened coffee pot with the stained glass lid was bubbling away to one side. Luke leapt up to help her to the table.

'Morning darling, how did you sleep?'

'Like a log. God it's good to be home.' She put her hand on her father's brown weathered one and gave him a tear-filled smile.

Luke leaned over and kissed her on the forehead. Ruth walked in at that moment.

'Mind if I join you? Hope I'm not interrupting.'

'Not at all,' they chorused.

'Bacon and eggs?' asked Luke.

'Yes please, I could eat a horse.'

'Sorry, we don't eat horses here,' he

laughed.

Ruth, Luke and Brigit sat and chatted over coffee before Ruth excused herself to go take a shower.

'So what do you think of Ruth then?' asked Brigit.

'Yeah, she seems really lovely. I like her.'

'Good,' said Brigit. 'I do too.'

Luke smiled knowingly but didn't say anything to alert Brigit to the fact that he knew she was probably thinking about matchmaking.

As promised, Luke spent the next two days totally devoted to his beloved daughter. Brigit decided not to tell her Dad about Jax and Samantha until she'd had a chance to talk things over with Jax first. She didn't want to worry him, she just wanted to enjoy being at home and try to forget everything else for a few days.

On the third day Luke and Ruth left for their ride after morning tea. Brigit, Stella and Rees were sitting around the in-ground pool on cushioned lounge chairs chatting when the phone rang. Stella jumped up to answer it. She brought the phone out to the poolside.

'Brig, it's for you. It's Jax.'

Brigit reached a shaking hand out to take the phone.

'Can you guys give me a little privacy for a few minutes please? Sorry, don't mean to be rude.'

'Of course, come on Rees, let's go make

some sandwiches.'

'Hello.'

'Brigit! God, how are you? I'm so sorry I didn't get to see you before you left. Couldn't you have waited for me in Darwin? I would have come with you.' He sounded annoyed, angry.

'Well Jax, when I saw you in bed with Samantha, I figured I was surplus to requirements and would probably get in the way. I wasn't going to be much use to you laid up in a cast for a while anyway so I came home,' she snapped back.

There was a stunned silence on the other end, then, 'In bed with Samantha, what are you talking about?'

'I woke up and looked out the window the other night and saw you creeping around to her hut. Is it over between us Jax? Just tell me. If you want her back just tell me and you will never see me again.'

Brigit thought she could hear Jax crying.

'Baby, please, I tried to tell you, it wasn't me you saw with Samantha, it must have been Stacey. Yes I went to see her but only to tell her to leave. There's nothing between us, honestly, she's bad news Brig, she really is. Please, please don't let her come between us. Look, how about I come down to see you. Please baby, I need to see you. I really miss you and you are so broken at the moment. I just want to look after you.' He was sobbing now and Brigit's heart went out to him.

'Well, if that's true you need to sort some stuff out with her. She's threatened me and says she will do everything she can to break us up. I'm frightened of her Jax. Did you know that she was in prison?'

'Prison? What? Where did you hear that?'

'She came to see me in the hospital. Said she'd had your baby in prison too.'

'Jesus Christ' he hissed. 'Okay, I'll sort this out. It sounds like a load of shit to me. Look, I'll talk it over with Mum and Dad and we'll do some digging, see what we can come up with. I promise you I will put this thing to bed one way or another. Sorry, bad choice of words,' he laughed through his tears.

Brigit let out her breath, relaxing a little as the news that it wasn't Jax who she saw in bed with Samantha that night, finally settled in her mind.

'Okay,' she decided, 'you go sort things out then maybe come down and see me. Oh, and Jax...'

'Yeah?'

'Be careful eh, she's a real piece of work.'

'You're telling me?' he said bitterly. Look, I knew she had her faults but I never saw this coming. Thank God I've got uncles and family and staff to back me up eh.'

'For sure. Good luck and keep me in the loop okay.'

'Will do. Love you babe.'

'Love you too,' she whispered as she slowly hung up the phone.

'Everything okay?' asked Stella as she and Rees appeared in the doorway with cold drinks trying to appear as if they hadn't been listening at the door. The ice chinked in the glass as Brigit reached for the orange juice being offered her.

'It is now' she sighed. 'Well almost anyway.'

Brigit filled them in on what had been going on, then asked them not to say anything to Luke, just for now. She wanted to wait until she'd got the full story from Jax. Then they could fill everyone in on all the details at the same time.

Stella, Rees and Brigit spent the next week lounging around the pool reading, playing board games, listening to their favourite music and chatting. Brigit was annoyed that she wasn't able to join the others in the pool and had to be content with being splashed occasionally by Rees. Luke and Ruth spent every day together and seemed to be getting quite close. Brigit was thrilled to see their relationship grow.

Jax turned up on the doorstep unexpectedly two weeks later catching everyone by surprise. Brigit squealed with delight when she saw him. She swung over towards him as fast as her crutches would allow and dropped into his welcoming arms.

'God I've missed you, why didn't you call

me?'

'I've missed you too babe, more than you will ever know. Sorry I didn't call, it's been a bit of a nightmare but I'm here now and everything is finally sorted.

'Really?' asked Brigit hopefully.

'Really,' he smiled, but he looked pale and worn out.

'How did you get out here?' asked Luke. 'You should have rung us, we would have come in and got you.'

'I wanted to surprise Brigit.'

'Well you sure did that. Here take a load off, you look beat. Wanna cold beer?'

'Yes please,' sighed Jax sinking into a dining room chair. 'It's been a rough couple of weeks.'

Once Jax had time to catch his breath and settle in he and Brigit went off to her room to get some privacy. They lay down on her bed together and talked.

'So tell me what happened. How did it go with Samantha?'

Jax turned away for a moment trying to hide the tears forming in his eyes.

'Babe, what is it? What happened?'

'Oh Brig, it was awful, really awful. It's a long story and I don't want to bore you with the details.'

'Jax, I want to know all the details, I need to know. We're in this together.'

He turned back and looked deep into her eyes.

'Do you have any idea how much I love you Mrs Jamieson? I was terrified I might lose you through all this? It's been so lonely without you these past few weeks, I don't ever want us to be apart again, ever, not even for one night, okay.'

She snuggled into him and placed a protective arm across his stomach.

'Okay Mr Jamieson, it's a deal. I'm sorry it's all been so rough on you. Hasn't been much of a picnic for me either.'

'I know babe, that's the bit that hurts the most. You know it was her who caused your horse to bolt eh.'

'Yeah she told me. She also came inside our house and took the letter you left for me on the table. I didn't know where you were. I only knew you had been with her that night, or at least I thought it was you, and I was really upset. That's why I went for a ride. To think things over. So what happened?'

'She was in a psychiatric unit down in Adelaide.'

'What? A nut house?' exclaimed Brigit raising herself up on one elbow so she could look down into Jax's face. Why? I knew she was a bit weird but not that crazy.'

'Turns out she hadn't been in prison at all, although it probably seemed that way to her. And no there is no baby. Thank God. When she left after we broke up she apparently went back to Adelaide to her family. She told them that I was going to follow her, that I just had to tidy up my affairs on the farm and then I would come down and we would go travelling together because I was filthy rich. And then when I didn't show up she became agitated. I didn't know it at the time but Mum said Sam phoned a couple of times and asked for me but didn't leave a message and she didn't want to talk to anyone else. Her brother said she started drinking and smoking dope and that her behaviour got pretty radical. Turns out she's a schitzo. Most of the time she was okay if she took her medication but if she went off it and something pissed her off, she would totally lose it. She got hooked on drugs and wouldn't take her meds so her family had her committed and that's where she'd been all that time.

'If she was so bad, why did they let her out?' Brigit interjected.

'They said she was making good progress on her medication and seemed to be coming right so the hospital started letting her come home once or twice a week on day visits. That was working really well for a month or two until she suddenly disappeared and they had no idea where she was.'

'Did you know any of her family?'

'I knew very little about her really. We had a bit of a fling for a couple of months over the summer when she first came to work for us.

Mum and Dad didn't like her and she knew it. She tried to butter them up but they could see right through her. They were very relieved when she left.'

'So what did you guys fight about, why did she leave?'

'You will have gathered by now that Samantha is an insanely jealous woman. She saw me sitting down by the river talking to one of the Jillaroos one day. She was absolutely furious and when we got back to the compound she rounded on the poor Jillaroo and slapped her face and screamed abuse at her. I stepped in to separate them and she turned around and slapped me in the face too,' he chuckled ruefully. 'That was a first for me, and I hope it was the last.' He looked at Brigit out the corner of his eye with half a grin tugging at the corners of his mouth.

'I suggested we go somewhere and sort it all out but she just glared at me and stormed off and I never saw her again. Willem apparently took her to the airport and we assumed she'd gone home. We weren't too concerned, we figured she'd calm down and come back, but she didn't. At least not until this year.'

He stopped talking for a moment and lay back staring at the ceiling as he relived the whole scenario.

'Wanna go for a walk?' suggested Brigit. 'Might help to clear your head.'

'Good idea.' He swung himself up and sat

on the side of the bed. 'What about your leg, you okay to be up and walking around?'

'Damn straight I am, you just watch me. Stella and I have been having races up and down the hallway. I nearly fell over yesterday,' she laughed. 'Dad wasn't impressed.'

'I wouldn't have been either,' admonished Jax.

He handed her the crutches and walked behind her as she deftly made her way outside. She stood and breathed in the cool fresh air.

'Take a deep breath Jax. Mountain air. Good for anything that ails ya,' she laughed.

And so he did. 'Mmmm, you're right, it does feel good to breath the air here, I'd forgotten. No heat, just fresh air, I could get used to this I reckon.'

They wandered around the grounds stopping every now and then for Brigit to point out some special plant or other that she had helped Gracie plant. They stopped at the swinging love seat in the gazebo and once seated Jax continued his story.

'When I went to see you at the hospital, I found out that Samantha had been posing as your sister and tried to prevent me from seeing you. One of the nurses told me how shaken up you were after her visit. Anyway after you told me that she said she'd been in prison, Dad and I went down to the Police Station to see if she had a record. That's when we found out that her family and the psych hospital had listed her as a missing person. She hadn't told anyone about working at Bullock Creek so they didn't know to contact us.'

'How did they find out then?'

'The Police gave us a contact number to call. Turns out the number was her brother's so we rang him. That's when we found out that not only had Sam not been in prison but that there was no baby either. It was all lies Brigit, all an attempt to get rid of you and get me back. The girl was totally delusional.'

'So what did you do?'

'Dad offered to fly a couple of her family and a doctor up to the farm to come and get her. When Dad and I got back from Darwin Samantha was back in her room and going to work on the farm as if nothing had happened, so we all played along with her for a couple of days until they arrived. As soon as she saw them though, she flew into such a rage, they had to sedate her. At the doctor's request Dad flew them all up to a mental hospital in Darwin where they could keep her locked up and sedated until her medication kicked in enough for them to fly her home. Shit it was awful.'

He was quiet for a while so Brigit put her hand over his and left him with his thoughts. Then she saw a tear roll down his cheek.

'What babe? What is it? '

'That wasn't the end of it,' he took a deep

breath.

'You mean there's more?'

He nodded. 'I was making plans to fly down to see you when the phone rang, Dad took the call. When he hung up he was pretty shaken. He said Samantha had hung herself in the showers with her bathrobe belt,' he let out a stifled sob. 'God Brig, I was gutted, how could this happen. I felt guilty. I know it wasn't my fault but a part of me felt so guilty. I felt I had to go down to Adelaide to the funeral so Mum and Dad and Uncle Jasper came with me. That's why it's taken me so long to get here.'

He laid his head on Brigit's shoulder as the tears flowed. 'But it's finally over sweetheart. Thank God, it's finally over.'

Chapter Seven

Birthday Party

Jax stayed with Brigit on the farm in New Zealand for two more weeks giving them both a chance to heal and get themselves back on track.

By the time they were winging their way back to the farm from the Darwin airport, Brigit had been away from Bullock Creek for almost six weeks. Willem circled the helicopter overhead to let everyone know that he was back with Jax and Brigit. They smiled and waved out the windows as everyone came running out of the buildings to wave to them.

'Oh my darlings you're finally here,' cried Janet running out to meet them. 'How are you both? Come on, let's get you both inside.' She fussed around and nudged them up the wide front steps to the shade of the veranda which had been set up for a party with tables and chairs arranged neatly in groups and table cloths held in place with brightly coloured homemade decorations.

'How's that ankle of yours now Brigit?' Janet asked once they were seated with their glasses of ice-cold home-made lemonade.

'I'm okay. My back has healed up really well, the ankle is only just out of plaster but everything looks good according to the doctor.'

'Well that's a relief. You had us all really worried you know. Now where are your things. Oh good, Daisy can you take them up to their room please. You both look beat, sit down and put your feet up for a while, there are nibbles on the table. Where's Ruth, didn't she come back with you?'

'Well, she may not ever come back Mum,' a secretive smile slid between Jax and Brigit.

'Why? What's happened?'

'It's nothing bad. She and Brigit's Dad hit it off so well she's going to stay on for a while, if that's okay with you guys?'

'Sure it is' called Sid as he came up the veranda steps. 'Girl deserves a good holiday. And a good bloke too, come to that.'

'Well, I wasn't expecting that,' laughed Janet. 'Good on them I say.'

After they'd all had a chance to catch up with each other's news Janet beckoned Brigit and Jax to follow her to the dining room.

'Come with me,' she smiled as she slipped an arm around Brigit's shoulders. There in the dining room was a beautiful table set for two with crystal glasses, a silver candelabra with pink tapered candles and fresh flowers in a crystal vase. A big banner strung across the wall read 'welcome home.'

Brigit sucked in her breath. 'Oh this is beautiful.'

'Sure is, thanks Mum,' said Jax kissing his mother on the cheek.

Jax and Brigit were waited on by a very attentive Daisy. They relaxed and enjoyed their meal and when Jax broached the subject of a road trip, that's all they talked about for the rest of the meal. They eventually finished their dessert and their bottle of wine and decided to venture out to join the others again. It was Sid Jamieson's 50th birthday. That was the reason Brigit chose this time to come back. They found Sid and Janet and the uncles lounging in the shade of the veranda imbibing in a variety of alcoholic beverages and feasting off plates of appetising refreshments.

Nearly fifty guests made up of family, friends and staff turned up to help Sid celebrate his birthday that night. The workers had also been invited to attend the celebratory shin-dig down in one of the large sheds which had been set up for the occasion. During the evening Brigit sought refuge from the stuffy crowded rooms inside and slipped out onto the gaily lit veranda. She leant against the white painted railing, noticeably peeling in places where it had been blistered by the relentless searing heat of the sun. From here she could see the shed and watch the revellers dancing and singing. Their music was almost loud enough to drown out the music playing inside the house. She took in all the festivities going on around her and the bright coloured lights strung up around the veranda and around the entrance to the shed. Solar lights lit up the driveway and gardens making it look like a spaceship in the darkness of the night. She took a deep breath of cool night air then, just as she turned to go back inside she heard a scream which caught her mid stride. She looked back towards the shed where she could see a couple of men fighting. She called for Jax and Sid. They both came running out followed by a growing group of men. They all raced down the steps across to the shed where the fight was escalating into an all-out brawl. Janet came over and put an arm around Brigit's shoulders.

'Don't worry dear, happens all the time, although not often on this scale of course.'

'What, you mean fighting and brawls?'

'Just fighting amongst the workers in general. It happens sometimes when you get a diverse group of people out here where there's not much else to do but work and eat and drink. It doesn't take much for trouble to brew, especially when there is alcohol in the mix. And a mix of races doesn't help.'

'Why? Are the Aborigines not well accepted?'

Janet hesitated. 'Let's just say some people are more tolerant than others.'

'I remember you telling me about Monti,' said Brigit.

'Ah yes, Monti, very sad, very sad indeed.' Janet seemed to be lost in her own thoughts for a moment and Brigit was surprised at the emotion in her voice.

'So do you know much about the Aborigines then?' Brigit asked.

Janet turned and smiled. 'Yes, a bit. The history of Australia was one of my favourite subjects when I was a school of the air teacher in my younger days. That's how I met Sid. I was teaching some of the children on the property here. I used to visit the out stations once a term to check up on the children and give them tests to make sure they were understanding and learning correctly and not just telling me what I wanted to hear over the radio,' she laughed.

Brigit was about to ask more questions when the volume of shouting from the shed escalated. There seemed to be an awful lot of pushing and shoving going on.

'Are they okay?' asked Brigit, getting alarmed.

Janet peered through the dark to see what was happening.

'It's okay,' she said, 'a couple of our men have just raised their voices to get everyone's attention. They'll be alright. I suspect that's the end of their celebrations for the night though. They will all be sent off to their quarters to sleep it off.'

Sure enough, within fifteen minutes, the shed had gone quiet with only a handful of people milling around cleaning up and putting the empties into bins. Sid and his 'gang' all ambled back to the main house. Once inside they picked up their drinks, turned up the music and the party carried on till the wee small hours.

Sid walked out onto the veranda the following morning. 'Where's Jax and Brigit?' he asked looking around at the visitors clutching cups of coffee and nursing varying degrees of a hangover.

'Don't know, haven't seen them this morning, probably still asleep,' answered Jasper with a yawn.

A breakfast buffet had been set up on a trestle table on the veranda so everyone could help themselves whenever they felt like eating. Some were piling their plates high with bacon, sausages, baked beans, hash browns and scrambled eggs, others just stuck with black coffee. It was quiet and peaceful out on the veranda after the rowdy partying the night before. Janet sat in a comfortable overstuffed old armchair chatting with one of the lady guests while Sid and his brothers tucked into plates piled high with food. Suddenly the radio leapt into life startling everyone within earshot.

'Boss, we got problems down by the gorge

on the eastern side of the river, Quadrant 16,' came the excited voice across the radio.

Sid took up the handset and pressed the button that allowed him to respond. 'What sort of trouble Vince, over.'

'Rustlers, over'.

'White or Aboriginal, over?'

'White bastards, about four of them. Got about twenty of our yearlings, over'

By now Jasper was on the intercom to the staff quarters calling for everyone to get ready to ride out as soon as possible. Suddenly the quiet of the day was filled with drama as guests stood back out of the way while the Jamiesons sprang into action. The women headed to the staff kitchen to make sandwiches and fill thermos flasks with hot water and grab cold drink bottles from the fridges. Once the horses were ready, the women carried the loaded saddlebags out to be fixed to the saddles.

'Thanks ladies,' called Sid.

'Jasper, Nick, Fred, I think we should take a group each and spread out but stay within view of each other. Don't know if these guys are carrying firearms or not, don't want to take any chances on anyone getting hurt. Where's Jax?'

'They're not in their room,' said Janet breathlessly as she ran back out to the veranda.

'Oh I saw them heading off early this morning in a jeep Mrs Jamieson,' called Daisy from the veranda steps.

'Damn,' said Sid pressing the radio call button on his hand-held radio.

'Jax…, Jax, can you hear me boy? Jax, it's Dad, come back, over.' He tried several more times before giving up.

'Janet, keep trying. Tell him to keep his head low, no heroics if he comes across the rustlers, okay?'

'Right, you guys get going,' she said, 'do you want me to call the Police?'

'No not yet, let's just get out there and see what's going on before we get too carried away eh. We might be able to resolve this peacefully.'

Nick and Jasper sniggered. 'Doubt it Sid, we're taking our guns, you got yours?'

'Yeah, but that doesn't mean we have to use them. Could be a case of mistaken stock identification.'

'Yeah right,' said the brothers in unison.

Jax and Brigit were enjoying the peace and quiet of the morning just sitting on the rim of the gorge watching the freshwater crocodiles sunbathing on the sun warmed rocks beside the softly flowing river below.

'Wow, this is amazing,' exclaimed Brigit. 'How far does this gorge go?'

'It cuts through the northern corner of the property pretty much. Awesome eh!'

Brigit's response was lost in a sudden burst of ricocheting gunfire that echoed through the gorge. Their hearts started pounding as they held their breath and flattened themselves to the ground, not sure which direction the shot came from.

'Who the hell was that?' whispered Jax. 'Shouldn't be any of our guys, nobody goes out shooting without us knowing about it.'

Brigit let out her breath. 'What do we do now?'

'Let's crawl to that pile of rocks over there and take cover, see if we can spot what's happening.'

They could hear hooting and hollering as four men on horses suddenly appeared on the other side of the gorge chasing a small herd of cattle.

'Fucking rustlers,' hissed Jax. 'Geez I hate those bastards, they steal from us all the time. Come on, we need to let Dad and the others know.'

He grabbed the handheld radio from the back seat of the jeep.

'Dad, it's Jax, can you hear me, over.'

'Jax, thank God son, where are you?' Sid came back breathlessly.

'At the edge of the gorge. Dad, we got rustlers, over.'

'I know son, Vince just called us up on the radio.'

'Vince? What's he doing out here?'

'Said he was going for a ride to clear his head. Just as well he did. Jax you and Brigit get the hell out of there and head home now. I don't want Brigit getting caught up in all this, do you understand, over?'

'Yeah, sure Dad, they're all yours. There's four guys I think and about 20 – 25 head of stock.'

'Any guns?'

'Yep, they're shootin all over the place and yahooing and carrying on like idiots, over.'

Sid was silent for a moment.'Okay, thanks son, report in now and again to let me know you are okay, over.'

'Wil do, over and out.' Jax picked up the binoculars, and crouching down behind the jeep, scanned around trying to focus in on the rustlers.

'There they are, the pricks.'

Brigit could see Jax was getting pretty worked up.

'Look…. Brig, umm, why don't you take the jeep and head back to the homestead. I wanna keep an eye on these guys so I can let the others know where they are.'

'But your Dad said…'

'I know sweets, dad's just wanting to keep you safe. You don't mind do ya? I'm sure you can easily find your way home, just follow our tracks back the way we came in?'

'Um, yeah, I think so,' she hesitated. But seeing the disappointment crossing Jax face she forced a confident smile.

'Yeah, I'm sure I'll be okay. Will you join up

with Vince?'

'Probably. You sure you'll be okay? Dad's gonna be annoyed that I didn't take you back but I really want to help deal to these bastards, they really piss me off.'

'I can tell,' smiled Brigit. 'Yes I'll be fine, you go get those thieves sheriff Jamieson.' She laughed, but her stomach was beginning to churn.

'Just follow our tracks back hon, you'll be okay. Call me on the house radio as soon as you get home so I know you are okay.'

'Sure will. You be careful and keep your head down too okay.'

He kissed her passionately before heading off in the direction of the disappearing rustlers, using the rocks for cover. Before she left, Brigit spotted Vince across the other side of the gorge also trying to keep out of sight of the rustlers. He and Jax exchanged hand signals and they both waved to Brigit as she turned the jeep and headed back towards the homestead.

Brigit was shaking like a leaf, and not at all confident she could find her way back. The wind had got up a little leaving a dusting of red dirt across their earlier tyre tracks. They were clear for about a kilometre until she came across another set of tracks. She stood up in the open jeep and looked around to see if there were any other vehicles nearby. Over to her left she spotted an old truck.

'Oh good,' she was relieved, 'must be the guys from the homestead. Maybe I'll stay with them and I can follow them back to the homestead.'

As she drew closer a scruffy old man came around from behind the truck and aimed a gun at her, she didn't recognise him. She screamed and swung the jeep around in the opposite direction and planted her boot. She ducked her head down as low as she could as gun shots rang out around her. A bullet hit her right rear tire blowing it out with a mighty bang. Too scared to stop she kept on driving, fighting with the steering wheel of the now difficult to handle vehicle. She didn't slow down to try and pick up any tracks, she just kept driving as fast as she could hoping like hell the truck wasn't following her.

It seemed like ages before she felt safe enough to slow down and look behind her. She drove the jeep round behind a large rock, stopped the engine and got out. She peered out from behind the rock but couldn't see any sign of the truck. There were no dust clouds indicating a vehicle might be coming her way, just an eerie silence. She took a look at the tire. The rim was badly damaged. She checked out the spare and decided she had better try and change it if the vehicle was going to get her home. She took out the jack and wheel brace but couldn't get the wheel nuts to shift. Hot and exasperated with sweat pouring off her brow she gave up and went to get some water. To her horror the water container hanging on the back of the jeep had been shot full of holes and all but a spoonful of water remained in the bottom. She felt close to tears. Jax had taken the backpack of food and the large water bottle they had brought with them from home because he knew Brigit would have the reserve tank if she needed it. Brigit rummaged through the jeep searching for anything edible. All she could find was an orange and a snack bar which Jax must have left for her. Sending him a grateful thank you, she sat in the shade of a nearby rock and devoured her snacks trying to decide her next move. She thought she should stay with the jeep and keep on driving it slowly on the rim until she was back on the track and likely to meet up with the men heading towards the gorge. She might get offside with the family for ruining the wheel but at least the jeep was easier to see than she would be on foot. She slid in behind the wheel and turned the key in the ignition. It wouldn't kick over, so she tried again. Nothing. She tried several more times becoming more and more anxious. Nothing. Finally the battery died completely. All she got was a tired click when she turned the key. She started to cry, the reality of her situation beginning to take hold. She climbed to the top of the rock and attempted to take stock of her position. Shielding her eyes she could see the truck way off in the distance and further to the south she could see a dust cloud of vehicles and horses. Her heart leapt at the sight. Thank God, there they are. She sat down on the top of the rock and waited until they got closer. They were heading towards the truck. She stood on top of the rock and began waving a white rag above her head to get their attention. Nobody seemed to be changing direction, there was no indication that anyone had seen her. She stood there waving until her arms ached. She yelled until she was hoarse but they kept slowly moving towards the truck. She watched them with a sinking heart.

'Too far away for them to see me now. Maybe I should just wait here until they come back. I can't be too far off the track, surely.'

She settled down in the shade and waited. By nightfall she realised she was on her own. She knew they would be out looking for her but where would they start. They didn't come back her way so she had no idea what happened or where they ended up.

'They must have gone back to the homestead by a different route,' she surmised.

Once the sun slipped down beyond the horizon it got very cold. She found an old blanket in the back of the jeep but not much else. She was chastising herself for eating the orange and snack bar all at once. But then, she reasoned, she didn't know she was going to be stranded out here overnight. Confident she would be found in the morning, she snuggled up on the back seat of the jeep and went to sleep.

The crows woke her up next morning as the sun quickly tracked its way up from the horizon. Brigit climbed up on top of her rock to see if she could see anything or anyone. The old truck was still there. She thought she could see small clouds of dust here and there, enough to suggest a couple of horses, but none of them were close enough for her to see clearly. She was very thirsty.

'They'd better get here soon,' she thought, *'can't risk dehydration. I'm not going to panic yet. I will be just fine, they will find me soon. They will have the plane up shortly.'*

She kept repeating these affirmations over and over to stop herself from panicking. Sure enough within half an hour she could hear a plane and a helicopter circling around.

'Thank God.'

She stood on the rock and began to wave her white rag again. Suddenly she lost her balance and slid down the face of the jagged rock, ripping at her skin as she fell. Her head hit a round marble shaped rock with a sickening thud. When she opened her eyes the sun was high in the sky and beginning its descent down the other side. She tried to sit up but her head was throbbing. She waited until it subsided a little then sat up and took stock of her injuries.

She cried out when she tried to move her injured ankle.

'*Shit, it feels like it's broken again. Damn.*'

She could feel dried patches of blood down the side of her face from a cut on her head. The blood had also dried in her hair causing it to become all matted together. Her head was throbbing. The rest of the cuts and scratches weren't too bad, red scabs had begun to dry over the cuts. She lay back against the rock wishing she had some water. She held her breath for a moment as she heard a helicopter getting closer.

'*Yahoo,*' she thought, '*At last. I'm going to be okay.*'

She tried to pull herself up on her good leg but the pain in her ankle brought her to the ground with a painful thump and the throbbing in her head intensified.

'*Maybe I can crawl out into the open*'. But the slightest movement made her feel sick with the pain.

'*At least they should be able to see the jeep,*' she thought. '*Shit, shit, shit, I really don't need this. Jax will be thinking he's married a real loser.*'

She lay back against the rock and listened to the helicopter, willing it to come her way. Then, with great despair she heard it getting further and further away from her in the opposite direction. She felt faint and put her head down between her legs, which didn't help the throbbing. A rustling sound brought her head up again, fully alert. '*What was that?*' Around from the side of the rock a snake came into view. Brigit sat rigid with fear and held her breath trying not to move a muscle, as Jax had taught her to do. The snake stopped as if it was waiting for something to happen. It did. A rabbit popped up out of a hole a few feet away and the chase was on. Unfortunately the rabbit lucked out, it sounded like a baby screaming. Brigit let out her breath and leaned back against the rock again.

'Poor bunny, but I'm glad it was you and not me.' She lay quietly allowing her heart to regain a slower rhythm again and willing the throbbing to subside. The sun was getting low now as she sat, silent and listless. She would be verging on panic if she wasn't so tired, hungry and thirsty. She drifted off for a while and when she awoke the sky was a deep navy blue and all the stars were out. It was a beautiful night.

'You'll be okay my dear. They will find you, tomorrow they will find you.'

Brigit started at the unexpected voice.

'Who's that?' She turned her head towards the voice and there sitting on the rock beside her was a man in a very old fashioned pair of trousers and shirt and a tatty old hat.

'Who are you?'

'Just an old friend my dear, just an old friend. I'm here to tell you to hang on, okay. Don't let go, just you hang on tight, you will be okay.'

'Are you going to take me home,' she mumbled drowsily.

'I can't my dear, but someone will come and get you tomorrow.'

'Why can't you take me?'

'You get some sleep now, I will stay with you for a while.'

Okay,' she whispered drowsily. 'Thank you.' And she was asleep again.

The Jamieson's were panicking at not having found Brigit. Jax was beating himself up so mercilessly that his parents had held off reprimanding him as they would have liked to. Instead they all focused on the search. The men had gotten into a real battle with the rustlers. Shots had been fired and the stock scattered in all directions. No one got badly hurt as most of the shots were being fired into the air as a warning rather than being aimed at anyone. When they first came across the truck the old man started to shoot at them. One of Sid's men snuck around behind the truck and come up behind the old codger and took him to the ground in a perfect rugby tackle. The others leapt off their horses to help tie the man up and leave him with the truck until he could be collected.

Sid had called Janet and asked her to phone for the Police as soon as Jax had said that guns were involved so by the time the group reached the rustlers, the Police were coming in from the opposite direction. There was a lot of dust billowing about as the stock, horses, riders and police vehicles all chased each other to a standstill. The whole thing ended without any loss of life and with the rustlers being taken back to the paddy wagon waiting for them at the gate. Sid sent three of his men off to round up the yearlings to try and calm them down and slowly walk them back towards the homestead.

'Get them as close to the homestead as you can so that we can check them over in the morning.'

It wasn't until the rest of them got back to the homestead that they discovered Brigit was missing. Janet wasn't expecting her and the men had been so wrapped up in their excitement that no-one had given her a second thought.

'I thought she was home, I had no idea she wasn't here with you Mum. Oh God, if anything happens to her, oh God.' Jax was beside himself with fear and worry.

'I told you to bring her back boy, now look what's happened. Next time do as I ask, please. I don't say things for nothing. You know damn well how dangerous it is for anyone to be lost out there, let alone someone as inexperienced as Brigit.'

'Can we get the helicopters back out there now. Please Dad, we gotta do something.

'Jax, there's nothing we can do tonight boy it's too darn late, we can't fly at night. We'll draw up a search plan for first light. Everyone try and get some sleep, we'll be starting at daybreak.'

Sid was distraught, Janet was in tears and Jax went to pieces, yelling and chastising himself and punching his fists against the door frames. He didn't sleep a wink that night, he just sat in a chair in the lounge crying and worrying about Brigit, fearing for her out there on her own. He couldn't help conjuring up all sorts of possible eventualities.

Everyone was on deck at daybreak without exception. Brigit was well loved by everybody on the compound and they were all there ready and waiting for instructions. When the day's searching didn't reap any results, fear started to build amongst the searchers. Everyone knew how potentially dangerous it was to be lost in the outback. Even more so, when Jax had tearfully confessed that he had taken all the food and the water bottle.

'At least she has the water tank on the back of the jeep,' he said hopefully.

That night as the family sat around coming up with plans and ideas, Sid decided to call the Police Station and suggested the cops ask the rustlers if they had seen her.

'Do you want a hand to search Sid?' asked the desk Sergeant.

'I'll let you know Dan, thanks, we're going out again at first light, there's plenty of us and we have the plane and the chopper.'

'Keep us posted and I'll go talk with these low-lifes for you.'

'Thanks Dan.'

'We need to go further afield tomorrow, much further than we think she might be,' suggested Sid. 'Obviously she's gone off track somewhere for some reason so let's widen the search and bring it back in to a central point. If that doesn't work we will go even further, and we will search the gorges. I'm just waiting on a call back from the cops in case those rustlers might have seen her.'

The words were no sooner out of his mouth than the phone rang.

'Yeah Dan. Did he now. Which direction? Okay, that gives us a lot more than what we've got, cheers. There's a what? What sort of a camp. Gold digging? Yah reckon? No, thanks for the heads up, I'll go check it out. Can you email the co-ordinates through to me. Thanks mate, I'll talk to you later.

Sid went back to the waiting group.

'That old geezer in the truck saw Brigit apparently. He confessed he took a couple of shots at her, didn't realise it was a woman. He said she took off south in a big hurry. He gave up watching her after a while, said she didn't seem to turn off anywhere.'

Sid and Jax went up in the helicopter leaving Willem and the others to go up in the fixed wing plane. They went way further south than they figured she could possibly be and then zig zagged their way back towards the gorge. Suddenly Jax let out a strangled scream which startled the living daylights out of his father.

'Dad, down there, look, the jeep, down there.'

They landed the helicopter close to the jeep. Jax leapt out before it even settled on the ground. Around behind the jeep he found his beloved Brigit. He shook her roughly to wake her up fearing she might be dead, but she mumbled and opened her eyes trying to focus against the bright sunlight. Sid came up with a water bottle and tilting her head up, dribbled a little water onto her lips. She sucked at it thirstily, her tongue out searching for more. Sid dribbled a little more into her mouth as Jax cradled her, sobbing and apologising over and over again. He gently lifted her and carried her to the helicopter. It was only a two-seater but he wasn't about to let her go, he cradled her all the way back. Sid radioed the good news to the homestead and asked someone to call the Flying Doctors. Just as they landed the helicopter beside the hanger at the end of the airstrip they heard a plane overhead.

'Gosh you guys were quick,' said Sid appreciatively as the doctors scrambled out of their aircraft.

'Actually we were just on our way back from a call when you guys called us. It was good timing.'

The Doctors checked Brigit over thoroughly. They dressed her head wound which fortunately wasn't deep enough to require stitches and they strapped her badly bruised ankle, deciding it hadn't been re-broken from her fall from the horse. They stayed with her for a couple of hours monitoring her vital signs. When they were satisfied that she was recovering from the dehydration satisfactorily and didn't need to go to hospital, they left on the proviso that if there was the slightest change in her condition they were to get her to Darwin Hospital without delay. Everyone promised. Jax shook their hands, tears in his eyes.

'Thanks guys, you've been great. You can rest assured she will be in good hands from now on. I might have let her out of my sight the other day but that won't ever happen again believe me.'

Sid slapped him on the shoulder.

'Okay son, I think you've beaten yourself up enough. Get over yourself, your wife needs you now.'

Jax sniffled and wiped his nose on the sleeve of his shirt as he looked sheepishly at his dad. The Doctors had given him a sedative when they arrived just to calm him down, he was such a wreck.

'Jax, take it easy on yourself okay, Brigit's fine, you need to get some rest too, doctor's orders,' said one of the doctors.

Jax allowed himself a smile. 'Yeah, you're right. Thanks again guys. Come on my darling, we are going to lie down together and sleep.'

And sleep they did, right through until morning.

'God I'm hungry,' mumbled Brigit as she tried to roll over. 'Ouch, shit, that hurt.'

Jax sprang straight up in bed. 'What?' You okay honey, what's the matter?'

Brigit smiled kindly at the concern on his face as his eyes filled with tears.

'It's alright sweets, just my ankle that's all, hungry mostly.'

Jax slumped back on the pillows and turned to face his beautiful wife.

'Do you have any idea how sorry I am and how much I adore you Mrs Jamieson. After all that you have been through with Samantha and the horse and now this, I am so, so sorry. You must be thinking we are jinxed or something.'

She smiled and put a finger to his lips to shut him up. Just then there was a knock on the door.

'Thought I heard voices,' smiled Janet carrying a tray of bacon, eggs, hash browns, hot buttered toast, orange juice and steaming hot coffee. Brigit sat up ignoring the pangs of pain.

'Oh Janet, thank you. Do you have any idea how good that looks and oh the delicious smells,' she laughed as she picked up her knife and fork and started on the bacon and eggs. Come on Jax, there's plenty here for both of us.'

'I'm just happy watching you eat for now my darling.'

Once the breakfast tray had been cleared away, the pair snuggled back down into their soft comfy bed and started to talk about the previous day's events. Brigit's heart went out to Jax as he told her of his despair at thinking that they might not find her alive.

Suddenly Brigit sat up. 'Oh, there was a man out there. That second night.'

'What man, where?'

'He was sitting beside me on the rocks telling me it would be okay and that you would find me tomorrow. And you did.'

Jax was puzzled. 'I take it you were hallucinating.'

'Well yeah, I guess, but he seemed familiar, like I knew him. Really strange.' She shrugged and flopped back down on the pillows again.

By the time they showered and emerged from their room, it was lunchtime and Sid, Janet and the three uncles were sitting around the kitchen table talking.

'I reckon it must be damned Braithwaite. Who else could it be?' Sid said addressing Jasper.

'What about Braithwaite?' asked Jax.

'Oh morning son. How are you two this morning?' He came over and gave Brigit a warm hug.

'I'm fine Sid, sturdy farm stock and all that,' she grinned

'You sure? You look a little pale.'

'Still just a little shaky but nothing to worry about. Seriously, I'm all good. What's for lunch?'

'Ah that's my girl. How about you my boy, you okay?'

'I'm fine thanks dad. Grateful as all hell that Brig is okay and thanks so much you guys, you were flippin awesome. So, what's this about Braithwaite?'

'When the Police came in to give us a hand with the rustlers, they passed a camp site with a small tent and fire pit. They figured it probably belonged to the rustlers, but the rustlers reckoned they knew nothing about it. The boys and I are going out to have a look, we were just going over the co-ordinates.'

'So what makes you think it's Braithwaite?'

'Apparently someone saw him in town a few weeks back buying some camping gear and a metal detector. You know how he always wanted to prospect for gold on the property.'

'You don't seriously think he'd come back here do you Dad? Not after what he did to Monti?'

'He might if he was hard up, he knows our operation, how we work, where we are likely to be. And I'm pretty sure he'd have a good idea where there might be some pockets of gold. He spent a lot of his free time away on his horse, camping out for days.'

Yes, I remember that. Can I come with you?'

'Don't you want to stay with Brigit?' asked Sid, glaring over the top of his glasses.

Jax threw a guilty look at Brigit. 'God, yes, sorry Brigit I wasn't thinking.'

'Oh don't be a goose,' she laughed, 'I know you'd love to go and have a look. Janet and I can have a quiet chat while you're gone.'

'It's too far to go on horseback, we'll take the choppers,' finished Sid as he rolled up the topographical map and headed for the door.

Within an hour the choppers were back.

'What did you find?' asked Janet as they came up the veranda steps.

'Pretty sure it was him. No sign of life there now, doesn't look like he's been there for some time,' said Sid, shucking off his dusty boots.

'So what makes you so sure it's him then?'

'Found this.' He tossed an old leather satchel to Janet. She looked inside.

'It's empty.'

'Look at the lettering on the front flap.'

Janet turned the flap down and could see where someone had rubbed a patch clean. 'W.E.B,' she read. 'Oh of course, Walter Ernest Braithwaite,' she felt a shiver run down her spine. 'It gives me the creeps to think that that man has been back on the property.'

'Me too my love,' said Sid seriously. 'Me too. I am issuing a photo to everyone on the property who doesn't know Braithwaite so that we can all keep an eye out for him. I would love to get that guy put away for life.'

Brigit sat quietly and listened to the conversation. Jax sat on the arm of her chair lovingly stroking her back.

'Kind of freaky that he's hanging around,' she whispered to Jax. 'Hope he doesn't come over our way.'

'Nah, the gold that he would be looking for is more in the area of where he was camped. We left everything as it was, apart from the satchel, and the guys will keep watch in case he comes back. But now Mrs Jamieson junior, if you are feeling up to it, I think we should think about heading home.'

'Oh no,' Janet perked up her ears. 'Not yet. At least give Brigit one more day of pampering. Perhaps go home day after tomorrow, what do you say?'

'I say yes, and thank you,' Brigit smiled warmly at Janet. I love being here, there's always so much happening.'

'We could make things happen back at our place too,' protested Jax.

'Now, now, you two, keep it seemly,' laughed Sid. 'So, who's up for a beer then? Brigit, glass of wine?'

'Lovely, thank you Sid,' she looked up at Jax and smiled triumphantly. 'You'll just have to wait won't you,' she winked.

Chapter Eight

Jax and Brigit's Road Trip

'Our very first road trip, just the two of us on our own, yahoo, can't wait', cried Brigit as she zipped up her overstuffed duffle bag.

'What the hell have you got in this thing Brig, it weighs a ton, good thing we're not flying, we'd be paying excess baggage,' complained Jax as he hefted her very heavy suitcase into the back of the wagon.

'Well, this is my very first road trip in the outback and I have no idea what to take,' she protested indignantly.

Jax laughed and grabbed her around the waist giving her a big hug. 'All you need my darling, are those sexy cut off shorts and a tight fitting t-shirt.'

Brigit feigned disgust then snuggled her head down into her husband's neck. 'I'm so excited hon, I've been looking forward to this ever since we first started talking about it.'

'Really? I would never have guessed.'

Brigit wriggled out of his grasp and did a quick check through the house to make sure everything had been packed into the back of the Land Cruiser. They weren't using the fold out camp trailer this time. Jax was treating her to the best motel rooms they could find along the way.

'Come on honey let's go,' shouted Jax impatiently gunning the engine.

'Coming,' she called back. She was having a last-minute chat with Jasper, who was going to be staying in the house while they were away.

'Don't forget puss likes his biscuits at breakfast time, not dinner time, okay.'

'For goodness sake Brigit, get your arse out of here before Jax blows a fuse,' he laughed as he pushed her out the door.

They tooted and waved as they drove off in a cloud of dust.

'Wow, three whole weeks, just you, me and the open road,' hooted Jax.

'I know, I can hardly believe it.'

'Got your map?'

Brigit reached into the glove compartment and tugged out the well-worn map she and Jax had been pouring over for weeks.

'Don't know why you don't use the GPS,' laughed Jax. It'd be much more reliable.'

'I don't like those things, I find a map much more accurate.

'More accurate? How can a map be more accurate than a GPS?' Jax couldn't help laughing.

'Because they keep saying *go to the nearest road, go to the nearest road*' whenever I try to use them around here,' laughed Brigit holding her nose to imitate the voice on the GPS. I suspect there are a lot of areas in Australia that aren't even on the GPS. Nope a map is much more accurate.'

Jax snorted. Brigit reached her hand round the back of his head and pulled his hair, hard.

'Ouch, that hurt.'

'Good, it was meant to,' she sniggered. 'So, we should be at Alice Springs by around eight o'clock tonight, all going well.'

'Should be. You booked us into *Lasseters* right?' asked Jax.

'Yep all booked.' Brigit saluted her husband and placed her hand on his knee. His hand covered hers and they rode in silence for a while, both smiling, enjoying the scenery.

Brigit broke the silence. 'I know we talked a little bit about it but I am struggling to get my head around this first part of the trip because it will all be in reverse when Rees and Stella come over to do the Adelaide to Darwin trip with us wont it?'

Jax nodded.

'So when we get to Port Augusta we change direction and head off to the Flinders Ranges.' Brigit was muttering away to herself as she ran her fingers along the red lines of her road map. 'God it's a long way to anywhere isn't it?' She looked up at Jax for confirmation. 'I mean, it's going to take us two days just to get to Port Augusta. You could just about travel the length of New Zealand in five days.'

Jax smiled. 'You could fit several whole countries on this continent. I think once you have done this trip you will have a better idea of its immense size. Must admit, it wasn't until I started flying with Dad that I really had any appreciation of the vastness. I had a pretty good idea of how big our property was of course, but from the air and flying to places like Darwin and Melbourne the distances from place to place just blew me away. I guess I've been lucky being able to see the land from the air.'

Brigit turned her concentration back to her map, turning it upside down to gain better perspective.

They stayed two nights at Port Augusta. Jax wanted to show Brigit through the Wadlatta Cultural Centre so that she could learn more about Australian History.

'That time lapse video of the history of the changes of the continent was absolutely amazing' oozed Brigit as they sat in the centre's café with hot coffee and muffins. 'I want to get some souvenirs before we go too.'

'Wilpena Pound. What a weird name,' mused Brigit as they pulled up outside their motel later that afternoon. 'What time is our

Gum Creek Station tour tomorrow?'

'Not sure, best we check with reception.'

'Jamieson, we're in for two nights,' Jax informed the receptionist.

'Yes you are, room 14 down the hall to your right. Now, I see you are booked in for a flight over the Pound day after tomorrow, your flight leaves at 3.30pm. You will need to board the shuttle bus outside the door here by 2.30pm for that.'

'What time is our Gum Creek Tour, we've booked in for tomorrow?'

The receptionist leaned back to check a timetable on the wall behind her. 'Tomorrow, um yep, nine thirty in the morning. Just wait over in the shop across the road and your guide will come and get you.' She smiled up at them as she handed them their vouchers for the tours. 'Have a nice stay folks.'

'Not what I expected,' remarked Brigit as they buzzed over Wilpena Pound in the fixed wing six-seater aircraft two days later.

'What did you expect?' Jax's voice came back through the headset.

'Not sure really, but I didn't expect it to look like a huge basin, it's really quite amazing.'

The pilot took them in an extended circle right around the Pound explaining its formation and history.

'Thank you,' breathed Brigit as the handsome young pilot helped her out of the plane. 'That was awesome.'

'You guys from New Zealand?' he asked.

'I am,' said Brigit smiling up into the sparkling blue eyes, 'Jax is from here. Why do you ask?'

'Oh I recognised your accent, I'm from NZ too, Invercargill actually, I used to work for Stewart Island Flights.'

'Really? I'm from Queenstown, a high-country sheep station up Skippers Canyon. My father and I ....'

'Brig, we gotta go honey,' Jax wrapped his arm possessively around his wife's waist.

'Oh, okay, sure. Well bye,' she held out her hand to the pilot. 'Don't know your name but thanks for the flight it was great.'

'Roger, and you're welcome, anytime.'

'Roger, what a stupid name for a pilot – roger Roger,' sneered Jax as they walked back to the bus. 'Radio communications with him must sound a bit weird – roger Roger,' he repeated.

Brigit stopped and looked at Jax. 'Why Mr Jamieson I do declaaya, I believe you are jealous,' she laughed, putting on her best Scarlett O'Hara voice.

Jax blushed and patted her bum as she got on the bus.

Next morning they set off through the Blinman and the Chambers Gorge to Balcanoona on to their two-night stay at Arkaroola.

'This place is owned by the Aborigines,'

said Jax as they drove in the gate of the tourist village.'

They pulled up outside reception and went to check in.

'Can't wait for dinner, I'm famished,' groaned Brigit as delicious smells from the restaurant followed them out the door.

The next morning they took the four-wheel drive Ridge Top Tour.

'Wow, what a view,' remarked Brigit, hands cupped around her coffee cup as she gazed out at the impressive view which stretched across to the far horizon. She looked back down at the road they had just driven up. I thought we had steep roads through Skippers but this bit coming up to the top here had my heart pumping a bit,' she admitted.

'Mine too,' confessed Jax, whispering in her ear, 'but don't tell anyone.'

Brigit laughed and swinging the camera up from around her neck took photos with one hand until Jax relieved her of her coffee cup.

'Okay, according to the map we go this way,' Brigit pointed.

'Yep, this should take us all the way to Marree and the old Hotel we used to stay in when I was a kid. Dad knew the owner years ago. I meant to ask Dad if old George was still there. Remember that video I showed you about Tom Kruse some time ago?'

'Which one, Top Gun?'

'No, not that Tom Cruise, Tom Kruse with a K. *The Back of Beyond* I think it was called. Remember, he was the mailman who delivered the mail between Maree and Birsdville for about 20 years back in the thirties. Took him about two weeks per trip. They didn't have roads back then, just miles and miles of flippin sand dunes. Can't imagine what it must have been like.'

'Yes of course I remember that, it must have been so cool for the people living out in the wops to see this man and his truck turn up every couple of weeks. I suppose he delivered food and stuff as well.'

'Yes, I guess so.'

'I often wonder what it would have been like living out here during those early years. Very different from now,' Brigit sighed wistfully.

'You sound as though you are disappointed Brig, don't you like our life now?'

'Of course I do. I just love to read about how people used to live all those years ago though. When I was in my cob cottage on the farm back home I used to pretend I was Elizabeth and would make preserves and cook meals for me and Gordon. I even furnished it with old furniture and some lacy curtains I found out in the shed.'

'So who's Elizabeth and Gordon? Are they the ones that used to live there hundreds of years ago?'

'Only one hundred and thirty something I think, but yes. It sounds a bit stupid when I say it now.'

'Not really, I know you've always loved historic places and old stuff, there's nothing wrong with a bit of make believe. Trey and I used to play make believe too as kids.'

Brigit shrugged and bit her lip. *'No use trying to explain that it wasn't really make believe,'* she decided, *if only he knew.'*

It was just on dusk when they drove in to Marree.

'Ah, there it is, Tom's old truck, the Leyland Badger. What stories that thing could tell,' muttered Jax as he drove past the truck and around to the back of the old pub.

They walked through the back door into the bar of the historic wooden two storied building. As his eyes adjusted to the dim interior Jax scanned around for the familiar face of his father's old mate. He wasn't disappointed. There in the corner of the room propping himself up on the bar was a grey haired man. He looked up and smiled as they came in.

'Well hello there, guess you folks is looking for a bed for the night huh?'

'Sure are, we did make a booking.'

'Good on ya. Hey Estelle, you got a booking for these folks?'

'If the name's Jamieson I sure have,' she called back pleasantly from the reception desk.

'Jamieson?' Enquired the old man. 'Not Sid's boy?'

'That's me', Jax flashed him a smile and held out his hand.

'Well I'll be,' he said pushing back his old worn-out hat and scratching his balding head. Thought you looked a tad familiar. Which one are you then?'

'I'm Jax, the eldest one.'

'Well whadya know. Ain't seen you since ya was knee high to a kangaroo.'

Brigit smiled at the old man, enjoying his delight at seeing Jax again.

'So how is your old man, haven't seen the coot for quite some time but I read about him now and again in the papers.'

'Keeping busy as always George,' said Jax extracting his squashed fingers from the old man's fist. 'This is my wife Brigit.' He stood aside to let Brigit come forward.

The old man smiled broadly. 'Well ya did alright for yourself there young man, didn't ya. Fine young specimen,' he laughed and winked at Brigit.

Brigit extended her hand to George. 'Nice to meet you, I've heard so much about you and your lovely hotel.'

'I'm pickin' you're a Kiwi girl, am I right?'

'I am, how did you know that?'

'He's got a keen eye for the Kiwi girls,' laughed Estelle.

'Come on then,' laughed George, 'let's get ya settled and we can sit and have a drink. You'll be wanting some dinner I expect.' Without waiting for an answer, 'Estelle, book these two in for dinner too will ya.'

'One step ahead of you George.'

'Aha, that's ma girl. Now, you wanna stay in the units out back or in the hotel, Lord knows we got the room this time of year.'

Jax glanced at Brigit. 'Hotel?'

'Yes,' she nodded.

'Good. Estelle, best room upstairs.'

'Yep, all done.'

'Been feelin a bit redundant around here lately, can't think why,' he winked at them.

The room upstairs had a window opening out onto a wide veranda which ran the full length of the hotel and faced the road coming into town. Brigit went out to take in the view. A few yards up the road to the left was a general store which she decided she must check out in the morning. The railway line was across the road and ran parallel to the Hotel. The old Leyland truck was parked up beside the water tank which was used to fill up the old steam engines. It stood alone and neglected now as a reminder of days gone by.

As Brigit walked into their hotel room, Jax leapt out from behind the door and threw her face down on the bed. She squealed in playful delight and tried to turn over but he held her arms over her head and lay full length over her body.

'Well miss Brigit, what are ya gonna do now?' he chuckled as he struggled to keep her from squirming away.

'Question is daaahling, what are *you* gonna do now?

Jax snuggled into her hair and kissed her warm neck. She relaxed and started to give in to him. He turned her over and kissed her, playtime had begun. They showered and changed before heading downstairs to join George and Estelle for dinner and drinks. By the time the night was over both Brigit and Jax were quite tiddly and giggled their way up the stairs to their room. Fortunately they were the only ones in the hotel so they weren't disturbing anyone. Next morning they woke up to a gentle knock on the door.

'Breakfast is ready on the veranda you two.'

They looked at each other and leaping out of bed, pulled back the curtain. There stood a small beautifully decorated table and two chairs with some silk flowers in a glass vase, two glasses of orange juice, coffee cups, silver coffee pot with matching milk jug and sugar bowl and a rack standing ready waiting for hot toast. A menu stood proudly beside the vase waiting for them to place their orders. They dressed quickly and went and sat down at the table.

'Oh my goodness,' exclaimed Brigit, ' eggs benedict, my favourite, yes please Estelle,' Brigit said enthusiastically as she glanced through the menu.

'Just make mine bacon and eggs please Estelle and thank you so much for this, it's great.'

'Love the chance to use the nice silver and good china,' she smiled at them, enjoying their appreciation.

'Let's stay another night, can we?' pleaded Brigit as she devoured her eggs.

'Funny, I was just thinking the same thing,' he said. 'I'll call the Birdsville Motel and change our booking.'

After breakfast Brigit left Jax and George in deep discussion about the viability of the live export market and made her way to the general store.

'Man they had a bit of everything in there,' she told Jax later when she got back.

'They have to really, it's a long way into town if you forget something.'

'Who's that guy over there by the motel? she pointed out the door.

Jax went over to the door. 'Ah, that's Talc Alf. You gotta meet this guy Brig, he's a legend.'

Alf, being the eternal socialiser and a bit of a show-off greeted them like long lost friends

'Here lovey, try some of my talc rock,' he placed some in Brigit's outstretched hand. This is what your talcum powder is made from.'

He was literally covered in the stuff and Brigit wondered how much of the grey in his hair was real and how much was talcum powder. Just then a bus load of tourists pulled up so Brigit and Jax slid away leaving Talc Alf to entertain his visitors.

The tourists, a group of senior citizens from New Zealand were staying the night in the motels out the back. They'd had a long day and turned in after an early dinner, leaving the dining room to Jax, Brigit, George and Estelle and one of the locals. They ate and drank and talked again until late into the night.

'Come on Mrs Jamieson,' said Jax eventually, 'another long day for us tomorrow.'

They were up and off bright and early next morning, after filling up their thermoses and packing the sandwiches and cake Estelle had kindly prepared for them. They travelled on in silence for several kilometres, Brigit taking in the vastness of the landscape. At one stage she turned around and looked out each window in turn.

'Stop the car,' she yelled.

'Bloody hell Brigit, you scared the bejeezus out of me. What's the matter?' he grumbled.

'I want to get out and take some video to send back home. You drive back up the road a bit and I will video you coming towards me. This is so cool, I want to do a full circle video showing there's absolutely nothing to see as far as the eye can see.'

Jax laughed and did as he was bid. Brigit stood on the side of the road and waited. A car appeared from the opposite direction as Jax drove away.

'What are you doing out here love?' the kind faced old man behind the wheel asked.

'Oh just waiting for my husband, he went to get some milk, said he'd be back before dark.' Brigit hid the camera behind her back desperately trying not to smile. The man looked a little alarmed.

He obviously hasn't seen Jax yet, he must think I'm nuts, she thought. Then looking up the road she exclaimed, 'Ah here he is now, got back sooner than I expected.'

The man also looked out his windscreen and saw the vehicle coming towards them. 'But where did he go? There's no shops for a hundred miles.'

'Oh I know, isn't he just the most thoughtful darling,' she smiled sweetly, then held up her camera to capture Jax on video.

'You're having me on aren't you, you little minx,' he said when he realised she was pulling his leg. He seemed a bit miffed but a bit of a smile started to appear at the corners of his mouth.

'Sorry mate, couldn't resist. See ya,' she called as she piled into the car. She laughed and waved as they took off.

'What's so funny?'

"Oh nothing, you had to be there really,' she said smiling to herself.

'Come on, give.'

'Okay, keep ya shirt on.' She told him what she'd said to the old man.

'That's naughty Brigit, you could have given the poor old guy a heart attack. You know you shouldn't joke about being lost or stranded out in the desert, it can be really serious.'

'Umm hello! I've been there done that remember, when those rustlers were down by the gorge.

Jax was quiet for a moment. 'Of course I remember,' said Jax soberly, 'I still have nightmares about it.'

'Really? 'Oh Jax don't be such a worry wart, everything turned out okay in the end.'

'But what if it hadn't. What if I'd lost you?'

'But you didn't Jax. You have to get over this. It's okay, you can't go on living in the past. A lot of shit has happened to both of us over the past couple of years but we can't dwell on it, okay!'

'Okay' he sighed. Speaking of the outback though, Dad used to tell us stories when we were travelling. True stories about the old pioneers and surveyors and the early landowners and the Aborigines. One I remember which got to me a bit was about this woman who lived with her husband and two daughters on a remote outback property somewhere in the Birdsville area. They owned the land but during a particularly long hard drought which lasted many years they had to sell up all their stock. They ended up with nothing. In the end the father would go off for weeks at a time to find work elsewhere leaving the mother and two little girls behind on their own.'

'For real?'

'Yep, they had nothing but a simple wooden two room shack that they lived in. They struggled to grow vegetables. They had to rely mainly on the hot salty artesian water.

'Why didn't they move?'

'They owned the land and couldn't really afford to go anywhere else. Nobody wanted to buy land during the drought. Anyway, one day the father came home after being away longer than he expected and found his wife running around the house demented and screaming. She'd gone quite mad.'

'What happened?

'They'd run out of food apparently. The mother didn't know if and when the father would come back with more food and she didn't want to see her babies dying of starvation so she killed them. She had only buried them the day before the father came home.'

'Oh that is so sad. Did it really happen or are you just pulling my leg?'

'It really happened and that's only one of

the many stories of hardship that hit people out in the outback desert. It was a hard life.'

'Then why did people come out here?'

'Don't know really, you would have to ask them. Dad was born on our farm as his father and grandfather were before him so I guess it's a given that it would be handed down from generation to generation until we run out of generations. I must admit, I wouldn't trade my life in the outback for anything. Oh I nearly forgot, have a look in the glovebox, there should be a small book in there.'

'This one?' she asked waving it in front of Jax's nose.'

'Yeah, there's a story in there called 'The Drover's Wife'. Mum gave it to me ages ago and thought you might like to read it. It's about a pioneer woman.'

'Cool. Do you want me to read it out loud or have you read it already?'

'No, read it out aloud if you like. I've heard it before but I don't mind hearing it again.'

Brigit flicked through the book, found the short story and began to read:

The Drover's Wife

The two-roomed house is built of round timber, slabs, and stringy-bark, and floored with split slabs. A big bark kitchen standing at one end is larger than the house itself, veranda included. Bush all round —bush with no horizon, for the country is flat. No ranges in the distance. The bush consists of stunted, rotten native apple-trees. No undergrowth. Nothing to relieve the eye save the darker green of a few she-oaks which are sighing above the narrow, almost waterless creek. Nineteen miles to the nearest sign of civilization—a shanty on the main road.

The drover, an ex-squatter, is away with sheep. His wife and children are left here alone.

Four ragged, dried-up-looking children are playing about the house. Suddenly one of them yells: "Snake! Mother, here's a snake!"

The gaunt, sun-browned bushwoman dashes from the kitchen, snatches her baby from the ground, holds it on her left hip, and reaches for a stick.

"Where is it?"

"Here! gone into the wood-heap!" yells the eldest boy—a sharp-faced urchin of eleven. "Stop there, mother! I'll have him. Stand back! I'll have the beggar."

"Tommy, come here, or you'll be bit. Come here at once when I tell you, you little wretch!"

The youngster comes reluctantly, carrying a stick bigger than himself. Then he yells, triumphantly:

"There it goes—under the house!" and darts away with club uplifted. At the same time the big, black, yellow-eyed dog-of-all-breeds, who has shown the wildest interest in the proceedings, breaks his chain and rushes after that snake. He is a moment late, however, and his nose reaches the crack in the slabs just as the end of its tail disappears. Almost at the same moment the boy's club comes down and skins

the aforesaid nose. Alligator takes small notice of this, and proceeds to undermine the building; but he is subdued after a struggle and chained up. They cannot afford to lose him.

The drover's wife makes the children stand together near the dog-house while she watches for the snake. She gets two small dishes of milk and sets them down near the wall to tempt it to come out; but an hour goes by and it does not show itself.

It is near sunset, and a thunderstorm is coming. The children must be brought inside. She will not take them into the house, for she knows the snake is there, and may at any moment come up through a crack in the rough slab floor; so she carries several armfuls of firewood into the kitchen, and then takes the children there. The kitchen has no floor—or, rather, an earthen one—called a "ground floor" in this part of the bush. There is a large, roughly-made table in the centre of the place. She brings the children in, and makes them get on this table. They are two boys and two girls—mere babies. She gives them some supper, and then, before it gets dark, she goes into the house, and snatches up some pillows and bedclothes—expecting to see or lay her hand on the snake any minute. She makes a bed on the kitchen table for the children, and sits down beside it to watch all night.

She has an eye on the corner, and a green sapling club laid in readiness on the dresser by her side; also her sewing basket and a copy of the Young Ladies' Journal. She has brought the dog into the room.

Tommy turns in, under protest, but says he'll be awake all night and smash that blinded snake.

His mother asks him how many times she has told him not to swear. He has his club with him under the bedclothes, and Jacky protests

"Mummy! Tommy's skinnin' me alive wif his club. Make him take it out."

Tommy: "Shet up, you little shite! D'yer want to be bit with the snake?"

Jacky shuts up.

"If yer bit," says Tommy, after a pause, "you'll swell up, an' smell, an' turn red an' green an' blue all over till yer bust. Won't he, mother?"

"Now then, don't frighten the child. Go to sleep," she says.

The two younger children go to sleep, and now and then Jacky complains of being "skeezed." More room is made for him. Presently Tommy says: "Mother! listen to them bloody little possums. I'd like to screw their bloody necks."

And Jacky protests drowsily.

"But they don't hurt us, the little shites!"

Mother: "There, I told you you'd teach Jacky to swear." But the remark makes her smile. Jacky goes to sleep.

Presently Tommy asks:

"Mother! Do you think they'll ever extricate the damned kangaroo?"

"Lord! How am I to know, child? Go to sleep."

"Will you wake me if the snake comes out?"

"Yes. Go to sleep."

Near midnight. The children are all asleep and she sits there still, sewing and reading by turns. From time to time she glances round the floor and wall-plate, and, whenever she hears a noise, she reaches for the stick. The thunderstorm comes on, and the wind, rushing through the cracks in the slab wall, threatens to blow out her candle. She places it on a sheltered part of the dresser and fixes up a newspaper to protect it. At every flash of lightning, the cracks between the slabs gleam like polished silver. The thunder rolls, and the rain comes down in torrents.

Alligator lies at full length on the floor, with his eyes turned towards the partition. She knows by this that the snake is there. There are large cracks in that wall opening under the floor of the dwelling-house.

She is not a coward, but recent events have shaken her nerves. A little son of her brother-in-law was lately bitten by a snake, and died. Besides, she has not heard from her husband for six months, and is anxious about him.

He was a drover, and started squatting here when they were married. The drought of 18— ruined him. He had to sacrifice the remnant of his flock and go droving again. He intends to move his family into the nearest town when he comes back, and, in the meantime, his brother, who keeps a shanty on the main road, comes over about once a month with provisions. The wife has still a couple of cows, one horse, and a few sheep. The brother-in-law kills one of the latter occasionally, gives her what she needs of it, and takes the rest in return for other provisions.

She is used to being left alone. She once lived like this for eighteen months. As a girl she built the usual castles in the air; but all her girlish hopes and aspirations have long been dead. She finds all the excitement and recreation she needs in the Young Ladies' Journal, and Heaven help her! takes a pleasure in the fashion-plates.

Her husband is an Australian, and so is she. He is careless, but a good enough husband. If he had the means he would take her to the city and keep her there like a princess. They are used to being apart, or at least she is. "No use fretting," she says. He may forget sometimes that he is married; but if he has a good cheque when he comes back he will give most of it to her. When he had money he took her to the city several times—hired a railway sleeping compartment, and put up at the best hotels. He also bought her a buggy, but they had to sacrifice that along with the rest.

The last two children were born in the bush—one while her husband was bringing a drunken doctor, by force, to attend to her. She was alone on this occasion, and very weak. She had been ill with a fever. She prayed to God to send her assistance. God sent Black Mary—the "whitest" gin in all the land. Or, at least, God sent King Jimmy first, and he sent Black Mary. He put his black face round the door post, took in the situation at a glance, and said cheerfully: "All right, missus—I bring my old

woman, she down alonga creek."
One of the children died while she was here alone. She rode nineteen miles for assistance, carrying the dead child.

It must be near one or two o'clock. The fire is burning low. Alligator lies with his head resting on his paws, and watches the wall. He is not a very beautiful dog, and the light shows numerous old wounds where the hair will not grow. He is afraid of nothing on the face of the earth or under it. He will tackle a bullock as readily as he will tackle a flea. He hates all other dogs—except kangaroo-dogs—and has a marked dislike to friends or relations of the family. They seldom call, however. He sometimes makes friends with strangers. He hates snakes and has killed many, but he will be bitten some day and die; most snake-dogs end that way.
Now and then the bushwoman lays down her work and watches, and listens, and thinks. She thinks of things in her own life, for there is little else to think about.
The rain will make the grass grow, and this reminds her how she fought a bush-fire once while her husband was away. The grass was long, and very dry, and the fire threatened to burn her out. She put on an old pair of her husband's trousers and beat out the flames with a green bough, till great drops of sooty perspiration stood out on her forehead and ran in streaks down her blackened arms. The sight of his mother in trousers greatly

amused Tommy, who worked like a little hero by her side, but the terrified baby howled lustily for his "mummy." The fire would have mastered her but for four excited bushmen who arrived in the nick of time. It was a mixed-up affair all round; when she went to take up the baby he screamed and struggled convulsively, thinking it was a "blackman;" and Alligator, trusting more to the child's sense than his own instinct, charged furiously, and (being old and slightly deaf) did not in his excitement at first recognize his mistress's voice, but continued to hang on to the moleskins until choked off by Tommy with a saddle-strap. The dog's sorrow for his blunder, and his anxiety to let it be known that it was all a mistake, was as evident as his ragged tail and a twelve-inch grin could make it. It was a glorious time for the boys; a day to look back to, and talk about, and laugh over for many years.

She thinks how she fought a flood during her husband's absence. She stood for hours in the drenching downpour, and dug an overflow gutter to save the dam across the creek. But she could not save it. There are things that a bushwoman cannot do. Next morning the dam was broken, and her heart was nearly broken too, for she thought how her husband would feel when he came home and saw the result of years of labour swept away. She cried then.

She also fought the pleuro-pneumonia—dosed and bled the few remaining cattle, and wept again when her two best cows died.

Again, she fought a mad bullock that besieged the

house for a day. She made bullets and fired at him through cracks in the slabs with an old shot-gun. He was dead in the morning. She skinned him and got seventeen-and-sixpence for the hide.

She also fights the crows and eagles that have designs on her chickens. Her plan of campaign is very original. The children cry "Crows, mother!" and she rushes out and aims a broomstick at the birds as though it were a gun, and says "Bung!" The crows leave in a hurry; they are cunning, but a woman's cunning is greater.

Occasionally a bushman in the horrors, or a villainous-looking sundowner, comes and nearly scares the life out of her. She generally tells the suspicious-looking stranger that her husband and two sons are at work below the dam, or over at the yard, for he always cunningly inquires for the boss. Only last week a gallows-faced swagman—having satisfied himself that there were no men on the place—threw his swag down on the veranda, and demanded tucker. She gave him something to eat; then he expressed his intention of staying for the night. It was sundown then. She got a batten from the sofa, loosened the dog, and confronted the stranger, holding the batten in one hand and the dog's collar with the other. "Now you go!" she said. He looked at her and at the dog, said "All right, mum," in a cringing tone, and left. She was a determined-looking woman, and Alligator's yellow eyes glared unpleasantly—besides, the dog's chawing-up apparatus greatly resembled that of the reptile he was named after.

She has few pleasures to think of as she sits here alone by the fire, on guard against a snake. All days are much the same to her; but on Sunday afternoon she dresses herself, tidies the children, smartens up baby, and goes for a lonely walk along the bush-track, pushing an old perambulator in front of her. She does this every Sunday. She takes as much care to make herself and the children look smart as she would if she were going to do the block in the city. There is nothing to see, however, and not a soul to meet. You might walk for twenty miles along this track without being able to fix a point in your mind, unless you are a bushman. This is because of the everlasting, maddening sameness of the stunted trees—that monotony which makes a man long to break away and travel as far as trains can go, and sail as far as ship can sail—and farther.

But this bushwoman is used to the loneliness of it. As a girl-wife she hated it, but now she would feel strange away from it.

She is glad when her husband returns, but she does not gush or make a fuss about it. She gets him something good to eat, and tidies up the children.

She seems contented with her lot. She loves her children, but has no time to show it. She seems harsh to them. Her surroundings are not favourable to the development of the "womanly" or sentimental side of nature.

It must be near morning now; but the clock is in the

dwelling house. Her candle is nearly done; she forgot that she was out of candles. Some more wood must be got to keep the fire up, and so she shuts the dog inside and hurries round to the woodheap. The rain has cleared off. She seizes a stick, pulls it out, and— crash! the whole pile collapses.

Yesterday she bargained with a stray blackfellow to bring her some wood, and while he was at work she went in search of a missing cow. She was absent an hour or so, and the native black made good use of his time. On her return she was so astonished to see a good heap of wood by the chimney, that she gave him an extra fig of tobacco, and praised him for not being lazy. He thanked her, and left with head erect and chest well out. He was the last of his tribe and a King; but he had built that wood-heap hollow.

She is hurt now, and tears spring to her eyes as she sits down again by the table. She takes up a handkerchief to wipe the tears away, but pokes her eyes with her bare fingers instead. The handkerchief is full of holes, and she finds that she has put her thumb through one, and her forefinger through another.

This makes her laugh, to the surprise of the dog. She has a keen, very keen, sense of the ridiculous; and some time or other she will amuse bushmen with the story.

She had been amused before like that. One day she sat down "to have a good cry," as she said—and the old cat rubbed against her dress and "cried too." Then she had to laugh.

It must be near daylight now. The room is very close and hot because of the fire. Alligator still watches the wall from time to time. Suddenly he becomes greatly interested; he draws himself a few inches nearer the partition, and a thrill runs through his body. The hair on the back of his neck begins to bristle, and the battle-light is in his yellow eyes. She knows what this means, and lays her hand on the stick. The lower end of one of the partition slabs has a large crack on both sides. An evil pair of small, bright bead-like eyes glisten at one of these holes. The snake—a black one—comes slowly out, about a foot, and moves its head up and down. The dog lies still, and the woman sits as one fascinated. The snake comes out a foot farther. She lifts her stick, and the reptile, as though suddenly aware of danger, sticks his head in through the crack on the other side of the slab, and hurries to get his tail round after him. Alligator springs, and his jaws come together with a snap. He misses, for his nose is large, and the snake's body close down in the angle formed by the slabs and the floor. He snaps again as the tail comes round. He has the snake now, and tugs it out eighteen inches. Thud, thud comes the woman's club on the ground. Alligator pulls again. Thud, thud. Alligator gives another pull and he has the snake out—a black brute, five feet long. The head rises to dart about, but the dog has the enemy close to the neck. He is a big, heavy dog, but quick as a terrier. He shakes the snake as though he felt the original curse in common with mankind. The eldest boy wakes up, seizes his stick, and tries to get out of bed, but his mother forces him back with a grip of iron. Thud, thud—the snake's back is broken in several places. Thud, thud—its head is crushed, and Alligator's nose skinned again.

She lifts the mangled reptile on the point of her stick, carries it to the fire, and throws it in; then piles on the wood and watches the snake burn. The boy and dog watch too. She lays her hand on the dog's head, and all the fierce, angry light dies out of his yellow eyes. The younger children are quieted, and presently go to sleep. The dirty-legged boy stands for a moment in his shirt, watching the fire. Presently he looks up at her, sees the tears in her eyes, and, throwing his arms round her neck exclaims:

"Mother, I won't never go drovin'; blarst me if I do!"

And she hugs him to her worn-out breast and kisses him; and they sit thus together while the sickly daylight breaks over the bush.

'What a gutsy lady,' marvelled Brigit.

'Reminds me of you sometimes,' laughed Jax leaning over and giving his wife a kiss on the cheek.

'Really?'

'Really.'

They arrived in Birdsville to be greeted by a large crowd of people milling around in the red dust. There were camels on backs of trucks standing tall, howling and spitting at anyone daring to get too close. Dogs, vehicles of every shape and size and air craft lined up row upon row on the airstrip. It was the beginning of the week of the Birdsville Races.

'Sid and Janet should be here by now shouldn't they?' Brigit was studying the crowd looking for familiar faces.

'Should be. They said they would fly up this morning so they should have arrived by now.' Jax made his way through the mayhem and drove down alongside the aircraft. 'There's the plane over there. I can see Fred and Jasper.'

Jax drove over beside the familiar aircraft.

'Good flight guys?' he asked as he and Brigit got out of the car.

'Yes it was, we took a detour to have a look at Lake Eyre. Plenty of water and birds there at the moment, it was quite something.'

'Wish I'd seen that,' said Brigit wistfully.

'You can if you want to Brig, we can take you up after the races if you are planning on sticking around that long. Don't want to lose our place in the line up here,' said Jasper indicating the long line of small aircraft taking up every available space along the fence line.

'Our plans are pretty flexible Jasper, thanks that would be great,' said Jax squeezing Brigit's hand.

Two days later Brigit emerged from the small private plane with a huge smile stretched across her pretty face.

'How was that?' asked Jax, as he came around under the wing from the other side of the plane.

'Oh wow, that was so awesome. Thanks Jasper,' she turned and gave him a big hug. 'It was neat that we could fly so low and not disturb the birds. It was really cool to see them all just hanging out around the lake. I have never seen so many pelicans in one place.'

Jax put his arm around her shoulders. 'I haven't either, I wondered why we hadn't seen many around this past year or so. Since the rain filled up the inland lakes that seems to be where they have all disappeared to. Jasper, I'm hangin out for a beer, how about you sweetheart, fancy a nice cold drink?'

'Lead the way,' she laughed, skipping along beside her husband.

The following morning after breakfast, Jax packed their gear into the back of the car.

'Geez it's about time you showed up. All the packing's done,' he scolded Brigit as she came bouncing out of the dining room. 'What have you been doing?'

Excitedly she explained. 'I've just been talking to some lovely old Kiwi tourists. They're on their way to Innamincka today too, they were the ones we saw at Marree.'

'Really? Quite a trek for oldies.'

'Oh I don't think they are that old. They

certainly seem like a spritely lot. They've come all the way from Adelaide and going back down through Broken Hill. They're having a blast. They're a hard case bunch.'

'Well, you'd better say goodbye to Mum and Dad and the others so we can get on our way. Now that the place has quietened down a bit we can have a look around before we go.'

About an hour and a half and 116km later they crossed the boundary into Cordillo Downs Station.

'Check your watch Brig, see how long it takes us to drive all the way through to the other side of the station. It's about 150kms I think?'

'Ten thirty, so how big is the whole farm?'

'Not sure, I think it was more than 7,000kms at one stage. They set a record in the 1880's of shearing 85,000 sheep in one season.'

'Bloody hell, I've never seen that many sheep in one place, let alone shear them. Must have been an impressive sight.'

'I reckon it was. We'll get to see the shearing shed they used, that's impressive too.'

After a stop for coffee and some fruit they set off again and lapsed into a comfortable silence, taking in the scenery. They were just pulling up by a river to stop and look at some old ruins when they spotted a small bus parked there.

'Oh Jax look, it's the Kiwi's I was telling you about. Come and meet them. They must have got away before we did this morning.'

They were delighted to see Brigit again and to meet Jax. They had a quick catch up before the driver hurried them along to get back on the bus.

'We've got a long way to go,' he explained, 'don't want to run out of daylight.'

As the bus drove off into the distance Brigit realised that it had suddenly gone quiet. She laughed. 'I just realised that the corellas have quietened down. Man they were making an awful racket when we pulled up weren't they. There must be hundreds of them.'

She walked over to take some photos of them while they were perched in the trees along the riverbank and away they went again, filling the air with their excited squawking. Having them flying around made for great photos though. Jax and Brigit wandered around the remains of the small settlement taking photos of each other posing amongst the old ruins of houses which once stood proud and strong. Brigit particularly liked the one where she was able to set the camera up on a piece of broken wall and get the two of them in the photo together. They set off again along the dirt track which showed a myriad of wheel ruts and tracks of previous travellers. Cordillo Downs boundaries are 116 km from Innaminka and 155 km from Birdsville so their whole journey for the day would be around 420kms. They stopped by another river later in the afternoon and had lunch and a swim under the shade of some willow trees. By the time they got going again it was getting on for four o'clock.

'Ah, there's the Burke and Wills tree turn off. If we go in to see it, we might run out of daylight but we could park up by the river for the night. Or else we could just keep trucking on. I figure we're about 100kms from Innaminka and we've got about 2 hours of daylight left.'

'Let's live dangerously' laughed Brigit, 'let's camp down by the river.'

'Bullah Bullah water hole, here we come then,' he said as they turned towards Cooper's Creek and the dig tree.

They were about halfway in when they came across the Kiwi tour bus again. 'Looks like they're in trouble,' said Jax. 'Not the best place to have a breakdown that's for sure.'

They both leapt out of the car and went to see what was happening.

'The trailer's lost a wheel', explained the driver. 'I'm happy enough to leave the darned thing here and forget about it but I haven't got enough room to fit all the luggage inside the bus.'

'No worries mate,' said Jax. 'we've got room to take some for you if you like.'

Before the driver could respond there was a yell from the group of passengers who were wandering around behind the bus chatting and taking pictures. They raced over to see one of the passengers lying on the ground.

'I think he's been bitten by a snake,' cried one of the ladies. It's my husband,' she explained to Jax as he tore open the man's trouser leg to take a closer look.'

'Yep, snake bite alright. Brigit go get our first aid kit, gotta get a tourniquet on this leg quick smart.' He turned to the driver. 'You got an Eperb and Sat phone with you?'

'Sure have. Soon as you said snake bite I set it off.'

'Good one. The flying doctors are in Broken Hill, we should be able to get one here pretty quickly. Here, their number is on the first aid kit.'

The driver walked away from the group and called the number. When he came back he wasn't looking too happy.

'They've got a major down south and won't have anybody here for about an hour they reckon.'

'Shit', said Jax, 'we really can't wait that long.' He was thoughtful for a moment. 'Brigit, didn't Mum and Dad say they were staying another night at Birdsville?'

'Yes they did, why?'

'Grab that Sat phone and call Dad. See if he can bring the plane up and pick this guy up and get him to Broken Hill. He'd get there a lot quicker than the doctors would.'

Brigit was on the phone before Jax

stopped speaking.

'Sid, Brigit here. We have an emergency. One of those Kiwi tourists we met at Birdsville has got a snake bite. The flying doctors are tied up on some major emergency down south, can you pick him up and take him to Broken Hill please? Fantastic. Yes we are at the Burke and Wills dig tree. The driver has set off their eperb. Can you, really? Great. See you soon.'

'Apparently he can hone in on the eperb signal,' she was impressed.

Jax and the driver loaded the injured man and his wife into the car and drove out to an area that would be more suitable for a plane to land. Sid's plane appeared 20 minutes later and landed in a cloud of red dust a safe distance from the car. Without stopping to make small talk, they loaded the man and his wife into the plane and Sid was off again banking right and heading straight for the hospital at Broken Hill. Jax headed back to the bus. He and the driver loaded as many bags as they could into the car, the rest they were able to get on the bus now that there were two empty seats. It was starting to get dark.

'I'm used to driving in the dark. Don't like it much but I'm happy to lead the way to Innaminka if you like?' he said to the driver.

'That would be great,' he said thankfully. 'Not comfortable being out here with these lovely old dears when it gets dark. Had hoped we'd be in by around five o'clock today but it's gonna be more like seven.

Jax smiled. 'They don't look too perturbed to me mate, they're singin.'

Both men laughed, hopped into their vehicles and the small convoy was on its way. They arrived in Innaminka as expected around seven o'clock. The motelier was very relieved to see them, she had been expecting them two hours earlier.

'Good to see you lot still smiling,' she said. 'Get yourselves into the dining room, grab yourselves a drink and some dinner. We can sort ya bags out for ya.'

'Hey,' said one of the travellers, 'Look, up there on the tele, looks like the All Blacks are beating the Aussies.' He laughed and stared at the men sitting stoney faced beneath the TV, their backs to the football game. 'Oooh, not happy boys?' he taunted.

He got a scowl from each of them in return.

'Go the Kiwis' he roared then wandered off into the dining room amidst cheers of support for their beloved footy team.

Brigit and Jax enjoyed having breakfast with their fellow travellers the next morning. The coach driver came in and told them that the man with the snake bite was okay and was expected to make a full recovery.

'When our group arrives in Broken Hill in

two days time we hope to pick them up from the hospital so they can carry on with the tour,' he added.

The group was delighted and effusively grateful to Jax and his Dad.

'All in a day's work,' laughed Jax. 'Just really glad we were there to help, could have been a bit messy otherwise. Now you lot take care out there in the wilds okay. We're heading off now, might see you in Tibooburra. We'll be off to Broken Hill the following day.'

'Yes we are too' said one of the ladies.

'Well have fun and don't do anything we wouldn't do.' He winked at them and gave Brigit a playful pat on the bottom as they walked out, raising a giggle from the group.

Brigit and Jax headed for home after a two-night stop in Broken Hill. They did see the Kiwi bus again on their second day and gave them a big wave.

Once they got back home and unpacked, they called Janet and Sid and caught up with all the news. Sid had stayed overnight in Broken Hill with the travellers in case they needed to be transported somewhere else. They didn't, but it gave Sid a chance to catch up with some of his mates in the flying doctor corps. They had quite a night from all accounts. Sid wasn't saying much about it in Janet's hearing.

'So what did you think of your first big

outback trip Brigit?' asked Sid when he got a chance to take the phone off Janet.

'Oh it was absolutely awesome Sid. Can't wait for the next one. I'm really looking forward to the trip we are planning for Stella and Rees when they come over, they'll love it. Their mother was a great traveller but so far they haven't been out of New Zealand yet.'

'Great idea,' said Sid. 'Where are you planning on taking them?'

'Jax suggested Adelaide to Darwin. He says that way we get to see two of Aussie's loveliest cities as well as some outback and hey let's not forget good old Uluru and Alice Springs.'

'Sounds like a plan.'

'Yes, we'll talk to Stella and Rees about it when we go over for Dad and Ruth's wedding. Are you guys coming?'

'Not sure yet, are we Janet. About Ruth and Luke's wedding? No, we'll have to see but we can talk about that another time, you kids must be beat. Get an early night and take the next couple of days off. We'll see you back on the job on Wednesday.'

Chapter Nine

The Wedding

Ruth Laurenson & Luke Williamson
request the pleasure of your company
at their wedding on

25th January 1999 at Duffield Station
RSVP by 10.01.99

They were simple invitations as there were only going to be a handful of family invited. On Ruth's side there was only Sid, Janet and Jax as her parents were unable to make the trip out from England. She was so excited that Sid and Janet were able to make it. On Luke's side were Brigit, Sandy, Selwyn, Stella and Rees of course and he'd also invited his brother Case and his wife Kate from Perth.

Sid and Janet were relieved that they were able to get away for a few days and fly to New Zealand. Jax and Brigit decided to fly over a week before the wedding so they could help with the preparations and then stay on for a couple of weeks afterwards to catch up with Stella and Rees and enjoy the change of scenery.

'I am so looking forward to this Jax. Dad and Ruth are perfect together, I couldn't be happier for them,' said Brigit excitedly as they sat at the table making table decorations. 'It will be so neat to have a 'Mum' again.'

Jax smiled and gave his wife a hug. 'I'm looking forward to it to. I haven't really spent much time on your high-country farm. It will be fun to help out while the newlyweds are on their honeymoon.'

The small intimate wedding was set to take place in the gardens at Duffield Station. Sandy had arranged for the local Women's Division garden enthusiasts to come in and tidy up the gardens for the occasion. There had been an excited hive of activity for a few days the week before and they had done a marvellous job, the grounds were picture perfect. The wisteria hung in glorious shades of lilac and white over the archway which would serve as the focal point for the ceremony and make a perfect backdrop for photos. The gardens bordering the backyard were dancing with a delightful array of colourful blooms of hydrangeas, rambling roses and dahlias. Perfectly formed blooms of aromatic roses graced every room in the house and Ruth had chosen pink roses and white gypsophlia for her hand tied bouquet.

Sid and Janet arrived two days before the wedding. Ruth was delighted to see them. She had only been back to the farm once since she left two years earlier. She had wanted to spend some time with Sid and Janet and the staff before signing off as their station nurse. It was a sad time for her, she had loved her life at Bullock Creek Station but she loved Luke and Duffield Station more, so the decision was easy.

Sid and Janet had a surprise gift for the couple.

'How would you two like to get married on top of the Remarkables Mountain,' Sid asked as they sat around with glasses of wine and beer discussing wedding details. 'I've been asking around and that seems to be the in thing to do. If you want to, it will be our gift to you both. Janet and I really didn't know what to give you.'

Luke looked at Ruth. 'Well darling, what do you think, would you like to get married on a mountain top?'

Ruth looked across to the mountains she had come to love so much and her eyes filled with tears. 'Oh Sid, Janet, thank you. That is a wonderful idea and Luke if you are okay with it, I would love to get married to you on a mountain top.'

Luke shook Sid's hand and gave Janet a big hug. 'Thank you so much, your generous and thoughtful gift is gratefully accepted.'

The 25th of January finally arrived. It was a truly remarkable blue sky day, perfect for a wedding on top of The Remarkables. Although there was no snow on the mountains at this time of the year, they were still – remarkable. The helicopter arrived at eleven o'clock as scheduled, with the videographer and marriage celebrant on board. They picked Ruth and Luke up from the paddock beside the house where many photos had been taken and flew them off to the mountain top. Sandy and Janet had tucked a small fold up table, lace tablecloth, two crystal glasses, a bottle of champagne and some nibbles into the back of the helicopter and alerted the celebrant that they were there.

The guests stood and waved the helicopter out of sight then went back inside to finish setting up the tables for the reception. Kate and Case had arrived the previous day and Kate was enjoying being back on the farm and catching up with the family.

'My gosh Brigit, the last time I saw you was at your wedding. How long has it been now, six years?'

'Yep, six years just gone,' she said proudly glancing across at her husband.

'You know you and Jax are always welcome to stay with us anytime.'

I know Aunt Kate and I'm sorry we haven't been to see you, but hey, you guys could come up and spend some time with us on the farm too you know. I'm sure the boys would love it.'

'They would, we would. , maybe Case and I should come up, I'll run it by him. As for the boys, they are busy with their young families now. So lovely having wee babies around again.'

'Gosh it's hard to believe the boys are fathers,' she laughed, 'I can remember them staying here for the holidays when they were teenagers.'

Brigit looked at her watch and went over to the window.

'Something the matter?' asked Kate.

'They've been gone an awfully long time,' Brigit anxiously checked her watch again. 'I thought it was only going to be an hour?'

'Oh, Brigit, I'm sorry I thought you knew,' said Sid coming in the back door. 'I had a quick chat with the pilot and asked him to extend the hire and take the newlyweds on a scenic flight over the Southern Alps after they tied the knot. I've been so caught up talking farming with Selwyn here that I forgot to tell you.'

'Oh, that's a relief,' sighed Brigit. 'So how long will that take do you think?

'To be honest I really don't know. It's a gorgeous day so maybe they will stay up longer. I left the timing up to them and the pilot.'

'Oh Sid, you are a worry. So what are we supposed to do about the hot food?' Janet was annoyed with her husband for not telling them earlier.

'Don't fret woman, it'll be okay. I'm sure they won't be gone for much longer.'

The guests waited patiently wandering around the gardens, sitting by the pool and enjoying the festive drinks and nibbles. After three hours had passed, Brigit took Jax aside.

'I'm worried hon, do you think we should call the helicopter company. It shouldn't take two hours to nip across to Te Anau in a chopper surely.'

Just as she finished speaking the phone rang. It was the Helicopter company.

'No cause to panic,' he assured them. 'Your folks are presently sitting on top of the Southern Alps in Fiordland while their chopper makes an emergency dash back to Queenstown with a badly wounded hunter. Once he's been off loaded, our pilot will refuel and head back up to get them. They are enjoying the adventure and the wonderful views by all accounts.'

Brigit hung up the phone and relayed the message to everyone. They laughed in relief and carried on with their drinks and nibbles and chatted amicably with each other. Brigit, Jax, Stella and Rees took the opportunity to get out of their wedding finery for a while and take a dip in the pool. Before long the rest of the guests decided to follow suit. It was way too hot to be standing around all dressed up.

By three o'clock Brigit was getting

annoyed. She went over and sat down with Kate on the sun lounger beside the pool.

'This is getting ridiculous,' she growled. 'Surely they should be back by now, the food will be going off in this heat.'

'I agree dear. It does seem an awfully long time doesn't it, maybe you should ring that company again.'

'Good idea, I think I will.'

She picked up the phone book, checked the number and dialled. When she hung up she went back out to Kate, ashen faced.

'Oh my God, Brigit, what is it?'

'You're not going to believe this,' she signalled everyone to gather round. 'The chopper pilot who dropped Ruth and Dad off on the top of the mountains knocked his head as he was checking the chopper while it was refuelling and he passed out. He hasn't regained consciousness and they want to send another pilot up to pick them up but they aren't sure of their exact location. They have tracking devices in the choppers but not to the pinpoint accuracy that is needed to find two people in such a vast mountainous terrain. Oh my God, what if they have to stay up there all night,' she fretted.

'Brigit!' Selwyn's voice was stern. 'Come on sweetheart, get a grip, you know darn well your Dad and Ruth are quite capable of looking after themselves on a mountain top. Hell they live on one for God's sake. Now did the guy at the office say if they had any supplies with them?'

Brigit wiped her eyes and took a deep breath.

'Umm, yeah, he did say something about a blanket and picnic basket but I didn't really take much notice.'

Just then they heard the sound of an approaching helicopter.

'Oh good, that must be them,' shouted Brigit excitedly. 'And here we are all sitting around the pool in our togs.'

Everyone laughed, relieved. But the pilot was the only person on board the chopper. Sid went straight over to talk to him as soon as the rotors stopped spinning. He came back with the pilot.

'Seems the other pilot has got concussion, and not cleared to fly. This is Merrick, the back up pilot'

'We are quickly running out of daylight hours folks, reported Merrick without waiting for any further introductions. 'I am happy to take someone up with me now as a lookout and see if we can find them with the information we have, otherwise it will be first light tomorrow morning and hopefully Wills will be conscious and able to pinpoint their location. We are so terribly sorry about all this. The company has never had this sort of thing happen before. We will be going out of our way to get them back as soon as we can, so, who's coming with me?'

'I will,' Sid stepped forward immediately. 'I've got choppers back home and I'm used to searching from the air, unless you want to go Sel?'

'No, you go' said Selwyn, 'I'll wait here and keep this lot in line.'

Sandy smiled to herself knowing that Selwyn hated flying, hence the fact that they had never ventured outside New Zealand. 'Plenty to do and see here in Godzone,' he'd always said to her.

The chopper returned with only Sid and the pilot aboard just before dark. Sid was bitterly disappointed.

'Didn't spot a damn thing,' he muttered. 'But I must say it's pretty awesome country up there, so vastly different from home. I can understand how you could easily lose somebody in that dense terrain.'

They watched the chopper disappear into the distance.

'He'll be back at first light to pick me up again and this time we should have more information. Let's hope that guy, Wills, is okay and can show us where they are.'

Kate and Sandy wrapped up all the food and refrigerated it hoping it would stay nice and fresh until they could re-set the reception table again.

Brigit tossed and turned fitfully during

the night.

'For goodness sake Brig,' said Jax irritably as the hours dragged by. 'They will be alright, you know that, just get some sleep, you don't want them to see you looking like a wreck in the morning do you?'

Brigit burst into tears. 'Oh Jax, I couldn't bear it if anything happened to them. I just can't imagine my life without Dad, you know?'

'I know honey, I'm sorry, come here.' He pulled her over and cradled her in his arms stroking her hair. Eventually he could hear the steady rhythm of her breathing as she fell asleep.

The chopper was back at five thirty in the morning as promised and Sid was ready and waiting. He had a chilly box full of food and drink which he loaded into the chopper as soon as it landed. He climbed aboard with a quick wave to those who were up and watching and they were off again.

Breakfast was a sombre affair. Nobody felt like talking so they ate in silence then wandered off to sit and wait. Selwyn and Sandy went out and checked on the stock. Once the dishes were done Janet took a book and sat in a sun lounger by the pool. Case and Kate took a couple of horses and went riding. It was another glorious day, clear blue skies and the promise of high temperatures again. By lunch time Brigit was getting rather fidgety.

'You'd think someone would contact us

wouldn't you?' she demanded irritably.

'No news is good news honey,' Jax attempted a smile.

'Not always,' she grumped.

Jax pulled her into a tight cuddle then picked her up and took her to the edge of the pool. 'Time you cooled down a bit I think Mrs Jamieson.' He threw his squealing wife into the pool and followed her in, clothes and all.

'That looks like fun,' laughed Janet, throwing off her sun top and joining them.

Stella and Rees walked round the side of the house just as all the commotion was taking place.

'Hey, what's happening? You heard anything yet?'

'Not yet,' said Jax. 'Just thought I'd cool my wife down, she was getting a little bit heated,' he laughed as he pushed her head under the water.

She surfaced and they started to splash water at each other. Rees took a running dive into the pool clothes and all, followed by Stella. As they were laughing and splashing each other with gay abandon a helicopter suddenly appeared up over the house just above their heads giving them all a huge fright. They looked up expectantly and were elated to see Luke and Ruth waving excitedly out the window. They cheered and waved and screamed delightedly from the pool as the chopper landed. Ruth and Luke ran from the chopper stripping off their finery and shoes and dived right into the middle of the group in the pool. There were hugs and kisses and tears as they all reunited. Sid, not to be left out, decided to jump in too. By now the pool was fairly crowded. Selwyn and Sandy came bursting breathlessly through the house to see if Luke and Ruth had been found. They couldn't believe their eyes when they saw everyone in the pool in their clothes, including the missing newlyweds.

"Any room for us,' they laughed, heading for the pool?

Just then Case and Kate came running in. They had seen the helicopter go over and raced their horses back to the homestead. The stunned looks on their faces had everyone in fits of laughter.

'So, did you actually get married before you went missing?' asked Sid as they were finally seated around the reception table celebrating the marriage of Luke and Ruth.

'We sure did,' smiled Luke, proudly showing off his new wife's wedding ring, we sure did. And don't ask us about the honeymoon night cos we ain't telling, are we darling,' he smiled conspiratorially at Ruth.

She blushed and lowered her lashes but no-one missed the colour creeping into her cheeks.

'My God, she's blushing,' laughed Sid.

'Well, in all the time I've known you girl, I've never seen you blush. Must have been quite a night.'

This only made Ruth blush even more.

'Oh leave her alone Sid, you're embarrassing the poor girl,' scolded Janet.

'Needless to say, we are sorry you all went through such a tough night not knowing where we were but believe me it was a perfect night up there among the stars. Actually it couldn't have been a more perfect honeymoon location could it sweetheart?' Luke smiled at his beaming bride.

'It was stunning up there, it really was,' sighed Ruth. Fortunately we had a blanket and some food so we were okay. Thank God Wills was able to fly though and was able to show Merrick exactly where we were. Not sure I would want to spend another night out there without food. There was fresh spring water nearby but we had no hunting gear with us of course. Oh and Sid, thank you so much for such a thoughtful gift. It might not have turned out as you planned but it will be a day and night we will remember for ever.' She reached over and covered Luke's hand with her own as they exchanged a look which excluded everyone else.

Chapter Ten

Stella and Rees's Road Trip

Stella and Rees emerged from the arrivals gate at Adelaide airport, breaking into excited squeals and smiles amid the tears when they spotted Brigit and Jax.

'Oh it's so good to see you guys,' gushed Stella. 'It's been ages.'

Rees pulled Brigit into a warm embrace fighting back tears.

They chatted excitedly as they made their way to the motel for their first night. Jax and Brigit hadn't really told the others exactly where they would be going on this trip, they decided in the end to keep the final itinerary a surprise.

'Leave it all to us,' Brigit had told them excitedly on the phone when they started to make plans. Trust us, Jax and I will take you on the trip of a lifetime.'

'So where are we off to first?' asked Stella as they sat on the floor of the motel eating fish and chips out of the paper.

'First stop Port Augusta,' announced Jax authoritatively.

'There's an awesome museum type place there called Wadlatta. You guys are gonna love it,' said Brigit with enthusiasm.

'A museum,' responded Rees with disgust. 'I hate museums, they are full of old shit.'

'Don't make any judgements until you see it Rees, believe me this one is something different and a real eye opener about what Aussie is all about. This continent has been around a very long time and has an amazing story to tell.'

'You sound like a blimmin tour guide,' laughed Rees, 'but I'll take your word for it. And it better be pretty darn good or…'

'Or what, little brother, or what?' Brigit threw a chip at him, he threw one back and that's how the food fight started.

They were all up bright and early and impatient to get on the road next morning. They visited the museum as promised and Rees had to admit it was 'a pretty cool place'. Brigit and Stella chose some souvenirs as they left.

'Hey Stella,' Rees threw his arm around her in a brotherly hug, 'we got a long ways to go yet so don't go filling up your bag with stuff otherwise we'll have to pay excess baggage to get home.'

'Then I'll just dump you off instead Mr excess baggage,' she tossed her head in mock irritation as she jumped in the car.

They made their way to Woomera for

their first overnight stop, taking in the typical tourist sights along the way. After they'd settled into their units and had dinner they sat in the air conditioned bar and had a few drinks.

'Rees has been talking with that barman for ages, what are they talking about?' Brigit asked Jax as he placed another round of drinks on the table.

'Oh just that Air Force test range we went past on the way in. Did you see it?'

'Can't say I took much notice,' confessed Brigit, 'I was too busy looking out for the motel, sounds a bit boring.'

'Not to Rees obviously,' laughed Stella. 'So what's on the agenda for tomorrow Jax, I wish you'd give us a list of where we're going.'

'Stella, chill okay, I just want to make each day a surprise. But I will tell you that tomorrow we will be going underground.'

'I don't like underground,' pouted Stella.

'See,' said Jax 'you are making assumptions. Just wait, I know you guys are gonna love this place.'

Stella was nervous about the day ahead and a little of it rubbed off on Brigit.

'How far underground do we go do you know?' whined Stella as she and Brigit dressed next morning.

'I dunno but I wish you'd just stop whinging about it Stel, you're pissing me off, let's just wait and see shall we.' Brigit yanked the unit door open and slammed it shut behind her.

'What's up with you?' asked Jax when Brigit thumped into their unit.

'Oh nothing, Stella's just being a scaredy cat that's all and it's just getting on my wick.'

Rees and Jax looked at each other and shrugged. 'Great, chilly silence, that's all we need,' complained Rees.

'It's that time of the month' Jax confided in a whisper to Rees.'

'Oh,' Rees's cheeks reddened.

Once they got on the road, Jax started to talk about Opals which caught the girls' interest and they eventually calmed down and made their peace.

'Are we going underground to find Opals?' asked Brigit?

'Nope, we are going underground to sleep,' gloated Jax hoping to draw a shocked expression from his wife. He wasn't disappointed.

'I'm not sleeping in any damn cave Jax. There could be all sorts of creepie crawlies down there.'

'Me neither' scolded Stella from the back seat.

'Good one Jax, here we go again, just tell us where we are going so we don't have to listen to these two complaining,' groaned Rees.

Jax pulled in to Roxby Downs. 'Okay everyone, let's grab a coffee and I will show you a map of where we are going then. No more surprises and no more bitching okay.' He was annoyed.

They ordered their coffees and poured over the map Jax had hidden under his seat.

'Coober Pedy?' queried Stella, 'that's a weird name.'

'It's a weird place,' said Brigit. 'My Aunt Kate has been there and told me a little bit about it, I'm really looking forward to seeing it for myself,' she added excitedly.

By the time they'd had their coffee Jax had calmed down and the group was once again back on a friendly even keel, much to Rees's relief, he hated disharmony. They stopped in Glendambo for lunch, taking the time to have a look around the small outback town before heading off on the final leg of their journey.

It was late afternoon by the time Jax pulled up outside the underground motel at Coober Pedy. As they walked into the reception area Stella was pleasantly surprised.

'Oh wow, this is underground? This is really cool; I can do this. Sorry Jax, didn't mean to be such a pain, I guess I should have had more faith in you huh.'

'Don't worry about it Stel, but no more pre-conceived panic attacks okay, trust me, I just want you guys to have fun and enjoy the trip.'

Stella walked over to Jax and putting her arms around his waist gave him a big hug.

'Thanks brother-in-law, you're the best.'

Next morning, after they had checked out all the opal shops and were sitting in a café enjoying cold drinks, Jax presented the girls with an opal ring each that he'd bought for them in one of the shops while they were ooohing and aaahing over sun frocks. The girls were delighted. They came at him from both sides and planted a big juicy kiss on both cheeks.

'Boy, some guys get all the luck, twice in one day,' complained Rees.

To which both girls did the same to him and laughed at his embarrassment. They cruised around Coober Pedy for a while before setting off on the main highway again.

'I actually like Coober Pedy,' remarked Rees thoughtfully. 'Great place to get lost if you don't wanna be found eh?'

'You planning on checking out of society Rees?' laughed Jax, glancing over his shoulder at his brother in law.

'Food for thought,' he grinned.

'Ayers Rock here we come,' said Stella excitedly as she checked their next destination.

'I think it's called Uluru now,' said Brigit.

'Officially it is Ayers Rock/Uluru,' explained Jax, 'and don't ask me why cos I don't know.'

Over the next five days the group enjoyed travelling and exploring the route to Tennant Creek. They traversed their way around the

Kings Canyon, stopping every now and then to take photos and marvel at the expansive scenery under clear blue skies. They also enjoyed cultural shows and experiences in Alice Springs during their two night stay there. Rees, who had a weird taste in music according to his twin sister, purchased a CD of didgeridoo music at the Starlight Theatre and insisted Jax play it on the car stereo as they travelled. He was pleasantly surprised to see everyone else was enjoying it too, tapping along with the haunting rhythms.

'What's this place called?' asked Brigit as she got out of the car at their lunch stop. There's aliens painted on all the walls, wicked.'

'Wycliffe Well,' said Jax, 'the guy that owned it was a UFO freak.'

'No kidding,' laughed Rees.

They grabbed a sandwich and coffee and sat down at a table by the window.

'Look, this is all about UFO sightings,' shuddered Stella as she wandered around the partitions completely covered in newspaper clippings going back many years.

'What's the matter Stella, don't you believe in UFO's?' smiled Brigit.

'Dunno, never really thought about it.'

'Jax, Jax, earth to Jax can you hear me?' demanded Brigit leaning over and jabbing Jax in the ribs.

'What? Oh, uh sorry.'

'You look like you've just seen a UFO,'

laughed Stella.

'Or a ghost,' whispered Brigit. 'Honey what is it?'

'Oh nothing. I just thought I saw a vehicle I recognised that's all.'

'So what did this vehicle ever do to you that's got you so shook up?' queried Rees putting his hand on Jax's shoulder.

Jax shrugged off Rees's hand and made an attempt to laugh it off. 'Ahh, nuthin, just thought it was some old bastard who used to work for us.'

'Owes ya money does he?' laughed Rees.

'Yeah something like that Reesy boy. Okay you lot, you finished your coffees? Time to hit the road.' Jax was eager to get out of the place.

They arrived at their motel in Tennant Creek just as the sun was beginning it's descent over the horizon. They freshened up then went off in search of a bar and some food. Sitting outside in the cool air with their beers and wine, the foursome talked about their trip.

'The highlight for me so far,' pondered Stella in response to Jax's question, 'was Uluru. What a cool place, or should I say, a hot place. I liked the accommodation too, that was pretty neat. What about you Rees?'

'Well, I did love seeing the 'red rock' but I was blown away by the walk around King's Canyon.'

Jax laughed, 'Yeah we know mate, you haven't stopped talking about it.'

'But it was so unreal, I've never seen anything like that before. I grew up on green mountains don't forget.'

'I know, just pullin ya tit mate.'

'Next stop Katherine,' Jax said as he stood up, stretched and yawned. 'Pretty long hot day again tomorrow folks so best we get some shut eye. Think it's your turn to drive first tomorrow isn't it Rees?'

'Yes it is,' confirmed Brigit.

The plan was always to get up early and get on the road before the day started to warm up. That meant as soon as it was daylight. Being mid-August the temperatures were cooler than the mid-summer temps that Brigit and Jax were used to, but Stella and Rees had come from snow on the ground back in New Zealand so they were certainly feeling the heat, not that they were complaining.

On their way to Katherine they stopped off at the Daly Waters Pub for a cold drink and a chance for Stella to buy some more souvenirs.

'Sis, I keep telling ya you're gonna need another suitcase at the rate you're going,' scolded Rees.

'I may never come this way again so why shouldn't I have some keepsakes,' she retorted defensively.

'Now, now, children, let's not squabble,' laughed Jax. 'Anyone for a swim? Next stop is Mataranka, there's a great swimming hole there.

Let me drive for a while Rees,' Jax held his hand out for the keys.

Stella got out her tourist map. 'Cool, there's an old homestead at Mataranka. I love the homesteads, don't you Brigit?'

'I live in one Stella,' she laughed glancing over her shoulder.

'Hey, that's not fair, it's not that old,' Jax feigned offence.

'Hey Jax, is that a lake over there?'

'What direction are you looking in Rees?

'Just over there on the right, can you see it?'

'Oh, yeah, looks like a lake alright, shall we go and have a look.'

He threw a wink at Brigit and she winked back with a broad grin, sharing a secret the others weren't privy to.

'I wouldn't mind a quick dip in a *cold* lake,' said Rees. 'Getting pretty hot and sticky. It's not that salty artesian stuff though is it?'

'Dunno Rees, best we take a look eh. Should be a turn off up here somewhere.' It was all he could do to keep a straight face. Brigit was desperately trying to stop herself from laughing out loud.

They travelled on for a short distance and turned off towards Mataranka.

'Doesn't seem to be getting any closer does it?' said Rees leaning over Jax's shoulder peering through the windscreen. Sometimes it seems to disappear altogether. Do you know the name of the lake, I'll look it up on the map.'

'Yes, it's called 'mirage' mate.'

'What?'

'Mirage, meaning it's not real, it's just an illusion, a heat haze.'

'Oh you rotten shit,' laughed Rees smacking him on the back of the head.

They arrived at Mataranka and changing into their swimming gear, dived into the clear cool pool. They stayed longer than Jax had intended but he figured they should still get in to Katherine around dusk or shortly thereafter.

Back in the car, refreshed and revitalised they headed back out towards the main road. They were almost to the main road when there was a loud bang.

'Damn,' muttered Jax, 'a bloody puncture.'

The nuts had been put on with a rattle gun at the homestead garage and by the time Rees and Jax had worked them loose and changed the tyre it was just on dusk. They were running well behind schedule.

'We'll need to get that tyre fixed first thing,' said Jax. 'Can't afford to be out here without a spare.'

'We're gonna be late getting into Katherine,' said Brigit checking her map. 'Do you think they'll hold our rooms for us?' she asked a little apprehensively.

'Haven't seen much traffic on the road

today and it's not peak holiday time so I think we'll be okay. Don't really want to use the Sat phone if we can help it,' said Jax.

My phones gone flat,' said Stella dejectedly.

'Seems I spoke too soon about no traffic on the road,' said Jax as he noticed car headlights looming up behind them. 'There are other people on the road tonight after all.'

The sun wasn't far off the horizon, the light was dim and would turn into full on darkness within a few minutes.

The vehicle came up behind them at speed then slowed down and tailed them for a couple of kilometres.

'Why doesn't he pass?' said Jax, annoyed at the headlights shining in his rear vision mirror.

Rees turned around to have a look but could only see the shape of a head behind the steering wheel.

' Looks like there's only one person in it.'

'He's pretty close, there's plenty of straight road for him to pass, I wonder what he's up to?'

Just then the vehicle sped past them. It was a white ute. Nobody noticed Jax's sudden intake of breath.

The ute pulled away into the distance and the group in the car breathed a sigh of relief and settled back down to their discussion about cell phones.

'Shit,' exclaimed Jax suddenly, jangling

everyone's nerves.

Up ahead they could see the red taillights of the ute. It was pulled over on the side of the road. As they got closer, they could make out the driver standing in the middle of the road flagging them down.

'Maybe he's broken down,' offered Brigit.

Jax hesitated. 'I don't like the look of this. You guys just keep your heads down and stay calm okay. Don't do anything stupid.'

Stella immediately crouched down on the floor between the seats and pulled a blanket over her head.

Jax pulled the car up in the middle of the road and waited until the driver of the ute came up to his window.

'What's up mate?' he pulled his cap down over his face and kept his head down.

The grey bearded man peered into the car.

'I want you to leave the keys in the ignition and get out. All of ya. NOW.'

Jax tried to negotiate with him.

'Look mate, we have to get to our motel tonight, maybe we can give you a lift. Where ya headed?'

'I said, get out of the car NOW.' He stank of alcohol and sweat.

Jax looked across at Brigit and his heart sank at the look of fear in her eyes.

He tried again. 'Is your ute broken down, maybe we can call someone for you.'

The man then produced a gun and held it against Jax's head. 'Listen sunshine, get your arse out of the car now.'

Jax drew in a startled breath.

'Stay in the car,' he whispered to the others, 'I know this bastard. I don't think he recognises me though, just trust me okay.'

He pretended to open the drivers door then put his foot flat to the floor in an attempt to drive away but the car stalled. A deafening shot rang out and Jax slumped forward onto the steering wheel. Brigit screamed and leapt out of the car to go and confront the man. Rees, who had been sitting behind Jax was stunned but managed to get out of the car to try and stop Brigit.

In the meantime Stella figured the man didn't know she was there so she stayed crouched down behind the seat under the blanket holding her breath and trembling like the last leaf on a tree in autumn.

The gunman swung around and aimed the gun at Rees as he got out of the car. Just as he fired, Brigit leapt on his back and grabbed him around the throat causing the bullet to hit Rees in the shoulder. Rees slumped to the ground. Brigit didn't let go her grip. She was really angry and the adrenalin was powering through her veins. She wanted to kill this bastard. She squeezed her arm around his throat as tight as she could, but he brought his head back with an almighty force and butted her full in the face. She dropped like a stone to the ground.

Stella's heart was pounding so hard she thought it would leap out of her chest. All she could do was listen to the terrifying noises outside. She heard the two gunshots and Brigit screaming, then nothing. Next thing the boot opened, giving her nerve jangled body another sharp shock. She could hear the man rifling through their belongings. She waited until she heard his car drive off before she emerged from her hiding place. She immediately got out and ran around to check on Rees. He was stirring.

Thank God you are still alive, she said, tears running down her cheeks. Then she turned and saw Jax slumped across the steering wheel.

'Jax!' she yelled, and pulled him back from the wheel. She screamed when she saw his staring eyes and the blood on his face. She put her fingers against his throat to feel for a pulse but she already knew the answer. He was dead.

'Brigit,' she called. Then louder, 'Brigit. Brigit where are you.' Stella began to run frantically around the car looking for her sister.

'Where are you, for God's sake. He's gone, it's okay to come out.'

There was nothing but deathly silence and Rees's laboured breathing.

'Get the sat phone Stella,' he gasped as he staggered to his feet. He was in a state of shock and running on survivor's instinct. ' It's in the boot.'

Stella ran around to the back of the car.

'It's gone,' she cried. 'He's taken all our stuff.'

'Bastard. We'll just have to drive on to Katherine. Where's Brigit?'

'I don't know, I can't find her.'

'Maybe she's run off and hiding somewhere, or unconscious or hurt. You walk along that side of the road with the torch, I'll walk along this side.'

'What about all that blood? Oh my God where did he get you?' Stella was dabbing tentatively at the blood soaking Rees's shirt.

'In the shoulder, hurts like a bastard but if we wrap it up tight it should be okay for now.'

Stella found the first aid kit under the passenger seat and with trembling hands dressed Rees's wound in the headlights of the car. When she'd finished they looked at each other and fell into each other's arms in tears as the reality of their situation began to sink in. Both of them were trembling so much with shock and adrenalin they could barely stand, their knees threatened to give way on them.

'Oh my God Rees, that bastard has killed Jax.'

Stella was staring at her brother-in-law through the windscreen. 'I just can't get my head around this, it's like a slow motion horror movie, I can't stop shaking. I can't believe this is really happening. But it is happening isn't it.'

Rees could see she was becoming hysterical.

'Look Stella, you've got to hold yourself together. At least we have each other and we are still alive, right?' he grabbed her roughly by the shoulders. He needed her strength and didn't want to have to worry about her losing the plot. He shook her roughly, 'we've got to find Brigit before that guy comes back, and then we've gotta get the hell out of here. 'Brigit, where the hell are you?' he called, looking around frantically.

They walked up and down along the roadside calling out for her.

Finally Rees said, 'You don't think that guy took her with him do you?'

The blood froze in Stella's veins.

'Noooooo. Oh God no, please don't let that be what's happened. Oh Rees, we gotta get help if that's the case. Oh no, pleeeeese God, not our beautiful Brigit!' Stella started sobbing.

'Stella, get a grip,' shouted Rees grabbing her roughly by the shoulders again. 'Stella I need you, don't fucking loose the plot on me now okay.'

Stella took a great gulp of air and glanced up at Rees. The fear and panic in his eyes brought another onrush of adrenalin as she wiped her eyes, blew her nose and nodded to him.

They were both alerted at the same time to a car coming their way. They held their breath as the headlights got closer.

'It won't be him,' Rees answered Stella's unspoken fear. 'It's coming from the other direction.'

They flagged the car down, it was two mine workers on their way home from two weeks at the mine.

'Geesus fucking Christ,' shouted one of the men, 'What the hell happened here?' He was instantly alert and jumped into action. He checked Jax's condition and felt sick when he realised he was dealing with a dead body.

"Frank, give us a hand here mate, we gotta get these poor bastards some help.'

Rees and Stella watched the two men in stunned silence. Working together the men eased Jax's body out of the drivers' seat and laid him out across the back seat.

'Frank will drive you into Katherine. You booked to stay at the motel are you?'

Stella nodded.

'I'm Steve, I've got a CB radio in my ute, I'll radio ahead so the cops can meet us there. You good to go Frank?'

'Yep. What are ya names guys?

'I'm Rees, this is Stella. We are on holiday from New Zealand. Our sister Brigit is missing, we can't find her.'

'Shit.' Frank went over to Steve. 'Looks like we might have an abduction mate. I don't have a good feeling about this at all.' He kept his voice low so Rees and Stella couldn't overhear them. Then he swung around.

'Come on let's get you guys out of here. We'll get someone out here with spotlights to find your sister, ok.'

They nodded numbly.

When they got to the motel the reception area was all lit up despite the late hour.

'Why didn't you bring them to the station?' asked the policemen leaning in the driver's window of the car.

Frank got out of the car. 'These guys are severely traumatised Brookie, I figured they needed to be somewhere more comfortable than your fucking police station.'

The policeman smarted at the response but said nothing. 'So what have we got then, Steve was a bit vague on the radio.'

'One dead, one missing and these two poor kids. Kiwi's.'

'Shit' said Brookie, this is all we need.'

Just then a middle-aged man wearing a stained white apron and a tired expression came shuffling out from the kitchen.

'Hey, what's up? Oh, shit, what's happened?'

Stella followed his gaze and looked down at her blouse, it was covered in blood.

'Oh, no, that's not mine. My brother-in-law has been shot dead and my brother has a gunshot wound to his shoulder. We think my sister has been kidnapped by a crazy man and....

"Whoa whoa, slow down a bit sweetheart,' Brookie jumped in to stem Stella's diatribe. The last thing he needed was this information getting out into the community and causing mass hysteria. This was a very small community, it wouldn't take much. 'Come on,' he said hastily, 'let's get you both inside.'

'It was a guy in a white ute.....' Stella continued, shock causing her to keep talking.

Brookie took her to a seat in the restaurant, ordered some water and facing her, placed his hand gently on her shoulder to get her attention. 'What's your name?'

'Stella, my name's Stella and that's my brother Rees. We're over here on a visit from New Zealand. That's my brother-in-law Jax Jamieson, he's married to my sis...' she choked on the word.

'It's okay Stella, here have some water.' He looked over her head and beckoned to a young constable standing by awaiting instructions.

'Alex, come take a statement from Stella while I check on Rees okay.'

'Sure. The ambulance is here, they've got him in the back, think they wanna get him to the hospital as soon as.'

By now there were several people milling around roused out of their slumber by flashing lights and the unusual hive of activity for this time of night.

'Okay everyone, let's give these poor kids some room. Go back to your rooms now, you can talk about it in the morning.'

Reluctantly everyone muttered their way back to their rooms and the place fell eerily silent except for the intermittent chatter of the police radio and the humming of a nearby generator and refrigerators.

'Rees, I'm Senior Constable Innisbrook. You can call me Brookie, okay? Now I know you must have been through something pretty traumatic so I won't bother you now, best we get you to the hospital. I'll bring Stella over shortly, she's keen to talk at the moment so we want to get down as much information as possible. She's likely to collapse when the adrenalin wears off so we'll get what we can from her then bring her straight over. We won't be long okay.'

Rees nodded absently, he was beginning to lose consciousness.

'Right, let's get this young man on the way,' demanded the ambulance officer as he beckoned Brookie out and slammed the doors. They left with lights flashing and the siren could be heard once they got out onto the main road.

Stella sat up. 'Where's Rees?' She rose from her seat, anxious to see her brother.

'It's okay sweetheart,' soothed Brookie, 'we'll take you to see him shortly, we just wanted to get as much detail from you as we can so we can start looking for Brigit, is that okay?'

Stella turned and focused on the Senior Constable as if seeing him for the first time.

'What? Oh, um, okay. She took the steaming cup of coffee being offered to her and stared at it absently.

'Good, now let's start at the beginning again, tell me everything you can about tonight while it's still fresh in your mind,' the constable coaxed gently.

Someone dropped a warm cuddly blanket around Stella's trembling shoulders but she didn't seem to notice. She was once again reliving the nightmare and pouring it all out to the policeman who was frantically taking notes.

'It was a man in a white ute.'

'What did he look like?'

Stella glanced up apologetically.

'I didn't see him, I was hiding under a blanket down behind the seat.'

'That's okay sweetie, Rees can fill us in on any blank bits, don't you worry. Clever you for staying out of danger, that was a very smart thing to do.'

Brookie was being beckoned from the doorway, the undertaker had arrived to take Jax's body away. Once he'd dealt with that Brookie returned to Stella.

'Come on young lady, I think we'll get you out of here. Alex would you grab their things from their car and put them in my car and then drive their car back to the station. Did you get any info from Frank and Steve?'

'No, they were keen to get home. Said they'd drop by in the morning tho.'

'Good, come on Stella, let's get you to the hospital and then we can call your next of kin.'

'Next of..? Oh, yes, Oh God, we have to let everyone know, oh, oh, umm…what do I do, have you got a phone I can use? Can I make a call to New Zealand, oh and …'

'Hey hey hey young lady, settle down, just take a deep breath okay.' Brookie gently guided Stella into the front seat of his car. 'There's a lot of things we have to set in motion now but we will do all that for you okay. You just need to give me the contact details of yours and Jax's families and we will make the calls for you. Are you okay with that?'

Stella was relieved, 'yes, thank you,' she breathed a sigh of relief. 'In my bag, there's a notebook with everyone's numbers in it.'

'Good girl,' said Brookie affectionately. 'We'll get it when we get to the hospital okay.'

'Okay' she nodded.

Chapter Eleven

The Search Begins

Luke roused himself from a very pleasant dream, looked across at the clock showing some ungodly hour in the morning and reached for the ringing telephone beside his bed.

What? Who? Who? Police? Where?

He sat bolt upright in his bed, his stomach lurched and his heart started to pound in his chest. Ruth stirred beside him.

'What's happened?' she asked.

'I don't know, it's the Katherine Police,' he said covering the mouthpiece. He listened intently as the voice on the other end continued. It took several minutes for the Police to relate what details they had to Luke, and to answer his questions. He was as white as a sheet and trembling by the time he hung up the phone. He turned to Ruth.

'Get us on the first flight to Darwin, now. Please.'

Ruth didn't hesitate; she'd caught the gist and urgency of the situation from Luke's end of the conversation. She leapt out of bed and headed for the lounge and the computer. By the time Luke had dressed and packed a bag she had it all arranged.

I've got us booked on the nine thirty flight this morning to Auckland, with a connecting flight to Brisbane. We'll have to change planes there but it's only an hour and a half lay over. What's happened?

'I'll fill you in on the way,' he mumbled, stuffing a sweater into his bag.

Luke called Sandy and Selwyn. They were on the doorstep out of breath and still in their pyjamas within minutes. Luke told them what he'd learned from the Police. Sandy started to sway as a low moan of despair welled up inside her. Selwyn put his arm around her and held her tight.

'Oh my God Luke, how can this be happening? Not to our babies please. I can't believe this, it's like a nightmare,' Sandy began screaming.

Ruth came in dressed and with suitcase in hand. Seeing Sandy falling to pieces she quickly went over and gave her a hug, both of them were trembling.

'We will do everything we can for the kids and keep you posted at every possible moment, okay,' she said looking from Sandy to Selwyn.

'Okay, you two just get on that plane, we'll look after things here. Sandy and I will be over as soon as we can get someone to look after the farm. Please give the kids a big hug from us and tell them we'll be there as soon as we can,' Selwyn's voice broke.

After hugs and tears all round Luke and Ruth were off.

'I'll drive,' said Luke as Ruth was about to hop in the drivers' seat.

'No, you're too upset,' protested Ruth.

'I need to concentrate on something, otherwise I will explode,' he was angry. He turned to Ruth as he clicked his seat belt into place, tears running unchecked down his tired drawn face.

'Jax is dead Ruth, I can't believe it. The cops would have phoned Janet and Sid by now to let them know about their boy. And Brigit.' He choked on her name as a huge wall of pain welled up in his chest. 'Oh God Brigit, please, please be okay baby, I can't stand the thought of losing you too.'

Ruth knew the 'too' was a reference to his late wife Ellen. She reached over and put her hand on his thigh, trying to comfort him. He was too caught up in his despair over Brigit that he hadn't considered that Ruth would be going through the same trauma and despair. She loved both Jax and Brigit as if they were her own family, and now to have lost Jax and with Brigit missing, it was an unbelievably difficult situation for both of them. Fortunately Luke knew the road like the back of his hand and navigated the winding high walled mountainous track expertly.

They arrived at the quiet airport way too early for their flight. Ruth tried to get Luke to sit in the café and at least have some coffee but instead he paced up and down like a caged lion as they waited for their flight to board.

It was a quick and uneventful flight from Auckland to Brisbane. Luke phoned the Jamieson's from Brisbane airport while they waited for their connecting flight to Darwin. Trey answered immediately.

'Trey, it's Luke. I'm in Brisbane waiting for my flight to Darwin. No I haven't heard anything except what the cops told me when they phoned earlier this morning. Trey, we are so very sorry to hear about Jax. We loved that boy like our own son and I know you two were very close. Where are your folks now? Okay. Any news on Brigit yet? Hey, yeah, that would be great, thanks. And Trey, tell them Ruth and I are on our way. Bye for now.'

Ruth's heart stirred as Luke spoke on their behalf about Jax. She was beginning to realise that maybe he noticed more than she gave him credit for. She wrapped her arms around him in a big hug and they stood like that for a while, crying softly.

By the time they arrived at Darwin Airport, Trey had set things in motion for them.

A young man stood right outside the arrival gates holding a placard with Luke's name on it.

'Hi Mr Williams, my name's Justin, we have the Jamieson's helicopter outside ready and waiting to take you both down to Katherine. Gidday Ruth, haven't seen you for ages, sorry it's such bloody awful circumstances.'

Luke stared absently out the window of the helicopter barely focusing on the stunning terrain that would normally have captured his undivided attention and before he knew it, they had landed at Katherine amidst a huge cloud of red dust. They were ushered immediately to the Police Station where it seemed all hell had broken loose. Janet and Sid spotted them the minute they walked through the door and rushed over to meet them. Janet threw her arms around Ruth's neck sobbing as Sid grabbed Luke's outstretched hand.

'Luke, so glad to see you, sorry it's under such circumstances. Come and sit down you must be exhausted.'

Luke sank into a chair beside Sid as Janet took Ruth off to grab some coffees.

'Sid,' Luke choked back tears, 'God I am so sorry to hear about Jax. I just can't get my head around all this. What the hell has happened, where's my girl?'

'Sid leant forward with his elbows on his knees, head hanging down, tears falling in tiny splats on the pale blue lino floor.

'I'm buggered if I know mate. I can't get my head around it either. We are just running on auto pilot at the moment trying to get to the bottom of this whole bloody nightmare. Stella and Rees are back out at the scene with the cops looking for Brigit and trying to gather what information they can.'

'I should be out there too,' Luke got to his feet.

'Sit down mate, they have been gone for ages they will be back soon. Let's just wait and see what they've got eh.'

Luke reluctantly sat back down and they both took the coffees Janet and Ruth offered them. The wives sat down in the plastic chairs alongside their husbands just as two police cars came into the yard. As soon as Luke spotted Stella and Rees he flew out the door and embraced them in a desperate hug of relief.

'God, are you guys okay? Rees, what's happened to you?'

'I'm okay Luke, I got shot but I'm alright, I just wanna help find Brigit.' He burst into tears as Ruth came out and gave him a hug. Luke pulled Stella to his chest and they both sobbed.

Constable Brookie called his men into the station to give the families some time to catch up before getting down to the business of finding Brigit. That was now their number one priority. Once he could see the group settling down a little he put them all into a police van and took them to a nearby motel where he had set up a large meeting room as an operational base.

'Much more comfortable than our small station,' he explained. 'This is your space to use as you see fit from now on. We have taken over this whole block of motel units, they are for you to stay in and use for as long as you like. The motel owners are pretty upset with what's happened and have generously waived all costs.'

Luke was humbled and made a mental note in his tortured mind to thank them at some stage. They sat around the room on comfortable chairs waiting to open the floodgates of questions and shared information. Brookie perched himself on the corner of the table, hands clasped together in front of him. Two constables leaned against the back wall while others hovered around the doorway conversing with each other and responding to the constant crackling voices on their radios.

'Firstly, I want to say how deeply sorry we all are for what's happened. Be assured we have every available resource at the ready to help us find Brigit and catch this creep who's turned your lives upside down. Now, I will fill you in on what we know at this point, feel free to ask questions at any time. Alex.'

The fair-haired young constable jumped to attention.

'Grab that whiteboard over there will you.

As you know,' Brookie continued, 'we took Stella and Rees back to the scene at first light this morning to see what we could find. We've had an aircraft searching overhead and a dozen men on the ground. Luke, I'm sorry but there was no sign of Brigit. I'm sorry to say that at this point in time we believe she has been abducted.'

Luke sucked in his breath and put his head in his hands. 'How could this happen? What the hell happened? This is really hard to understand, does this sort of thing happen often in the outback or what?' he was getting himself all worked up.

Ruth put her arm around his shoulders and he allowed himself to lean into her.

'Sorry Luke, yes it has happened a few times over the years unfortunately. The combination of long, lonely roads, wide open spaces and low life rotten scum bags doesn't help.'

Luke went pale and swore under his breath at the thought of Brigit being held by some rotten low life scum bag. He fought down the bile rising in his throat and gagged. Ruth quickly handed him a glass of water.

'Luke, sorry that was insensitive, I apologise.'

Luke nodded. 'Carry on mate, I'll be okay,' there was a tremor in his voice.

Addressing Stella and Rees Brookie said, 'thanks kids, you did a great job this morning.

Rees you're looking a bit peaky, think it might be a good idea if you guys go with Sally here and check into your rooms and take a break eh. We'll keep checking in on you and bring you some lunch soon.'

They both nodded, gave Ruth and Luke a hug and went off with the policewoman. Brookie waited until they left the room then turned to Luke and Ruth.

'Brave kids, but I don't think the reality has hit them yet, better keep a close watch on them.' They both nodded. 'Now, we have a description of the vehicle, a light coloured utility driven by an old man with grey hair and a beard, that's about all the kids could give us at this stage but it's better than nothing. We currently have aircraft flying all over this area searching for any sign of the ute. We have men in cars and two helicopters visiting all the nearby and outlying stations. We are also door knocking all over town looking for every scrap of information we can gather so we can try and piece this thing together and we have another operations room set up at the police station. There is a car at your disposal, you are welcome to come down to the station at any time and see what's happening there, although we will be keeping the ops room here fully informed. In the meantime I think it's best that you grab yourselves some lunch, sit and talk with us if you want to and try and get some rest. Alex will be stationed in this room with the radio and will let you know the minute there's anything to report.' Brookie eased himself from the corner of the table, shook the men's hands, nodded to the ladies and left. The four of them sat in silence for a while, Alex lurking uncomfortably in the background. Ruth looked around and spotted him.

'Where's the dining room Alex? I think it's time we all got something to eat. Come on you lot, we aren't going to be any use to anybody if we don't look after ourselves,' she said, putting on her nurses voice.

Chapter Twelve

Braithwaite

Brigit stirred and stretched, the movement causing her to cry out as a stabbing pain grabbed at her temples. She gingerly opened her eyes, the blinding daylight making it hard for her to focus. The smell was awful, stale alcohol, sweat, and a nauseating odour of cooked food. Her stomach retched and she tried to sit up in case she vomited but found herself restrained. She lay back down, her head throbbing. She lay still with her eyes closed for a moment trying to gather her thoughts. Then as the events of the previous night started to take shape in her mind she opened her eyes in panic. Her eyes felt swollen and her nose throbbed so much she feared it might be broken. She focused as much as she could through the slits in her eyes but didn't move any further until she could make out where she was.

The roof was bare wood, no lining, and very basic. She could see daylight coming through the cracks. She turned her head gently to one side, a rough-hewn wooden wall. When she gently turned her head to the other side she was startled to find someone standing beside her bed looking down at her. He had a long grey beard and he reeked of alcohol and body odour which didn't help Brigit's headache and nausea.

'Finally woken up eh? You been out for a while, thought I musta kilt ya.'

Brigit was too terrified to speak, she was trying to make sense of the situation. Where the hell was she, and who the hell was this smelly old creep. The old man shoved a water bottle in her mouth and she sucked on it greedily. It tasted funny but she was too thirsty to care. She gratefully gave in to the drowsiness which started to overtake her and her mind became a tumbled mess of fractured pictures and flashes of gun shots and blood and... Jax. She let out a mighty howl of absolute despair as she relived the picture of Jax being shot. The man got such a fright he fell backwards off his chair. She quietened down again and fell into a drug induced sleep.

Brigit stirred hours later. Her ankles were anchored down spread eagled and tied to the corners of the bed. She tried to sit up but her legs were stiff and sore and she could only pull herself up on to her elbows. She spotted the old man and started screaming abuse at him, dredging up all the foul language she could think of. She was terrified, furious and angrier than she had ever been in her life. The man stormed over to her, yelling at her to shut up, but she was in full flight. He struck her hard across the face and she slumped back down onto the bed, out cold. When she woke up again it was dark. Her eyes didn't seem to be as swollen as before but her head still hurt and she now had a very sore jaw and cheek. She moved her body, testing the restraints, and another pain raced up inside her. She raised her head and looked down at her near naked body and with dawning horror realised the man must have raped her while she was unconscious. She was overcome with disbelief at this unimaginable horror she found herself in. It was deathly quiet, except for the sound of snoring. Must be that grey bearded bastard she thought. She lay quietly in the dark straining to hear anything that might give her an indication of where she might be and if there was anyone else there. Nothing made any sense. She allowed herself to think again of Jax. Her logic was telling her he couldn't have survived a shot to the head at point blank range but she didn't want to dwell on that. What if he was still alive, what if by some miracle... but she stopped herself and instead thought about Stella and Rees, hoping they were okay. She remembered the gun going off a second time but wasn't sure of the outcome. She remembered nothing after that. Then she thought of her father. Poor Daddy, he must be frantic with worry. I wonder if anyone knows where I am, I wonder how long I've been here, I wonder how long it will take for them to find me. I wonder if I will still be alive when they do. She started to cry as everything began to overwhelm her. She didn't want to wake the old man up so she stifled her sobs in the dirty smelly bed coverings.

When daylight started to creep through the cracks in the walls she was able to take better stock of her surroundings. With great effort she pulled herself up to a sitting position straining against her leg restraints. Her shorts and panties were nowhere to be seen. The ropes pulled hard on her ankles causing her to wince in pain but she wanted to take in as much as she could before the old man woke up. The leg ties looked to be leather thonging and were bound in tight knots. She leaned forward to try and untie one but she couldn't reach. The knots were down below the bed, tied to the legs of the bed frame. Her legs ached, it was a very uncomfortable position and she felt very exposed and vulnerable. She leant back down on her elbows where it was a little less painful and looked around. It was a small, roughly built one room wooden hut with one rectangle window at the far end which let in the sunlight. In the shaft of light dancing with dust mites Brigit could make out a bench with untidy shelves above it covered in various pieces of old crockery, tin cups, paper, and cardboard containers. A small portable gas stove sat at the end of the bench. There was one plain small table in the middle of the room and two simple wooden chairs. Over in the corner the old man was slumped sound asleep in an overstuffed armchair with a wooden crate beside him serving as a small table upon which sat several empty beer bottles. Brigit shuddered with repulsion. She swore that if she was able to, she would run a knife through him without a second thought. *I wouldn't care if I spent the rest of my life in jail for murder*, she thought, *I could cheerfully kill that bastard right now.*

The old man must have sensed something for his eyes suddenly flew open staring at Brigit and giving her such a fright that she gasped and swore at him. His eyes quickly checked her restraints to make sure she was still tethered as he settled back into his chair with a lecherous smirk.

'Well well well, my pretty little spitfire has finally woken up again has she?'

'You bastard,' spat Brigit, 'how low can you possibly go. You've shot my husband and raped me while I was unconscious. What sort of a low life creep are you. Bastards like you should be hung out to dry you creepy old shit.'

The old man grinned back at her tirade.

'Check it out sweetheart. There you are all tied up and at my mercy and here I am alive and in control and getting just what I wanted. A pretty little girl to fuck any time I want. Now you tell me who's got it wrong eh!'

'It's only a matter of time before someone finds us,' she spat back at him.

'Finds us? Out here? Sorry darlin but ain't nobody gonna find us way out here. We are miles from anywhere and nobody knows about this place but me. Built it myself, been living here undetected for years so forget about being rescued, ain't gonna happen.'

Brigit's heart sank to her stomach in absolute despair.

'Then why have you got me tied up if there's nowhere for me to go?' she pleaded.

'That's just so's I can have ya whenever I want ya, he laughed. But, if ya co-operate, I could loosen them off a bit and who knows, ya might eventually get to like it here after a while.'

Brigit leaned over the side of the bed and retched, realising as she did so that there was nothing in her stomach.

'You're probably pretty hungry. I'll fix ya somethin to eat.' He untied one of her leg restraints and loosened the second one. He hauled an old, chipped chamber pot out from under the bed. 'Use this, we ain't got no dunny.'

'How long have I been here?' she asked.

'Two days. Ya bin out to it most of the time.'

'That's because you've been drugging me you old bastard,' she spat.

She flexed her aching muscles and rubbed

the stiffness out of her legs, cringing with the pain. With one tie removed and the other one loosened Brigit was able to stand awkwardly on the floor. She turned to see if he was watching but he was engrossed in whatever he was cooking on the stove. She squatted down and relieved herself in the pot. She winced at the stinging sensation which she figured must be from him forcing himself on her. The thought was overwhelming enough to cause her to retch again. The smell of cooking food didn't help either but she knew if she didn't eat and drink, she would die.

Maybe I'm gonna die anyway and I'm just prolonging the agony, she thought.

After a breakfast of salty bacon, eggs, toast and coffee with powdered milk, Brigit's strength and resolve were beginning to return. *Damned if I'm gonna let this bastard kill me,* she thought. *My life ain't over yet, I'm not going down without a fight.*

Chapter Thirteen

The Search continues

'I never expected quite this many cops,' observed Luke as he and Sid drove into the station the following day.

'I know,' said Sid humbly, 'as a family we've always had a good rapport with the police. We've helped out on a lot of search and rescues over the years using our aircraft and staff, I guess they just want to pay some of it back, especially as there's also a deceased family member involved. He choked on the last few words and went quiet.

'We'll get through this,' Luke tried to offer some comfort. 'Why don't you guys go back home, you must want to make arrangements for Jax?'

'That can wait, my friend. Janet and I talked about it, we want to stay until they find Brigit, we're in this for as long as it takes.'

'Thank you,' said Luke quietly, 'I really appreciate that.'

Once inside the station the pair were swept up in a tide of intense activity as they made their way into the operations room.

'How are you two doing?' asked Brookie kindly as he beckoned them in and shut the door quietly behind them.

'Hanging in there mate, hanging in there,' said Sid. 'We'll go home and collapse once we've found Brigit.'

'Right, now Luke, are you up to answering some questions about Brigit? We want to get a picture in our minds about her which might help. From what we've heard from Stella and Rees, she's a feisty young thing so we're hoping she will be able to stand her ground with her captor.'

Luke couldn't help but smile. He took a well-worn photo from his wallet and with trembling hands passed it to Brookie. 'Yep she's feisty alright, gets it from her late mother.'

'Good, that's something positive to hang on to. Do you think she's got the guts to try and fight her way out of a hostage situation or do you think she might use her head and try to outsmart him somehow, play the long game?'

Luke thought for a moment. 'Brigit's a smart girl, I'm picking she'd try both tactics. She's always been a quick thinker, likes a challenge and gutsy as all hell. She's surprisingly strong too, comes from working on the farm all her life I guess.'

'I agree with Luke, Brookie,' chipped in Sid. 'From what I've seen and learned about

Brigit over these past few years she's never ceased to amaze me at the way she's bounced back from adversity. I have every hope and confidence that she'll be trying to get herself out of whatever situation she's in. Brigit is not a victim, I'll tell you that here and now.'

Luke smiled. Sid obviously loved Brigit too and certainly had a lot of respect for her.

'Good' said Brookie. 'Sally, get some copies of this photo run off and get the original back to Luke okay.'

'Sure boss.'

Sid and Luke became engrossed in the radio communications and watched with fascination as information was written up on a white board. A sudden commotion outside the door caught their attention. Luke looked up and saw Selwyn and Sandy through the window and leapt to his feet. He threw the door open, grabbed Sandy in a big hug and then turned to Selwyn. They both grinned shyly at each other for a moment, shrugged and then gave in to a comforting bear hug. Wiping their eyes they followed one of the constables into the lunchroom.

'So what's happening?' asked Sandy, 'where are the kids?'

'The kids are okay, they're back at the motel resting. I can take you there now if you like?'

'Maybe someone else could take us if you

want to stay here, we don't want to drag you away.'

One of the community volunteers was in the room making coffee.

'I can take you to the motel,' she said.

Luke waved them off and went back into the ops room.

By midday the following day the news of the kidnapping had gone nationwide on all the local networks and the press was rolling in to town in droves. Rees had been going through mug shot folders all morning and had also described the old man to a police sketch artist who drew what Rees considered to be a remarkable likeness of the man they were looking for.

On the third day of the search one of the checkout operators from the local supermarket came into the station.

'I might have something of interest for you Brookie,' she said secretively.

'Come into the interview room Nancy, what have you got?'

'Well this morning this guy came into the shop and bought some groceries. He had these scratch marks down his face. I seen him before but he's not a regular, comes in about once a month. He's always dirty and smelly like he lives rough, you know?'

'So apart from the scratch marks what

makes you think he might be of interest?'

'Well, it's just that this morning he bought more groceries than he usually does. And not the sort of stuff a guy usually bothers about, you know?'

Brookie smiled. 'Girlie stuff you mean.'

'Well, yeah. He got some woman's deodorant and some soap and toothpaste. Normally he just buys food and booze and cigarettes and stuff.'

'How many times have you seen him then?'

'Like I said, he comes in about once a month, guess he's been in a dozen times or more, can't be sure.'

'Would you recognise his photo if you saw it?'

"Yeah, course I would,' she said confidently.

Brookie took her into another room and pulled out six or seven photos that Rees thought might be the man. He put the photos in front of Nancy.

'Any one of these?'

'That's him,' she pointed immediately to one of the photos.

'Are you sure?'

'Sure I'm sure. That's the guy that was in this morning, bet my life on it.'

'You don't happen to know his name do ya?' Brookie asked, double checking to make sure she'd picked the right man.

'Nope, he always paid in cash, no cheques or nuthin.'

'Thank you Nancy, you've been a great help, well done.'

Nancys chest puffed up with pride as she walked out of the Police Station.

Brookie jumped in the car and headed to the motel. He found Sid, Janet, Luke and Ruth in the meeting room.

'Don't suppose you've ever come across this guy?' he asked Sid, holding up the photo.

Janet went pale as Sid grabbed the photo.

'That's bloody Braithwaite,' he gasped 'what the hell...? Do you think this is the guy who's got Brigit?'

'Could be, he was seen in town this morning with scratch marks down his face.'

Brookie picked up the hand piece on the radio sitting beside him and relayed a message.

'Get a copy of that photo that Nancy identified out to everyone in town and use the press too. The man's name is Braithwaite, looks like he's our man. I'll get back to you with further details. Turning to Sid he said, 'okay, think you better tell me everything you know about this bastard Sid. For starters did he own a ute?'

'Yes he did, a white one.' Sid was shaking with rage, his fists were clenched so tight his knuckles were white. He couldn't sit still so he started pacing. Janet didn't know whether to try and comfort him or leave him be. She stood up then sat down and stood up again only to find her legs were shaking too much to support her. Ruth sat beside her and put an arm around her shoulders. Sid continued to pace, pouring out Braithwaite's history as an employee and as a murderer.

'So this is the same guy who killed poor old Monti then?' Brookie frowned as he realised the type of man they were dealing with and the danger Brigit was in.

'Do you think this is aimed directly at you or just coincidence?'

'How the fuck would I know?' snapped Sid. He looked up and caught the shocked expression on Janet's face. He turned to Brookie and took a deep breath.

'Sorry. Look all I know is that he's a bad bastard and I can't stand the thought of him having Brigit.'

He looked apologetically at Luke and Ruth.

'I'm so sorry guys. If this is aimed at us and he has dragged Brigit into it I will never forgive myself.' He sunk to his knees and howled.

Luke was stunned, his head was whirling with a myriad of fearful thoughts.

'Do you think he might be looking for money Sid? 'a ransom?' queried Brookie carefully. 'Look I'm sorry to push you on this but we gotta get this guy, and soon.' Brookie helped

Sid to his feet.

'Could be, I don't know. He wanted to dig for gold on the property and we wouldn't let him. Who knows what's going on in his bloody head?'

Rees wandered into the room just then. 'What's happening?' he asked alarmed at the fragile expressions on everyone's faces.

'We know who we are looking for now,' offered Brookie, 'a guy called Braithwaite. He used to work for the Jamiesons.'

'Oh,' Rees was deep in thought, 'shit, I forgot. When we were at Wycliffe Well Jax got a bit spooked about a guy in a white ute but I didn't think any more of it.

'That's okay son, is there anything else you can remember about that?'

Rees hung his head. 'Yeah, when the guy came up to the car window that night, Jax said he thought he knew him, I am so sorry.'

'Don't fret son, it's good you've remembered now, it's all starting to add up. Did the man say what he wanted?'

'No, just what I told you before. He just told us to get out of the car and then when Jax tried to drive off he fired his gun.'

The owner of the motel had been hovering at the door and overheard the conversation. He disappeared and came back with a bottle of brandy and some glasses and quietly placed them on the table beside Brookie and left.

'Good idea,' said Brookie, 'thanks mate.'

Lunch was also brought in and placed on the table. Everyone ate in silence mindlessly popping food into their mouths and chewing, paying little heed to the constant babble on the radios. They were becoming immune to it.

'Got him,' crowed Brookie suddenly causing everyone's hearts to start racing. 'He bought bullets this morning and someone saw him turn off down Dobson's track, I've got cars heading out that way now.

Sid leapt out of his chair and grabbed Luke by the arm. Let's get in the helicopter, I'm not sitting around here waiting anymore. If it's Braithwaite, I want to get to him before the cops do, I've got a score to settle with that bastard.'

'Sid, don't do anything rash...' began Brookie. But his words fell on deaf ears as the two men rushed out of the building.

'What am I looking for Sid?' asked Luke as he fumbled the binoculars out of their case once they were airborne and on their way.

'A small shack, a dust cloud from a vehicle, the ute, just anything that might be worth a look. See if you can pick up any tyre tracks in the dirt too, I'll go as low as I can.'

Chapter Fourteen

Fight for Life

Brigit spent the night and the following day trying to form some sort of plan in her mind. The first thing she needed to do was to gain the old man's trust if she wanted him to let her out of the restraints.

'Do you have a name?' she asked him.

'Course I have a name. Walter Ernest Braithwaite at your service ma'am,' he smiled as he bowed low before her. 'And yours?'

Brigit ignored the cold chill that ran through her veins at the mention of the name Braithwaite. Surely it couldn't be the same man who killed Monti. She kept as calm and collected as she could and tried not to let on that she might know him.

'My name is Brigit,' she said defiantly and then with emphasis, 'Brigit Jamieson.'

'Ahh, so I did get me a little Jamieson did I. You must be Jaxon's wee misus then are ya?'

'You know the Jamiesons?' Brigit's heart was pounding in her chest.

'Everybody knows the Jamiesons,' he

crowed.

'I'm a Kiwi but I'm married to Jax Jamieson.'

'Not any more you ain't, I shot the little bastard, he's dead just like those damn Jamieson's killed my Sam.'

Brigit's head was reeling.

'You don't know Jax is dead for sure you bastard. He's probably still alive and when he comes for you, you're gonna regret what you've done, big time.'

Then something he said started to register.

'Sam? Who the fuck is Sam?'

'Samantha.'

'Holy shit, Samantha was your daughter?'

'My niece, but near enough to a daughter, now I got you instead. Fair's fair don't ya think? They killed her and now I killed their precious boy and as a bonus I get a pretty little girl to play with.'

Brigit leaned over the side of the bed and vomited all over his shoes. He drew his arm back and swiped a back hand across the side of her head sending her flailing back down on the bed, unconscious once again.

When she came to, she lay still for a moment gathering her thoughts before letting on she was awake. The side of her head was throbbing and she had a splitting headache.

She raised her head slightly. Walter was sitting in the corner of the room drinking, he looked moody and thoughtful. Brigit hardly dared move a muscle, she sat with her own private thoughts not wishing to stir him up anymore in case he got violent again.

At least while he's pre-occupied he's leaving me alone, she thought.

Finally Walter got up and started preparing some food for dinner. Brigit sat up then and watched him. She was still tethered by one foot but hoped she might be able to talk him round, although in his current demeanour she wasn't quite sure what he might do now. He brought her some food and set some down on the table for himself. He was facing her so she started talking to him trying to calm him down.

'Do you know the Jamiesons personally Walter or do you just know of them? You seemed to know my husband, Jax.'

He dropped his fork down on the tin plate and glared at her.

'I used to work for them.'

'What? When?'

'A few years ago,' he said vaguely. 'I killed one of their stockmen and took off. Guess you know all about that though, being married to Jax and all.'

'Oh!'

'What do ya mean, Oh. Have they said anything about it?'

Brigit was in two minds as to whether to tell him the truth or to lie to put him at ease. She opted for a lie.

'Can't say I've heard anything about it Walter. I've spent quite a bit of time with the family but can't say I've ever heard anything about you. Maybe they've forgotten all about it eh!'

He shrugged his shoulders and picked up his fork again.

'Maybe you're right, it was only an Abo after all.' He cleaned up the food on his plate mopping the last of it up with a piece of bread. Walter then went over to his chair, sat down and slowly downed half a bottle of whiskey before falling asleep. Brigit breathed a sigh of relief and eventually fell into a fitful nightmare laced sleep herself. She woke up next morning just as the sun was coming in through the dusty windowpane. She watched the dust mites in the shaft of light for a while, her mind working overtime. She eased herself up quietly and relieved herself on the chamber pot. Walter was still asleep snoring loudly. Brigit fiddled with the leather thonging around her ankle. It was very tight but she decided if she kept working at it she might just about be able to work it loose. Then what?

Maybe I could then tie and untie it at will, giving me control of one thing at least, she pondered.

She was making some headway when Walter woke up. He looked across to make sure she was still there then got up and went outside to relieve himself. He didn't speak and neither did she. After breakfast he sat down and started writing something on a scrap of paper.

'I gotta go get some supplies,' he muttered.

'Where from? How far do you have to go? How long will you be?'

'I ain't telling you nothin girlie so quit with the questions. Ya think I'm stoopid or something, I know exactly what you're trying to do. I'm going out for supplies and ya better hope I come back cos if I don't, you'll probably die out here on your own so don't get any fancy ideas about runnin away. I'm takin all but a small bottle of water and the only vehicle so yer stuck here, okay. Just settle down and relax and if yer good I might bring ya back somethin nice. But before I go, I want somethin nice from you.'

He walked over to the end of the bed and undid his trousers. He hadn't given Brigit her shorts and knickers back so she was still naked from the waist down. She tried to fight him off so he tied her free leg to the bed and crawled up between her spread-eagled legs. Her skin crawled with repulsion and she screamed at him not to touch her but his eyes were glazed over with lust. She reached up and clawed her fingernails down his cheeks leaving deep welts and drawing blood in places. If she could mark him in some way, it might draw some attention to him when he went into a shop. He was furious. He slapped her hard across the face. She leaned over and clamped her teeth hard down on his forearm. He cried out in alarm and slapped her again. Tears welled up in her eyes, she was in a lot of pain but she wasn't giving up. He got up off the bed and walked outside. She breathed a sigh of relief thinking she'd won but he was back in a moment with rope. He tied her arms to the corners of the bed and tied one piece of rope tightly across her throat so she couldn't move. All she could do was watch as his red streaked face and leering eyes loomed over her and he shoved himself roughly inside her. Tears streamed down the sides of her face as she gritted her teeth and closed her eyes to the dreadful assault being acted out on her.

At last it was over. He pulled himself up off her prone body and looked down at her. For a moment he looked almost ashamed at what he had done. He quietly untied the ropes and one leg restraint and left. Brigit could hear the vehicle drive away.

She pulled herself up and sat on the edge of the bed sobbing. She felt used and dirty and would have given anything to be able to scrub herself in water so she could try and get rid of his god awful stench and the foul sticky semen that was running down her thighs. When the sobbing finally stopped, she pulled herself together, her survival instinct was kicking in. She started working on the lashing around her ankle, it would take some time to work it loose. She looked around the room and spotted a knife on the bench. She stood up at the corner of the bed and grabbing hold of the bed frame, pulled with all her might. It gave a little, so she tried again. The bed was pretty solid and heavy so it took several goes to get it to move close enough for her to reach out for the knife. It wasn't overly sharp but did have a bit of a serrated edge. She worked at the leather strapping until it finally gave way and she was free, she was overwhelmed with relief. She found her shorts and knickers and put them on then rummaged around for something to eat before making her way outside to check out her surroundings.

She stood on the step of the hut and had a good look around. There were no trees or any sign of a water supply, just a pile of rocks which she assumed were an attempt to conceal the hut. There was nothing but dirt and a bit of sporadic vegetation all the way to the horizon. Brigit wasn't surprised by her surroundings but she was disappointed not to see a stand of trees within walking distance which could indicate a river which she could follow and which would hopefully lead her to a road or a homestead. She slumped dejectedly down on the top step and gave way to despair for a while, then she pulled herself to her feet and went back inside the hut to see if she could find anything useful. She started rummaging along the shelves before starting on a ragged old chest of drawers in the corner of the room. She pulled the drawers out one by one and strewed the contents on the table. There were some smelly old clothes in the top drawer which she tossed aside in disgust. The second drawer though, was much more interesting. There, amidst some yellowing old paperbacks was a small gun. Brigit's heart leapt in her chest. She quickly checked the chamber, damn, no bullets. *Maybe that's what he's gone into town to get*, she thought ruefully. She checked the last drawer but it was empty. She sat down at the table and studied the room for hiding places.

Suddenly she heard a noise and her blood ran cold, it was a vehicle. She raced to the door which hung at an angle on two of its three leather hinges. She peered out and spotted a cloud of dust, he was on his way back. She scrambled around the hut running her hands along the uneven ledges looking for a hiding space. Meanwhile the vehicle was getting closer and closer, she began to shake. What would he do if he found she was free and had been roaming around and found the gun, what if he used it on her.

He stood in the doorway of the old wooden shack his shadow falling across the foot of the bed touching the leather strapping that had bound Brigit to the dirty old wire wove. When he came inside and saw the place had been turned upside down he turned and glared at Brigit.

'What the hell have you been doing?' he demanded as he dropped the packages on top of the mess on the table. He bent down to pick up a packet that had fallen on the floor and Brigit saw her opportunity. She raced out the door to the ute. Walter was right behind her. He grabbed her around the waist and threw her to the ground, rolled her over and pinned her down. He leered at her, spittle dribbling from the corner of his mouth.

'Like it rough eh, I'll teach you to disobey me, I am your master now and don't you forget it.'

He held both her hands on the ground above her head with one hand and reached down to pull off her shorts and panties. She fought and kicked and bit but he just held on tighter. He ripped at her clothes and managed to get her shorts and panties off before undoing his trousers and roughly pushing her legs apart thrusting himself inside her, relishing the control he had over her. When he'd finished he got to his knees to do up his fly which gave quick thinking Brigit a chance to bring her knee up hard into his groin. He drew in a sharp breath and doubled over. Brigit twisted over on to her stomach and tried to crawl away from him but he reached out and grabbed her feet, twisting her on to her back again.

'Wanna play some more do we?' he slapped her hard across the face causing her lip and nose to bleed. She grabbed a hand full of sand and threw it in his face. He roared in anger but his grip eased off just enough for her to attempt another escape. She managed to get to her feet this time and started to run but once again he launched himself on top of her bringing her crashing face first onto the ground. He stood up and hauled her up by the hair to her feet. By now she was on full alert, the adrenalin was pumping, she was fighting for her life.

'It's him or me now,' she thought angrily.

She reached up and pinched the skin on the insides of his arms. He yelped and before he knew what was happening she had grabbed her hair and yanked as hard as she could to release his hold. She swung around and brought her knee up hard into his groin again and as he doubled over she grabbed the back of his head and pulled his face down onto her up-thrusting knee just as she had been taught in self-defence classes. He groaned loudly as blood began pouring out of his nose and he crumbled to the ground. Brigit wasted no time, she raced back into the house and frantically searched through the packages.

'Ah, bullets, thank God.'

She quickly grabbed the gun which she'd hidden under the mattress and managed to load it. She walked back outside, took a deep steadying breath and with shaking hands aimed the gun at Walter. As he began to rise to his feet she fired a shot which went straight through his shoulder.

'That's for Rees, she said slowly and deliberately.'

Then she aimed at his crotch. 'And this one's for me she snarled menacingly.'

'Nooooo,' he yelled as the bullet forced it's way into his body tearing at the skin and muscles. He was writhing on the ground in agony now. Brigit was enjoying taking control of this piece of shit that had been terrifying her for the past few days.

It's payback time,' she snarled. Her adrenalin was pumping, the blood pounded through her veins as she stood over him with nothing but pure hatred running through her like fire.

'My beloved husband and Monti may never walk this earth again but neither will you, arsehole,' and she shot out his kneecaps. Walter's petrified screams tore through the air. Brigit stood and watched him writhing in the dirt like an animal. She felt like she was standing outside her body watching a movie. It just didn't seem real, this wasn't her, was it? Her legs began to shake uncontrollably and the bile started to rise in her throat. She staggered over and leant against the side of the hut and threw up before slowly sinking semi-conscious to the ground, the gun still in her trembling hand.

She could hear a strange noise in the distance. It sounded like a large buzzing insect. It got louder and louder and there was dust flying everywhere and her hair was being blown about. Then she heard someone calling her name, it sounded like.....

'Daddy?'

Chapter Fifteen

Darwin Hospital

The first thing Brigit saw when she opened her eyes was her father standing over her, tears coursing down his face.

'Daddy? What are you doing here? Where am I? What's happening?'

'Hush sweetheart, you're safe now, you're in Darwin Hospital.'

'Really? What happened?'

'You've been given a sedative, you may not remember anything just now?'

She groggily squeezed her father's hand. 'Daddy don't cry, I'm okay.'

'I know Sweetheart, you just relax and get yourself better so I can get you out of here and take you home, okay.'

'Home? Why are you taking me home? Where's Jax…'. Suddenly reality hit her and the events of the past few days started to come back like snapshots in an album. She sat up and started retching. The nurse who was monitoring her quickly held a cup out to her to be sick into.

Luke's heart was breaking.

As Brigit lay back on the pillows the tears started to cascade down her pale cheeks.

'Oh my God Daddy, Jax is dead isn't he? That bastard killed him didn't he?'

'Yes my darling, I'm afraid he did, I am so sorry. Never in my wildest dreams did I ever see this coming. My precious baby, I am so sorry.'

'Daddy this is not your fault, neither of us saw this coming, how could we?'

Brigit haltingly, painfully related her experience to her distraught father. It tore him apart to think of that creepy old bastard with his dirty paws all over his precious girl. If Sid hadn't killed him by now, he certainly wanted to. When she'd finished talking, she sunk back down on the bed, her face as pale as the pillows supporting her.

'So how on earth did you find me Daddy?' she asked sleepily.

'I'll tell you all about that tomorrow darling, but right now I think you need to sleep.'

She'd become quite agitated and upset as she told Luke of her ordeal so the nurse had been quietly adding a sedative to her drip to give her some peace.

'She'll sleep through the night now Mr Williams, why don't you try and get some sleep too.'

Luke went back to the motel he and Ruth, Sid and Janet, had checked into while they waited for news of Brigit. Sandy and Selwyn had flown home the night before with Rees and Stella amid promises from Luke and Ruth that they would be kept up to date with Brigit's progress.

'How is Brigit? Janet asked Luke as they sat down by the pool.

'She woke up for a few minutes but she got upset so they had to sedate her. They told me she'd be out to it for the night now so we'll go in first thing in the morning.'

'Will she be okay do you think?' asked Ruth, I just wonder if she is strong enough emotionally to cope with this, I know how she was when she and Jax had that break up over Samantha.'

'I'm hoping she will be okay sweetheart, she's strong like her mother.'

'God, this is bringing back all those memories of when her mother was here in the same hospital after the plane crash,' he sobbed to Ruth. But worse than that is that Brigit told me what happened to her. I swear if I ever get my hands on that guy I will kill him. It's just as well you and I were focused on getting Brigit here to the hospital and left him lying there in the dirt Sid, otherwise he would be a dead man. 'I certainly wouldn't want to be in that bastard's shoes when the cops got there.' He smiled a little and Ruth looked at him quizzically. 'You should have seen what Brigit did to him Ruth, she shot him, several times, but didn't kill him. I think if she had wanted him dead she would have shot him in the head but she didn't, I just think she wanted him to suffer.

'God she's got guts alright,' said Sid. 'Does she know that Jax is gone.'

Luke nodded. 'Yes she does but I don' really think it has sunk in yet.'

Ruth asked the waiter to bring some Brandy and poured Luke a large glass and offered some to Sid and Janet. They sipped at it as Luke relayed the rest of Brigit's story to them glancing around to make sure no-one else was in earshot.

'Luke how long before we can take Brigit home?' asked Ruth when he'd finished talking.

'I'm not sure sweetheart, it all depends on her now, how quickly she can recover enough for the Doctors to let her out. I think her wounds will be okay, it's just the emotional trauma that concerns them most.'

'Just let us know when you are ready to go Luke, I insist on paying for your air fares back to New Zealand and ....uh uh no arguments,' he said, raising his hand to stop any protests, 'it's the least I can do please,' he urged.

'Thank you,' Luke replied humbly. 'I'm not sure if she will want to come home or go back to live at Bullock Creek though, I haven't asked her that question yet.'

'Whatever she wants to do Luke, we will make sure you are all taken care of, okay. You are our guests and you are family. We want to do everything we can to help you. We are doing this for Jax too. He would have wanted that.'

Sid's eyes filled up with tears. He stood up then and said goodnight and he and Janet walked slowly back to their room arm in arm, leaving Luke and Ruth clinging to each other sharing their own grief.

Chapter Sixteen

The Aftermath

Luke watched Brigit closely as she gazed absently out the window of the small plane while it circled over the Jamieson homestead.

'It's gonna be hard my darling, really hard, but I know you can get through this, we're here with you, we will get through this together, okay.' She turned and smiled at him but said nothing.

They landed on the dirt runway close to the homestead and were greeted warmly by Sid and Janet who had come home the week before.

'How is she?' asked Janet quietly when Brigit was out of earshot.

'Not really sure Janet,' said Luke, frowning in concern. 'She's certainly not her old self and she seems overly cheerful for someone who has just lost a husband and gone through so much trauma. I'm really quite worried about her, Ruth is too.'

He watched as Ruth and Sid led Brigit into the house.

'She doesn't want to talk anymore about

what happened and if we ask her anything she says she can't remember. The doctor said it wasn't uncommon for people to block out traumatic events, especially women who have been violated the way she has been.'

'Come on dear, let's get you inside. I'm guessing a cold beer would go down well.'

Luke smiled. 'You're getting to know me so well Janet.'

There were more mourners and well-wishers at Jax's funeral than Janet and Sid had anticipated. They decided to hold the service in the small stone chapel on the property a short distance from their homestead. Until now the chapel been host mainly to Sunday services once a month when the local pastor called, or weddings and christenings. It only held thirty people, the rest of the mourners were seated in a very large marquee set up right outside the door of the chapel so that everyone could see and hear what was going on. The Jamiesons were humbled by the outpouring of grief from so many areas of the community. People came from all over the country and the Police presence was overwhelming. The funeral had been delayed so that Brigit could attend, which unfortunately gave the media plenty of time to inveigle themselves upon the proceedings. They were there in droves but the Police helped to keep them from getting too close and further upsetting the family. The Jamiesons were disinclined to issue trespass notices and instead relied on the Police to keep the news hounds at bay.

The day passed in an achingly painful haze for both families. Brigit sat stoney faced and mute during the whole procedure. She didn't shed a tear, not even when she turned to see Luke and Ruth softly sobbing into their handkerchiefs. Luke, Trey, Sid and the three uncles were the pall bearers. At the end of the service Brigit walked behind the coffin arm in arm with Ruth as if she was in a trance, she simply didn't appear to register what was happening. When the hearse had rolled slowly out of sight up the dirt path taking Jax to his final resting place in the family cemetery, Ruth began to fall apart. Luke spotted her and came quickly over to gather her up in a big comforting hug. He looked at Brigit over Ruth's shoulder and his blood ran cold, there was absolutely no emotion. She was looking at her father with questioning eyes as if she didn't understand what was going on.

During the days that followed, Luke, Ruth and the Jamieson's started their healing process. They talked a lot, about everything. They cried over the silliest little things and they hugged and comforted each other. Brigit would excuse herself whenever they started to discuss Jax or the kidnapping. She was happy to sit and chat about the farm and ordinary everyday events but beyond that she didn't seem remotely interested. She was becoming more and more withdrawn.

'Just give her time Luke, I'm sure she will process all this when she's ready,' Janet suggested.

'I'm really concerned though Janet,' responded Ruth. 'I haven't seen her cry once since we brought her here. She hasn't been grieving with the rest of us, she doesn't want to talk about Jax or what has happened to her.'

'I agree sweetheart, I think she's far from okay. But I do hear her crying and tossing and turning and groaning in the night, it's heart breaking. I don't know what to do about it, I think she needs professional help. I want to get her back home as soon as possible but I don't want to push her.'

'Why don't we take her back to the house she and Jax were living in and we'll help her pack up her things. That might stir things along a bit,' offered Ruth.

Brigit showed no sign of emotion as they pulled up in front of the home she'd shared with Jax. She waltzed in and picked up the cat as if nothing had happened. She was alarmed to see Nick and Jasper in the house.

'Oh, what are you guys doing here?' she demanded.

Ruth caught their eye and shook her head,

holding her finger to her lips to indicate to them not to say anything. They got the message.

'Gidday Brig, nice to see you. Nick and I were just feeding the cat and making sure everything was okay before you came home. You okay then?'

'Mwaa thanks guys, aren't you just a couple of big old softies.' She gave them both a big hug.

Ruth ushered the men out of the house promising she would seek them out later and fill them in on what was happening. Brigit showed her father around the house but when they got to the bedroom she stood in the doorway a little confused.

'What is it sweetie, you okay?'

"Hmm, what? Oh yeah, I'm okay. Hey how about a coffee, I'm parched.'

Luke put the kettle on and sat down with Brigit at the table. 'Brig, sweetheart, listen to me, I want you to come home with us, with me and Ruth.'

'When?'

'As soon as you are ready.'

'Why?'

He hesitated for a moment. 'Well.... I could do with a hand on the farm, I miss having you around the house. It's been ages since you were last there, why don't you come home with us when we go back?'

Brigit turned as Ruth walked in.

'Dad wants me to go back and help him on the farm, says he misses me,' she scoffed. As if. He's got you to keep him company now,' and she laughed.

'Well,' said Ruth pausing to allow her mind to come up with an excuse to get Brigit home, 'I'm not that good at the stock work. To be honest I would much rather be at home than out on the farm so your Dad could do with another hand.'

Luke appreciated what Ruth was saying. It wasn't true but he would go along with anything to get Brigit to come home.

'Seriously Dad, you need my help?'

'I've really missed having my right-hand girl beside me darling, nothing would please me more than to have you back in the saddle working a muster with me again.'

'Oh Dad, you are such a softie. Actually, it would be great to have a change of scenery for a while, get me away from all this heat and dust. So when did you say you were heading back home?'

Later that night Brigit phoned Janet and Sid and told them the news.

'Oh Brigit that sounds like a lovely idea, it's about time you went home for a visit.'

'You sure you don't mind. I mean, there's still plenty to do here.'

'Oh don't you worry your pretty little head about that my precious girl, you know Jasper and Nick will be more than happy to look after things while you are gone.'

'Okay, I guess that's settled then.' She turned and gave Luke and Ruth the thumbs up.

They clasped each other's hands under the table, relieved.

Chapter Seventeen

Back Home

Brigit barely spoke on the long flight home from Darwin. Luke didn't prompt her for conversation, he left her in peace. She brightened up considerably when they drove in through the gates of Duffield Station though.

'It seems so long ago since you were last home Brig,' said Luke.

'Yes, it's been a while,' she sighed. 'Thanks Daddy, this was a good idea, I have missed this.'

Sandy, Rees, Stella and Selwyn came running down from their house up the track. They all clambered around Brigit suffocating her with hugs and kisses. She loved every minute of it and was soon laughing and chatting amiably with the twins.

Luke was relieved. Maybe this was just what Brigit needed, to be home. Brigit was delighted to be back in her old room again and before long was almost back to her old self. Apart from the nightmares and not wanting to talk about Jax or the traumatic events that happened in Australia, she seemed okay.

'Stella and Rees tried to talk to Brigit about the first part of their trip,' said Sandy one morning when she and Selwyn, Luke and Ruth were sitting at the homestead kitchen table having a cuppa and a catch up, 'but she told them she couldn't remember anything.'

'It's probably the memory block the doctor was talking about,' Luke replied.

'Maybe she has dealt with it in her own way and is moving on,' offered Sandy.

'I would agree except for the nightmares,' said Luke. 'I often hear her crying in the night but when I go in to check on her she appears not to know what's going on, it's as if she is still asleep. Even when she screams it doesn't seem to wake her up. If I try to wake her, she just rolls over and goes back to sleep. When it's really bad I curl up beside her and cuddle her until she is settled again. It's heartbreaking Sandy, I just don't know what to do.'

'Have you thought about a psychologist?' asked Ruth.

'A shrink? Whatever for? She's not crazy.'

'No, no of course she's not crazy Luke but sometimes when people have difficulty dealing with traumatic events, they just need a little help to come to terms with it,' Sandy explained.

'She's right Luke, I think it's time we looked at getting psychological help for Brigit,' said Ruth.

'You really think that might help?'

'Won't do any harm to try will it.'

'Guess not. I'll make a few calls on Monday and see if I can talk to someone about it.'

'From what you tell me Mr Williams, it sounds like your daughter might be suffering from posttraumatic stress disorder, more commonly known as PTSD.'

'I know what that is,' said Luke, 'but I thought it only happened to guys who came back from the war.'

'No, not at all, it's more common than you think. When people suffer such trauma as your daughter has, it can be too painful for them to remember or think about so the mind blocks it all out. A bit like a self-imposed amnesia I suppose.' The doctor's voice was soft and he sounded like a gentle man. Luke liked the sound of him.

'So how do we fix it doctor?'

'That's a hard one to answer. If she is willing to come in and see us, we can certainly make an assessment and see if counselling or hypnotherapy would work for her.'

'And what if she won't go?'

'Then it's just a matter of time Mr Williams. She may come through it and eventually allow herself to remember. Once she is strong enough you could always take her back to the scene of the events with a psychiatrist on hand and see if that shocks her back to reality. It's a bit harsh I know, but it often works. She needs to grieve for her husband and allow herself to get angry and grieve for what she lost out there in the desert. I wish you luck Mr Williams, I hope I have been of some help and please let me know if I can help further.'

'Thanks doc.'

When Luke broached the subject of counselling or therapy with Brigit later that night she was annoyed.

'I'm not nuts Dad for God's sake, what makes you think I need a shrink?'

'Hey hey Brig, I'm sorry, please don't get upset, I am just worried about your nightmares that's all.'

'Nightmares? Everyone has nightmares Dad, why should I be any different?' she stomped off to her room like a petulant child. And that was it, subject closed.

Chapter Eighteen

Recovery

Spring started to blossom on Duffield Station after a long cold winter. Daffodils were in full bloom and the farm was alive with the delightful bleating of baby lambs.

'I love this time of the year,' gushed Brigit as she rode around the paddocks with her father checking the newborns.

She smiled at the little ones leaping around on all fours chasing each other, their little tails waggling crazily behind them.

'Looks like we have a good crop of lambs this year.'

'Yes, it's looking very promising,' agreed Luke. He was pleased to see the colour in Brigit's cheeks and a smile on her face. It had been three months since Luke and Ruth brought Brigit home. She never mentioned going back to Australia and Luke and Ruth never brought the matter up either.

'Dad.'

'Yes sweetheart,' Luke stopped and turned in his saddle to face Brigit sensing she wanted to tell him something important.

'Dad, I want to move back to the cottage.'

Luke wasn't expecting that.

'I love the cottage Dad,' she'd explained. 'I feel at home there. Besides, I don't want to come between you and Ruth.'

'You don't come between us sweetheart, we love having you here, you're our baby,' he chuckled.

'Oh Dad, don't be an old goose, I'm too old to be anyone's baby,' she protested, 'I just need some space to myself and you know how much that place means to me. It's my home.'

Luke paused for a moment to think.

'On one condition.'

'What's that?' Brigit was hesitant, not sure what Luke had in mind.

'You cook a meal for Ruth and I at the cottage once a week, and you still join the rest of us for the traditional Sunday Roast. Deal?'

'Deal,' agreed Brigit, 'I can live with that.'

But Luke still wasn't happy with the idea of Brigit moving out. 'I'd much rather have her here in the house with us where we can keep an eye on her,' Luke discussed with Ruth later that night as they lay cuddled up in bed. 'But if she's going to be happier in the cottage then I guess that's the best place for her, we'll just have to be extra vigilant.'

Selwyn and Sandy carried on working on the farm as they had before Brigit came home. Rees and Stella were busy with their studies so Ruth was the only one who had to make adjustments to her old routine. She loved working with Luke on the farm but was more than happy to move over and let Brigit take up the reins again like she used to before she married Jax and moved to Australia.

'I miss having you out there with me darling,' Luke complained one night over dinner. 'Don't get me wrong, it's awesome having Brigit with me but I miss you out there too. Might see if I can create more work so the three of us can work together.'

Ruth smiled. 'That would be great hon, but if Brigit gets the least bit upset about it, I'm happy to pull back. Besides, I am developing a passion for gardening, the spring flowers are glorious.'

'Yes I've noticed,' smiled Luke, 'the gardens are looking fantastic, you are doing a great job.'

As the weather warmed up Luke and Ruth saw less and less of Brigit. When she wasn't out working with her father, she was either cleaning, bottling, doing the gardening around the cottage, or she was off riding somewhere.

'Brigit was up at the shepherds hut yesterday,' commented Selwyn as they saddled up one morning. 'Looked like she had been there for a while.'

'Yeah I know Sel. She has been up there for

a couple of days. I went up to check on her but she said she was okay, said she wanted to spend some time with her mother.'

Selwyn shot a concerned look at Luke and then with a sigh of relief said, 'Oh, you mean the Angel monument. For a moment there I thought she must have really lost the plot.'

'No, I think she's okay. She seems happy enough but she's still not back to her old self. I really miss the old Brigit.'

'We all do mate, we all do. Life can be so bloody unfair sometimes.' He turned and mounted his horse before Luke saw the tears in his eyes.

'Oh, she gave me this, said she found it down in the gully below the shepherds hut.' Selwyn handed Luke a small rusty item. 'What do you make of it?'

'Looks like a piece off a horse's bit,' said Luke turning it over in his fingers.

'Where did you say she found it?'

'Down in the gully below the hut.'

'What was she doing down there? It's as steep as buggery.'

'She scrambled down to free up a ewe that had got stuck in some brambles apparently.'

'Yeah, that sounds like Brigit.'

'She said the strangest thing though.'

'What was that?'

'She said she didn't know what to do with it. She didn't want to throw it away but she said something about it made her cry.'

'Luke's blood suddenly ran cold.

'The gully below the hut you said?'

'Yeah that's right.'

'Sel, that's the gully where Elizabeth found Gordon. Remember, from what she wrote in her diaries? Gordon's horse slipped and went over the edge. You don't suppose this is….'

'Could be I suppose. I know something about it upset her.'

Luke thoughtfully popped the item into his pocket.

Chapter Nineteen

Visit Down Under

Another year passed and spring returned to the farm again. Luke had been in regular contact with Sid and Janet and after a year of pestering, they finally accepted Luke's invitation to fly down for a visit.

'What did Brigit say when you told her they were coming?' asked Ruth when Luke returned from seeing Brigit.

'She just said, that's nice. I don't know how I thought she'd react but I thought it would be a little more than, 'that's nice'. It will be interesting to see how she reacts when they get here.'

Everyone was excited at seeing Janet and Sid again. Ruth and Sandy had been baking all morning, Stella and Rees were on vacuuming and window cleaning duties and Selwyn was out cleaning the pool. As soon as Stella spotted Luke's car coming up the driveway she alerted everyone with a squeal of delight and they all rushed out of the house to greet their visitors.

Sid and Janet were all smiles as they climbed out of the car. 'Oh it's so good to see you all again, it's been forever,' gushed Janet.

'And who's fault is that?' scolded Ruth as she hugged Janet tight. 'Luke's been asking for you to come down for ages.'

'I know,' said Janet, 'It's just been a really tough year for us, there's been so much to sort out, you know.' Her voice broke and Ruth immediately regretted what she'd said.

'I'm so sorry Janet, I wasn't thinking.'

Janet smiled and kissed Ruth on the cheek. 'It's okay sweetheart, we are doing well, really.' She looked around. 'Where's Brigit?'

'Oh she's off on one of her jaunts,' laughed Stella. 'She disappears up to the shepherd's hut for days on end. Only comes back when there's work to do.'

'Better than taking off when there's work to do I guess,' added Rees.

Janet shot a concerned look at Luke. He lifted his shoulders in resignation and ushered her into the house.

They were all sitting around the table talking at once when they heard a horse galloping towards the house.

'That'll be Brigit.' Luke glanced out the kitchen window.

Next thing the screen door swung open and a pink cheeked, wind-swept Brigit breezed into the room.

'Oh' she said. 'Hi, I didn't know you were here. How are you?'

Sid and Janet got to their feet and took turns gathering Brigit into a loving hug.

'How are you sweetheart?' Janet held Brigit at arm's length.

'Umm, yeah, I'm all good thanks,' she seemed a little bewildered. 'What are you doing here?'

'Don't you remember darling, Ruth and I have been trying to get them to come for a visit for ages.'

'Oh yeah, silly me. Any more tea in the pot?'

Brigit didn't seem to notice the stunned silence at the table. 'So did you guys have a good flight?' she glanced over her shoulder as she reached for the tea pot.

'Yes, it was good, no delays thank goodness,' said Janet.

Slowly the conversation picked up again but nobody spoke about Jax or the events of the previous year while Brigit was there. She sat down with her cup of tea and joined in with the conversation for a little while but as soon as she'd finished her tea she made some excuse about having something to do and got up and left.

'She's still not herself is she?' Janet was looking at Luke.

'No she's not Janet, and I don't know if she will ever be. I guess life has a way of changing people. I really miss her, the real her I mean.' There was a deep sadness in his eyes.

Whenever Brigit wasn't around Janet, Sid, Ruth and Luke talked about the traumatic events of the previous year. This time the emotions weren't quite so raw and they were able to talk a bit more freely amongst themselves.

One night Ruth invited Sandy, Selwyn and the twins to join them at the homestead for a big roast dinner. Brigit also accepted the invitation. The conversations that night swung around and covered a variety of topics but care was taken to avoid any mention of Jax and the kidnapping. Stella and Rees were particularly interested to hear what was going on in Australia. They had been disappointed that their trip of a lifetime had been cut short so tragically but had been reluctant to venture back again on their own.

'You two kids thought about coming back to Aussie sometime soon?' asked Sid as if reading their minds.

Rees looked at Stella. She turned to see Brigit's reaction. When there was none, she turned back to Rees and shrugged her shoulders.

'Yeah we'd like to go back, wouldn't we Rees. We'd like to see some more of the country. Not sure when we'll get the chance though, I'm looking for a job at the moment, Dad says I gotta start earning a living,' he laughed.

'Well, how about covering both options and coming to work for me. Think you could handle being a jackaroo?'

'I'd sure love to give it a go.' He glanced at his father 'whaddya reckon Dad?'

Rees had no idea that Sid had already talked to Sandy and Selwyn about offering him a job. They were a little hesitant at first but Sid convinced them Rees would be in good hands and would be given ample opportunity to learn as much as he wanted. In the end the parents decided it was too good an opportunity to pass up so they agreed.

'Well if it's okay with Sid then I guess it's okay with us.' said Selwyn.

'Oh my baby boy,' Sandy cooed, 'I will miss you so much.'

'Stop it Mum, you're embarrassing me. Thank you Mr Jamieson, how soon can I start?'

'Call me Sid, and you can come back with us when we leave day after tomorrow if you like, if that's okay with you folks of course?'

'Looks like you better start packing then,' Sandy sighed.

'We'll have a spare room to turn into an office now,' laughed Selwyn.

'Dad,' protested Rees, 'I'm not even gone yet.'

'What about you Stella?' asked Janet noticing her forlorn expression at losing her brother.

'I'm studying dress designing. I'm hoping to eventually get work in a fashion house somewhere but I really need to work in a boutique for a while and get a feel for the industry.'

'I might be able to help you there,' offered Janet. 'How would you like to live in Melbourne?'

'Melbourne? Really? I would love to go to Melbourne.'

'My sister lives there, she's in a large flat all by herself. She's a widow and quite the fashionista, I'm sure she'd love to take you under her wing, it would give her something to focus on. I'll call her later on tonight and see what she thinks if you like.'

Stella beamed at her mother. 'Oh dear mama, looks like you might be losing us both' she laughed, clapped her hands in delight. 'Hope you don't suffer too bad from empty nest syndrome.'

'Not a chance' laughed Selwyn. 'Your mother and I will love having the house all to ourselves. Who knows what we will get up to,' he winked at his wife.

'Eeeww, too much information,' scolded Stella covering her ears.

Selwyn glanced anxiously at Sandy, this part of the conversation wasn't pre planned. He was a little concerned at her losing both twins at once.

Luke had also been watching Brigit while all this was going on. She showed no emotion and while everyone sat making plans she quietly got up and left. Luke looked across to Ruth, she'd been watching Brigit too.

'Wonder what she's thinking?' Ruth pondered after everyone else had gone to bed.

'Don't know, but I hope she's alright,' sighed Luke.

The following day was a blur of sorting and packing and getting ready to go. Sid and Janet apologised to Luke for causing such mayhem.

'Actually you have done us a favour Sid. The kids have been unsettled since the trip last year and heaven knows there's not enough work for them both on the farm, especially now that Brigit is back. She works herself to exhaustion some days, I think sometimes she does it to stop herself from thinking about things.'

'Is she going to be alright Luke? She's certainly not the same old Brigit is she?'

'No, Janet, far from it I'm afraid. All we can do is wait and hope she will work through it somehow. I had hoped your trip might have triggered things for her, but it doesn't seem to.'

That afternoon Luke took Sid and Janet for a drive up the mountain to the shepherd's hut. It was their last day and the weather was perfect. The air was still, the sky clear blue, the daffodils were out and of course there was the wonderful spring sound of lambs. As they drove up the mountain in the jeep, Janet giggled in delight.

'Oh look at those precious wee lambs bouncing around. You'd think they had springs on their feet,' she laughed.

'Yes Spring has always been Brigit's and my favourite time of the year, how could you not like Spring time eh.'

They arrived at the hut and as Sid and Janet wandered around taking in the expansive views down into the valleys below, Luke set a fire going in the tin trough outside the hut and made billy tea.

'My I can see now why Brigit used to get homesick,' sighed Janet as she looked out across the valley. The air is so fresh and crisp isn't it, certainly nothing like the air back home. So what is this monument you have here Luke, this beautiful Angel?'

'Oh, that's in memory of Brigit's mother, Ellen. You know she died shortly after Brigit was born and this was just something we wanted to do. This was Ellen's favourite spot, she used to love coming up here and we thought it might be somewhere for Brigit to come and be with her mum.'

'What a lovely idea,' said Janet, walking over to get a closer look, 'Ellen would have loved this idea of giving Brigit somewhere special to come and 'talk' to her. Speaking of Brigit, I haven't seen her today.'

No sooner were the words out of her

mouth when Brigit came bounding over the ridge behind them, riding like the wind, hair blowing in the breeze. She brought the horse to a prancing halt beside the hut.

'Oh hi guys, I didn't know there was anyone else up here.'

'Thought I'd bring them up and show them the view and have a cuppa. You want one?'

'Sure, thanks Dad,' she said as she slid down off her horse.

'You look bright eyed and bushy tailed,' he laughed, 'how was your ride?'

'Great. I've just been up to check the pastures over the back, it's looking promising. That recent bout of rain has greened it up nicely.'

Sid and Janet looked at each other and smiled. 'Guess it's good to have your side-kick back eh,' laughed Sid.

'It sure is,' smiled Luke with pride. 'I certainly missed her while she was away. Oh by the way Brig, Stella is leaving with Sid and Ruth and Rees tomorrow. The arrangements have been finalised for Stella to go and stay in Melbourne.'

'Wow,' Brigit blew out a breath, 'well, that's a big change in a short space of time, I'll miss the twins,' she said thoughtfully.

Brigit took the mug of tea Luke offered her and walked over to the Angel monument. She sat in her favourite spot beneath it as she had done hundreds of times before and stared down into the valley.

'You okay Brig?' called Luke after a while.

'Yep, just discussing it all with Mum, she's all good with it so I guess I am too,' she laughed over her shoulder. 'So what time are you guys heading back tomorrow?'

'We have an early flight in the morning,' said Janet.

'Oh, well I guess we should say our goodbyes now in case I miss you in the morning,' said Brigit. She pulled herself to her feet, walked over and handed her empty cup back to her father.

She hugged Janet and then turned to Sid. She looked intently at him for a moment and tears started to form in her eyes. 'I really miss you, you know,' she whispered. She hugged him tightly then abruptly turned, mounted her horse and was off. Sid watched after her, tears streaming down his own cheeks.

'I miss you too sweetie,' he whispered back.

'You okay darling?' Janet touched his arm.

'I'm fine,' he sniffed, 'I just miss that girl you know. She was the daughter I never had.'

'Yes, she was for both of us,' Janet agreed.

Later that night Luke went up to the cottage to see how Brigit was doing. They sat together on the wooden bench outside under the kitchen window.

'Guess it's just you and me against the world again eh Dad.'

'Don't forget Ruth,' he said.

'Oh of course I didn't forget Ruth, but you know what I mean.'

'Yes, I do know what you mean. Have you ever thought of going back to Bullock Creek Station? I know Sid and Janet would have you back there in a heartbeat if you wanted to go back.'

'Don't be silly Dad, why would I want to go back there? I love it here. I'm back to stay,' she smiled glancing up at him, 'you don't get rid of me that easily.'

She reached over and gave him a hug.

'Wanna glass of wine?' he asked, 'I'll grab a bottle if you've got one in the fridge.'

'Nope, you stay there Dad, that's my job.'

'Actually, that's my job,' laughed Ruth as she came in the front gate with a bottle of wine and some nibbles in a basket. 'Brigit, you are a farm hand now, you don't get to do the household stuff. You coming down to join us for dinner tonight?'

'Yes I'd love to, thanks Ruth. Did I ever tell you how good it is to have you as my Mum?'

'Awww thanks Brig. Have I ever told you how much I enjoy having you as a daughter. Now, have you given any thought to coming back to live in the homestead with us?'

'To be honest Ruth I feel at home here in

the cottage. Hope you don't mind.'

'Not at all, just as long as you are comfortable here. You know you are welcome home any time though, okay.'

'Yeah I know, thanks'

Ruth broached the subject of Brigit living by herself in the cottage the following evening. It was the first time she and Luke had had the house to themselves for over a week and they sat out by the pool with a glass of wine and watching the sun go down.

'Actually Ruth, she seems happier in the cottage than anywhere else, I'm happy for her to stay there, said Luke. 'You know how much she's always loved that cottage, right from the time she was a little kid. I still remember the time when she was about four years old and she dragged Sandy up to "her" cottage to ask where "her" books were. The books she was referring to had belonged to Elizabeth Tregowarth who lived there over 100 years ago. It freaked the hell out of Sandy I can tell you. She came back looking like she'd seen a ghost.' Luke laughed at the recollection.

'I remember you telling me about Elizabeth and Gordon. Of course, they used to live in that cottage. Funny that Brigit feels so at home there isn't it. So what did you make of Brigit referring to the diaries as 'my books'.

'I dunno, I've thought about it from time to time but I'm still puzzled by it. Grace reckoned it was something to do with reincarnation or something but that was sort of brushed under the carpet, Grace knew I wasn't into any of that woo woo stuff.'

Just then Sandy and Selwyn called out as they came bustling through the back door.

'Oh good. Glad you two are both here. Sel and I have been talking and we've come up with something we want to run by you.'

'Come and sit down, help yourselves to a wine Sandy. Sel there's plenty of cold beer in the fridge.'

Selwyn with beer in hand and Sandy with a glass of wine plonked themselves down on the sun loungers which they had turned away from the pool so they could sit and face Ruth and Luke.

'Okay you two, what are you up to?' smiled Luke. 'You look like Cheshire cats.'

'How would you feel about us going away too? We want to get a motor home and tour around Australia, something we've often talked about. Now that the kids are over there, and with Brigit being home, we thought it might be a good time to go.'

'Can't say I'm surprised,' said Luke, 'ever since you did that camper van trip down south a couple of years ago you've never stopped talking about doing the same thing in Australia. Couldn't think of anything worse but if that's what spins ya wheels, go for it,' laughed Luke.

'You're sure you don't mind?'

'Nah, Brigit and Ruth and I can run the place here with the help of the contractors, and if we need a hand we only have to ask the neighbours. I will bloody miss you though you old coot. And you too of course Sandy,' he gave her a wink. 'Gonna be awfully quiet around here without you, the place just won't be the same.' Luke was quiet for a few moments as the reality set in.

'Stay for dinner,' suggested Ruth.
'Only if you let me help,' Sandy insisted.

Chapter Twenty

Full Circle

The days were getting noticeably cooler as Brigit, Ruth and Luke settled into a comfortable daily routine. Another year had gone by and the shearers were due any day. The weather had been pretty stable so there should be no delays this year. The same shearing contractor had been coming to the farm for several years now and with the exception of the odd 'newbie' coming and going, they were pretty much the same hard-core bunch of workers. They were a fun group who worked hard and played hard.

Ruth was curious to see if Adam would be back again this year. He was an unusual young man who seemed older than his years. Luke found him one day standing at the gate of the old cob cottage.

'Wanna go in and have a look around mate?' he'd asked the young man.

Startled by the unexpected voice at his side Adam had shied away. 'Ah no it's okay, thanks,' he'd mumbled and had gone back to the shed.

Ruth had noticed that the young man had taken a bit of a shine to Brigit last year, not that Brigit would have noticed. She was still lost in her own little world and barely spoke to, or interacted with, anyone outside the family.

When the shearers finally arrived, Ruth was delighted to see Adam leap out of the second van as it pulled up. There was something about the young man that fascinated her. She decided she would make a concerted effort to get to know him this year and perhaps wave him under Brigit's nose a little.

'I see young Adam is back here again this year Brig. Last year when he was here your Dad found him standing outside your gate staring at the cottage. Maybe he was hoping to catch a glimpse of you.' Ruth and Luke were lingering at the cottage gate saying goodnight to Brigit before heading down the track to the homestead.

'Oh Ruth you're not trying to match make are you? Some people are just fascinated by old cottages, maybe he is too.'

'Well, maybe you could take him in and show him around sometime then.'

'Doubt it,' she laughed, 'my cottage is a male free zone.'

'Is that by choice or by circumstance?'

'By choice. There's no way I'm getting mixed up with any man again.'

'Why? What's so awful about men?'

'Not men in general, just any man who

wants to get too close.'

'It's been three years since Jax died honey, don't you think it's time to get back on the horse, so to speak.'

The colour drained from Brigit's face to the point that Ruth feared she might pass out.

'Brigit, sweetheart, I'm sorry, I didn't mean to upset you.'

Brigit slowly sunk to her knees letting out the most god-awful howl. Luke crouched down in front of her and pulled her into his arms.

'Let it out honey, just let it all out, you can't bottle up your pain forever, it will kill you.'

The three of them were kneeling on the ground beside the little white picket gate which was standing open in welcome. They hung on to each other as if for dear life while Brigit opened the flood gates of bottled-up emotion.

When Brigit had been quiet for a while, Luke gently scooped her up in his arms, carried her in to her cottage and carefully laid her down on the couch like a baby. Ruth took the lavender angora wrap from across the back of the settee and draped it over her. Sleep well my angel, sleep well Luke whispered,' kissing her on the forehead. They quietly slipped out the door pulling it closed behind them.

They didn't see Brigit until morning teatime the next morning. When she walked in it looked as if she had been crying all night. Her eyes were red and swollen, her face was puffy and she sounded as though she had a head cold. Luke pulled her into his arms and gave her a great big bear hug, she hugged him back real tight.

'Oh my darling, are you okay?'

'Better than I have been in a long time, thanks Dad, thanks Ruth.'

'For what?'

'For helping me to let go. I've been doing a lot of thinking. I don't know what's been happening to me, I just couldn't feel anything or remember anything, but it all came rushing back last night. At least the part about Jax did. I'm not sure I'm ready to face the other stuff yet, not on my own anyway. So I've been thinking, is that offer of going to see Sid and Janet still on the table? I think it might be a good idea for me to go back there for a visit, put things to rest.'

'Now there's my girl, my beautiful, brave girl, cried Luke, eyes glistening with tears. 'Yes of course it is, as soon as the shearing is finished we'll head over for as long as you like. Actually this is exactly what the psychiatrist suggested when you first came home.'

'What psychiatrist?'

'I rang one when you first came home to talk about the nightmares you were having and that you just weren't yourself. He said he thought you had post traumatic stress disorder and suggested that I take you back to the scene to help you get over it. He said you had probably blocked it all from your memory, like selective amnesia or something.'

'Makes sense I guess, and yeah it does describe where I've been doesn't it. The kidnap thing is still pretty hazy in my mind, I'm not sure I really want to remember it but I guess it would be best if I do. Do you know, I have no idea what happened to that guy.'

'That's because we opted not to tell you. Every time we brought the subject up you would walk away so we stopped talking about it in front of you.'

'So what did happen after you found me?'

'Shall we go over there first and see what happens and then we can sit down with Janet and Sid and fill in the blanks together. How does that sound?'

'Scarey, but I'm up for it, let's do it. I'm gonna ring Sid and Janet right now.'

There was only one day's delay in the shearing programme due to a sudden downpour on the fourth day, but fortunately there were enough dry sheep in the yards to keep the crew going, albeit at a slower pace. Brigit took notice of Adam this time, since her father and Ruth had drawn her attention to him. She liked the look of him, in fact he seemed rather familiar to her.

During a lunch break on the slower paced fourth day, Adam found the courage to venture over to where Brigit was sitting outside her cottage.

'Mind if I join you?' he called from the gate.

'Not at all,' she called back, indicating the seat beside her. 'My name's Brigit Jamieson, what's yours?'

'Jamieson? I thought you were Luke Williams's daughter.'

'I am but Jamieson is my married name.'

'Oh.' The disappointment on his face stirred her heart.

'I am a widow, my husband died three years ago.' After all this time it felt strange to talk so freely about Jax, but it felt good too, even if it was bittersweet.

'Oh,' he said again, still standing.

'Please, sit down, I promise I won't bite,' she smiled kindly at him.

'Tregowarth, my name is Adam Tregowarth.'

Brigit felt a chill run through her veins. 'Did you say Tregowarth?'

'Yes, that's right. One of my ancestors used to own this farm, Gordon Tregowarth. He was my great grandfather's brother. From what I can gather he died after falling down a gully on his horse somewhere on the farm. I assume this is the cottage where he and his wife Elizabeth lived? My family often talked about it.'

Brigit was sitting stock still staring at him, her mouth hanging open. He stopped talking and looked up at her, smiling.

'Sorry, have I said something wrong?' He couldn't stop smiling, her open-mouthed expression was priceless. Suddenly she snapped out of herself and shut her mouth.

'Oh, wow, I certainly wasn't expecting that.' Her heart was pounding. 'It was my mother who found Elizabeth's diaries when she first came to the farm with Dad, before they were married. She and Dad returned them to your family. It was a very long story, did you ever read the diaries?'

'Yes, I've read them, they were awesome.'

'Come with me.' Brigit stood up and held her hand out to Adam. He followed her eagerly into the house not sure what to expect. She took him into the tiny parlour and brought him to stand beside her in front of Elizabeth and Gordon's wedding photo above the mantelpiece. They both stood still hardly daring to breathe as a familiar electricity charged between them. Their arms were touching, he let his fingers reach out and intertwine with hers.

'I feel like I've come home,' he whispered.

'Me too,' smiled Brigit.

Chapter Twenty One

Closure

Sid picked Luke, Brigit and Ruth up from the Darwin airport in the helicopter and flew them back to Bullock Creek Station. They weren't prepared for the welcoming committee that awaited them. The whole extended family and a large group of staff were standing out in front of the homestead waving as they landed. A huge banner saying 'welcome back Brigit' hung across the veranda.

Brigit was swallowed up in a wave of hugs and kisses which left her breathless and overwhelmed. Luke was quite overcome, he hadn't fully considered how much this family had loved Brigit too. Brigit coped with all the attention better than Luke had hoped, he was so proud of her. It was great to see Rees looking so happy and healthy. It took Brigit a moment or two to piece together why he was there as she hadn't really taken much notice of what was going on when Rees and Stella had left.

The party went on long into the night before they all sank gratefully into their comfortable beds. Janet had been sensitive enough not to put Brigit in the room she had shared with Jax. She didn't wake until late morning, sheepishly creeping out of bed hoping to grab a shower before anyone spotted her. She knew there was going to be a lot of talking going on for the next few days. Sid had called Brookie, the cop who had been in charge of the kidnapping case and informed him Brigit was back at Bullock Creek for a couple of weeks and was willing to address what had happened to her. The Police had wanted to talk to Brigit soon after the kidnapping but by then she had refused, saying she couldn't remember anything. Fortunately, Braithwaite had confessed to everything so they didn't really need her testimony but they said it would be good to put a full stop to the end of the story, if Brigit ever felt up to it.

'Daisy, Abigail, oh my God you are still here,' Brigit hugged the women as she walked into the kitchen following the aroma of fresh coffee and bacon.

'Sure are, where else would we be girl, this is home. Now what would you like to eat?'

'Bacon and eggs for me please Daisy,' said Luke as he came into the kitchen behind her, and eggs benedict for my girls if I'm not mistaken.'

Brigit laughed, 'oh Dad I only have that when I'm out, I don't expect Daisy to cook that for me.'

'If its eggs benedict you want my girl, then its eggs benedict you will have,' she laughed.

They finished breakfast and were sitting on the veranda with their coffees when Sid and Janet came back from the sheds.

'Well hello you three, hope you slept well,' called Sid as he came up the steps.

'We sure did, how about you?'

'Always do Luke, always do,' bragged Sid. 'Brigit, look who's flown back from Canada just to see you.' He stepped aside and Brigit caught sight of a tall young man coming up the steps behind him. He looked so much like Jax she caught her breath.

'Trey? Oh my God, is that really you?' She leapt out of her chair and flew into his arms giving him a big hug. 'Oh my gosh, I haven't seen you in forever,' she cried. 'Where have you been? What have you been doing?'

Trey set her back on her feet and sat her down, taking the recently vacated chair beside her. 'Well you know I got married eh.'

'Nooo. Really? When?'

'About two years ago now, I did write.'

Brigit hung her head. 'Sorry Trey, I've been pretty remiss with my mail.'

'Hey, I know what's been happening with you, I do understand you know. Anyway Alice didn't want to stay on the farm, she's a city girl so we ended up getting work with the Volunteer Service Abroad scheme. We based ourselves in

Canada after a holiday there and we just go wherever we are needed.'

'So what do you do exactly?'

'Oh there's quite a few options really. At the moment we are building houses in the Pacific Islands.'

Daisy appeared with cold drinks, freshly brewed coffee and fresh baked scones. Everyone sat around with their refreshments and caught up on the gossip and staff comings and goings and what the rest of the family members had all been up to over the previous three years.

'I can't believe it's been three years,' exclaimed Brigit, 'I feel like I've been living in a fog all this time.'

'I guess in a way you have,' said Janet, we are just so relieved that you are getting back to your old self again, it's good to see, we've really missed you,' she reached over and patted Brigit's hand.

'Not quite there yet though am I? I've still got to work my way through all that horrible kidnapping stuff. I haven't allowed myself to think about it too much but I know I have to face it sooner or later, that's if I am to get over it all and move on with my life.' She looked shyly across to Ruth. 'Now that I have something to look forward to eh,' she was referring to Adam.

'I talked to Brookie this morning Brigit,' interrupted Sid. 'Do you remember him, he was head of the operation.'

'Sorry, no, I really don't remember much at all. I don't think it's that I can't, I think it's more that I don't want to because I know once the memories start, I won't be able to stop them and I will have to relive everything all over again.' Her eyes welled up with tears. 'I'm really scared, you know.'

Luke reached out and took her hand. 'Brigit, we will all be there right beside you, holding on to you when you decide you are ready to go through with this. There is no pressure, you can do it all in your own time, you won't be doing it on your own. You will be safe I promise.'

She sniffled and wiped her nose. 'Thanks guys, I guess there's no reason to put it off any longer. So what's the plan?'

'Well, the Police would like to hear as much as they can from you, mainly so they can fill in any details that Braithwaite may have omitted to tell them. They would like to take you back to that part of the road where you were held up, just out of Katherine, and go from there. Of course you won't remember the trip out to the hut but hopefully it will all come back to you when you get there.'

Brigit got out of the Police car and walked around to the front of the car, trying to cast her mind back to that fateful night that took her beloved Jax from her. To start with it was like snap shots in her mind. Quick darting flash backs. But as she stood looking around it all started to piece together and make sense.

'He came up behind us then passed us and pulled in front,' she began. She continued to tell them what she could remember. She felt quite drained by the time she'd finished. Janet saw how pale and strained she looked.

'Let's go into town and grab some lunch and have a break,' she suggested, 'Brigit looks done in.'

'I'm okay, I don't want to stop now, but a break and some food would be good.'

After lunch they all piled into two vans. Sid, Janet, Luke, Ruth, Brigit, Trey, Nick and Jasper, Brookie and a young constable, who was their driver, were all in one van. The other van carried seven members of the Police who were involved with the operation at the time and a local newspaper reporter.

'You weren't kidding when you said I wouldn't be doing this on my own,' laughed Brigit nervously. 'Sure hope I don't let anyone down.'

'Brigit,' cut in Brookie, 'we have absolutely no expectations of you at all. We just want to be there with you and take the opportunity of putting this all behind us. This deeply affected every one of us on the case and you know us cops, we love a happy ending. I have a psychologist and a doctor on standby if you need them?' He reached out and squeezed her shoulder, 'I can have them come with us if you like.'

Brigit hesitated for a moment. 'No, I have my family here, that's all I need.'

They turned off the tar sealed road and followed the dirt track, Dawson's track. It took them half an hour to reach the hut, such was its remoteness. As they drew closer, Brigit, who was sitting in the front seat, could feel her pulse starting to race. She felt a little lightheaded and took a swig of her water bottle but didn't take her eyes off the hut as it loomed into view. Sweat was pouring down her neck and she dabbed at moisture forming on her brow. Luke reached over and touched her gently on the shoulder.

'You okay hon?'

She nodded but didn't take her eyes off the hut. When the van came to a halt she sat looking out the window for some time. Nobody moved. Nobody said a word. They remained quiet and just let Brigit find her own way. Finally she took a deep breath and slowly climbed out of the car, never once taking her eyes off the hut. She walked over and stood in front of the ramshackle wooden building, trembling, willing herself to go in. She knew it would be painful but she also knew she had to do this. She walked up to the door, opened it and stood in the doorway until her eyes adjusted to the dark interior. Once she stepped inside the memories came flooding back. She sat on the edge of the bed, her knees trembling. She allowed the unwelcome thoughts to flow into her mind. Then she could feel the emotions start to rise up and take over. She rocked back and forth clutching her arms to her chest, moaning, tears streaming down her face. Luke made a move to go to her but Ruth held him back.

'This part is for her to do on her own Luke, just give her a moment or two, she'll be okay, she knows we are here and that she is safe.'

Suddenly Brigit jumped up and with a mighty howl ripped the dusty old mattress off the bed and dumped it on the floor. She kicked at it and jumped on it as if she was jumping on top of the old man himself.

'I woke up tied to this fucking bed,' she fumed. The notebooks were out and the pens clicked on as Brigit's words started to tumble out. She walked around the room, talking, touching, reliving every awful moment of her horrendous experience. Luke couldn't listen to the parts where the old bastard raped her, he had to walk away. The bile still rose up in his throat whenever he thought about it.

The note takers were crowded in the doorway for a good half an hour before Brigit told them she wanted to go outside. She sat on the doorstep and told them about the fight they'd had, when Braithwaite returned from town just before Sid and Luke turned up in the chopper. The whole group were visibly moved as Brigit recounted her story. She told it tearfully and emotionally but she put it across so well that everyone felt as though they were watching it happen right in front of them rather than just hearing about it. When it was all over, everyone stood and clapped.

'You are one hell of a gutsy young lady Brigit,' Brookie didn't bother to try and hide his tears.

Luke came over and hugged her real tight. 'How do you feel my darling.'

'Actually Dad, I feel like a load has been lifted from my shoulders, I feel like I can breathe again. Brookie, is there any reason why I can't burn this bloody place down.'

'Absolutely not,' he grinned, 'Peter, grab some petrol and let's help Brigit burn this place to the ground. Actually I think it will help bring closure for all of us and Braithwaite certainly won't be back here again.'

They pulled the vehicles back out of the way and Janet grabbed some cold drinks she had thoughtfully stowed in the van along with some delicious home baked cookies. Brigit took immense delight in striking the match and setting fire to the old hut. It gave her a great deal of satisfaction to see the flames lick up and take hold of the dry ageing timber. The group sat in silence, each with their own thoughts and memories watching the flames devour and destroy the scene of the hideous crime. It didn't take long to reduce the hut to a smouldering pile of ashes. Brookie went and sat beside Brigit and filled her in on the rest of the story.

'Obviously the bastard lived,' laughed Brigit, 'I didn't try to kill him you know, I only wanted to hurt him like he'd hurt other people.'

'Oh you hurt him alright,' laughed Brookie, 'you hurt him real good honey, couldn't have happened to a nicer bloke. He's in a wheelchair now cos funnily enough his kneecaps don't work anymore. Oh and he'll never have sex again, seems he's lacking something in the nether regions. The shoulder wound did heal though.'

'I almost feel guilty,' admitted Brigit, 'I said *almost*,' as Brookie started to protest.

'Well, the creep got life for Monti's murder and a consecutive life sentence for Jax's murder and another twenty years for what he did to you so he won't ever step foot outside prison again, not in this lifetime anyway.'

A week later Brigit was back to her beautiful vibrant feisty self, which was an enormous relief to everyone. It was their final dinner together at Bullock Creek Station before Luke, Ruth and Brigit were due to fly back to New Zealand. Luke took Brigit aside and sat her down on the bed before they went into the dining room. He put his hands on her shoulders and looked intently at her.

'Brig, did you know you were pregnant

when you were kidnapped?'

'What? No. What makes you say that?'

'When you were in the hospital the doctor came and told me that they were sorry they couldn't save the baby. He said you were nine weeks.'

'Oh.' She was quiet for a moment, deep in thought. 'Jax and I had been trying for ages to have a baby and I'd almost given up. That would explain the nausea I guess. Oh, how sad is it that I couldn't have brought a little Jax into the world.' She started to cry and Luke held her close.

'Sorry darling I wasn't sure if you knew or not. You never asked about it so I wasn't sure. I guess it was nature's way of dealing with things though eh. With all that you've been through, the PTSD and all that, you may not have coped with a baby.'

She pulled away and reaching for a tissue, blew her nose.

'That's true. Let's not tell Sid and Janet eh. They've had enough heartache just losing Jax, they don't need to know they lost a grandchild too.'

'Agreed,' said Luke. 'That's why I told you now before we left in case you wanted to tell them. But you are right, they don't need any more heartache.'

Chapter Twenty Two

Back to the Future

Luke, Ruth and Brigit were back and well settled on the farm by the time Christmas came around. Sandy and Selwyn parked up their motorhome in Melbourne and flew back to New Zealand with Stella for the holidays. Sid and Janet insisted Rees go back home for the Christmas holidays too. He was looking forward to being in a cooler climate for a while. Like Brigit he had had trouble adjusting to the intense summer heat in the outback.

It was a wonderful family reunion. They all spent many long summer days and beautiful evenings together at the main homestead hanging out around the pool and sharing their experiences. They were all thrilled to find that Brigit had broken through the barriers that had bound her since the kidnapping and Jax's death and they sat enthralled as she re-told her story.

'Oh Brigit,' Sandy had tears in her eyes, 'I had no idea. Your Dad said you told him what happened but he couldn't bring himself to talk about it. Oh my precious girl, it must feel so good to be able to talk about it now and get it off your chest.'

'It does Aunty Sandy. I still get a chill down my spine when I think of that guy but it also gives me a kind of strength and courage to know that I survived what he did to me.'

'I'm glad sweetheart, I really am. Your mother would have been so proud of you, you know. She was a very brave young woman too, you are so much like her.'

Brigit smiled, failing to hide the swell of pride she was feeling.

'Brigit, I will never forgive myself for not trying to save you that night.' Stella was in bits all of a sudden. 'If only I hadn't hidden down behind the seat, if only.....'

'Hey Stella, stop that.' Brigit was on her knees beside Stella's chair.

'Don't you ever ever blame yourself for what happened. Do you hear me.' She grabbed Stella by the shoulders and shook her harshly. 'Don't you ever regret surviving and doing what your instincts told you to do. I am so relieved it was only me he took. He could quite easily have shot and killed you too or taken both of us but you were brave and sensible enough to keep yourself out of danger. Don't you ever doubt that. From what I've heard you did an amazing job in helping the Police to find me which is something you wouldn't have been able to do if you were dead, right?' she shook her again. 'Right?' she demanded.

Stella wiped away her tears. 'Right,' she snuffled.

'Again. I didn't' hear you,' demanded Brigit, this time with a smile.

'Right,' shouted Stella.

'That's better. You are my beautiful sister and I could not imagine how my life would be without you, now come here and give me a hug.'

'God it's so good to be able to talk about this with you Brig, it's been really hard having to watch what we say all the time.'

'I'm really sorry too Stel, let's hope we can now put all of this behind us.' She turned to Rees.

'And that goes for you too Rees, you did an awesome job, thank you. So you want some hug therapy too.'

'No, no, I'm all good,' he laughed and dived into the pool before Brigit could get to him.

'Men!' she laughed.

'Well, speaking of men,' Luke cleared his throat.

'What?'

'Are you going to tell them about Adam or shall I?'

'What's this? Have you got yourself a man Brigit?' cried Sandy excitedly, 'oh this is good news.'

'Wait up a minute folks, Adam is a shearer that's all. We got chatting when they were here last and it appears he is the great-grandson of

Gordon Tregowarth's uncle. You know, the one who used to own this farm hundreds of years ago. Elizabeth was Gordon's wife, the one who wrote those diaries that Mum found.'

Sandy's face went white as a sheet. 'Oh my God that's so spooky,' she exclaimed, 'I've got goosebumps. So has he read the diaries then? Does he know the history?'

'Sure does. I took him into the cottage to see the photo of Elizabeth and Gordon and he said he felt like he'd come home.'

Sandy stared across at Luke. 'What do you make of this Luke?'

'First I've heard of it,' he looked at Brigit. 'You didn't tell me any of this.'

'What's the big deal? He's probably so familiar with the story that it feels like he's been there before that's all. What are you guys looking so spooked about? I've always thought of that place as if it was mine too.'

'Are you going to tell her, or should I,' Sandy challenged Luke.

'I will,' said Luke hesitantly.

'Brigit, Gracie and I discussed this subject many times. You know she was really into all that psychic and reincarnation stuff.'

'Would someone please tell me what's going on,' demanded Brigit excitedly.

'My, aren't we being demanding today, good to see you have your spirit back miss,' laughed her father. 'Okay, but first I think I'll grab myself a beer. Sel?'

'Yeah I'll have a beer thanks mate.'

'You ladies want a wine?' they all nodded.

'Beer for me thanks Uncle Luke,' called Rees from the pool.

They settled themselves by the pool with a supply of drinks and nibbles and Luke began to talk.

'Brigit, do you remember as a little girl you used to spend a lot of time at the cottage? You claimed that it was yours and you hated anyone else being there.'

'Uh huh. Yes I've always loved it but I'm not sure why.'

'Do you remember dragging me up to the cottage one day to show me the gap under the windowsill and ask where the books were?' ventured Sandy.

'Oh yeah, that's right,' she giggled, 'I'd forgotten all about that. For some reason I knew that if I pulled on the windowsill it would come away from the wall and reveal a space underneath. I expected to find some books in there. I don't know why. I know I was annoyed that there was nothing in there though.'

'You have no idea the effect that had on me Brig, I nearly had a damned heart attack,' laughed Sandy.

'Why?'

Luke carried on with the story. 'We all brushed the incident under the table but it niggled away at Grace, she just wouldn't let it go. She believed that you were the reincarnation of Elizabeth Tregowarth, that's how you knew those books were there.'

'Really? For real?' Does that sort of thing really happen? I mean, do we come back after we die? Oooh, now I've gone all goosey,' she rubbed her arms.

'Who knows darling, I know Grace certainly believed we do,' said Sandy.

Everyone went quiet for a moment, lost in their own thoughts.

'So if that was the case, then what about Adam, do you think he might be Gordon, come back?'

'Look, let's not even go there shall we. We could tie ourselves up in knots without really understanding what we are talking about,' offered Luke, wanting to put an end to the whole subject, but before he did he said, 'by the way, do you remember this?' Luke opened up a small wooden box on the mantel piece and took out the rusty bridle bit Selwyn had given him. Brigit took it from Luke and her eyes welled up with tears.

'For some reason I figured this was off Gordon's' horses bridle. I found other bits of metal and leather there too but I left it there. It had been dug up under where the ewe had been struggling, I couldn't bring myself to dig any further so I left it. Perhaps we could go back and do some more digging some time.'

'Or perhaps not,' laughed Selwyn nervously.

'Gordon's Uncle!' Brigit suddenly exclaimed. 'It was Gordon's Uncle, oh my God, it really was.' She jumped up excitedly and went and grabbed an old box of photos Elizabeth's family had left with Ellen before she died. Coming back outside she plopped down on her sun lounger scrabbling through the box.

'There, it was him, I'm sure it was him,' she pulled out a small well-worn photo of a man wearing old breeches with braces over a loose fitting shirt and a floppy leather hat.

'Brigit!' Her fathers voice snapped her back to reality. 'What in the darn fool blazes are you talking about? What was Gordon's Uncle?'

'You know when I got stranded out in the desert when Jax and I went out to the gorge that day and the rustlers came and I got shot at and all that,' she paused for a breath. Luke nodded. 'Well, that second night when I thought I might not make it, a lovely old man came and sat on a rock beside me and told me that I would be okay and that Jax would find me in the morning. He said he would stay and look after me during the night. I thought he looked familiar but I couldn't place him. It was Gordon's Uncle, the one who left Duffield Station to Gordon in his Will, how weird was that?' She stopped talking and stared at the photo, excited by her sudden realisation.

'Aaagh, this is all a bit much for me,' Rees

got out of the pool. 'Might go back to the house and get something to eat.

'Wait for me Rees, this is all a bit too creepy for me too,' said Stella grabbing her sun top and slipping it on over her swimsuit.

'The twins were never really into all this stuff,' laughed Sandy, 'bit like their father eh Sel.'

'Oh I don't know,' said Selwyn thoughtfully, there has to be more to life than just ending up in a grave as worm fodder otherwise why would we bother? There are so many theories out there, which one do you choose to believe?'

'Which ever one speaks to your heart I suppose,' said Sandy thoughtfully.

'Let's leave it at that shall we,' Luke reached for another beer. 'Anyone else for another drink?'

Ruth had been sitting quietly beside Luke during this discussion and went and sat beside Brigit. 'This is really fascinating,' she commented. 'It's not something I ever came across until Luke started to tell me little bits and pieces. Must admit, it does give me goose bumps and something to think about.'

Brigit laughed and got up to leave. As she passed through the kitchen she paused for a moment deep in thought then called out, 'hey wasn't there a carving of a heart with Elizabeth and Gordon's name on it at the back of this dresser?'

Luke glanced at Sandy. 'We never told her about that did we?' he whispered.

Sandy shook her head. 'Don't think so.'

'Yeah probably honey, we'll have a look sometime.' Luke called back over his shoulder.

'Okay, laters guys,' she sauntered out the door leaving Sandy and Luke gaping at each other in stunned silence.

Chapter Twenty Three

Adam

The young man stood on the doorstep of Duffield Station homestead twisting his well-worn cap nervously in his trembling hands.

'Adam? Don't just stand there on the steps man, come on in, sit down. What can I do for you?'

'Hi Mr Williams, I..'

'Call me Luke, please.'

'Okay, Luke. Um, you know I've been coming here for three years now and I've gotten to know Brigit quite well,' he blushed.

'Carry on,' Luke tried to hide his smile. He knew darn well Adam and Brigit had been sleeping together for the last two weeks, although Brigit never let on.

'Well, Mr.. I mean Luke, I would like to ask your permission to ask Brigit to marry me, if that's alright with you I mean. I promise I'll take good care of her and...'

'Yes.'

'What?'

'I said yes Adam, you have my permission.

I would be delighted to have you as my son-in-law. That's if Brigit will have you?'

'Do you think she might say no?' His face had such a hang dog look it made Luke laugh.

'Adam, I have no idea what my daughter might say but if she gives you a hard time you come and talk to me and I will put in a good word for you, okay. You obviously haven't spoken to her about this yet.'

'No. Do you think I should wait?'

'I will let you trust your own instincts on that one Adam. Good Luck.' Adam sprinted out of the house like his pants were on fire.

'You're a braver man than me Adam Tregowarth,' he smiled to himself as he watched Adam sprint up towards Brigit's cottage.

A fortnight later the shearing was over for another year and no engagement announcement was forthcoming. Luke was a little disappointed. 'Perhaps the poor man lost his courage, he thought. Can't blame him, Brigit can be quite a handful when she wants to be. The last van pulled away from the shed and out onto the driveway with Adam waving solemnly from the back window. Brigit seemed genuinely upset when he left and in the weeks that followed she was just not her bright and bubbly self.

'You missing Adam?' Luke ventured one afternoon as spring began turning everything a luscious shade of deep green.

'I am a bit. We talk on the phone a lot, but yes I am missing him.'

'Why don't you ask him to come and stay? They must be just about finished shearing by now.'

'Actually I was thinking the same thing. He said they had one more farm to do and would be finished in about two weeks. Would it be okay if he came then?'

'Of course it would sweetheart, you are welcome to have your friends come visit any time you want. The more the merrier really, now that Sandy and Selwyn and the twins aren't here.

'Yes, I really miss them. It's not the same around here is it?'

'No it isn't.'

The day following his last day of shearing Adam appeared at the door of Brigit's cottage. The moment she saw him she flew into his arms wrapping her legs around his waist and covering him in kisses. He stood her gently down on the door sill and went down on one knee.

'Brigit Williams, Jamieson, will you do me the awesome honour of becoming my wife, *please!*'

He produced a small ring box from his pocket and opening it presented her with the most beautiful antique diamond ring Brigit had ever seen.

'Oh my God Adam, it's simply gorgeous, and yes, yes yes I will marry you. Oh my God, I'm,

I , I don't know what to say.'

'Then shut up and kiss me.'

He picked her up and carried her across the threshold of the cottage, kissed her again and stood her back down so he could place the ring on her finger.

'Look at that, a perfect fit, but how did you know my ring size?'

'I didn't. But there is a story to this ring.'

'It looks like an antique, is it?'

'Yes, it belonged to Elizabeth Tregowarth and now all these years later it is going to be on the finger of another Tregowarth, here, on the same farm.'

Brigit felt a chill run down her spine.

'Elizabeth's ring? Really? How did you come by it?'

'Well it was the strangest thing. I was telling Mum and Dad that I wanted to propose to you and Mum got all excited because there is only my brother and me and she'd always wanted a daughter. She went into the bedroom and came back with an old jewellery box and pulled out this ring. After Elizabeth died, her parents decided that the ring should come back to the Tregowarth family and as my great, great grandfather was Gordon's nearest living relative he ended up with the ring which he kept and handed down the line. So now here it rests with you my darling.'

Brigit felt so lightheaded she had to sit

down.

'Are you okay, you look really pale?'

'I'm fine,' she smiled up at him, I'm just overcome by all of this, it is so out of the blue, you turning up unexpectedly, the proposal, the ring...'

Adam got her a drink of water and sat down beside her, his arm draped comfortingly across her shoulders.

'Wow, wait till I tell Dad and Ruth,' she giggled.

Later that night after a sumptuous roast meal Luke, Ruth, Brigit and Adam sat out by the pool drinking champagne. They had been on the phone most of the afternoon telling everyone the good news.

'Adam, welcome to the family young man. I can't tell you how thrilled I am to have you here. Now, I have a proposition to put to you. How would you like to come and work for me. Once you and Brigit are married you can live in Sandy and Selwyn's old house and be my right-hand man. What do you say?'

Adam was taken aback. 'Oh, wow, I wasn't expecting that. I was freaking out about what you were going to think about me taking Brigit away from the farm but this is fantastic. Yes, please, I accept, thank you.'

'Actually Dad, I think we'd rather live in the cob cottage for now if that's okay, what do you think Adam?'

'Couldn't think of a more perfect place to start our new life together,' he smiled lovingly at Brigit.

Luke looked across at Ruth with a huge smile on his face. 'Looks like we are finally a family again Mrs Williams. Another generation begins on Duffield Station.'

'Oh, I almost forgot' said Adam leaping to his feet. 'I've got something for you, from the family.

He raced out to his car and came back in with a brown paper package.

'It's not Elizabeth's...' began Luke, his mouth hanging open.

'Yep, her diaries. We had a family gathering a few weeks ago and the diaries came up in conversation.' Blushing, he looked across at Brigit. 'We were talking about you my love, and the cob cottage. Anyway, the family felt it would be nice if we put the diaries back where they were found and as you and I will be living in the cottage I thought that would be the perfect thing to do, bring them home.'

Brigit's eyes welled up with tears as she gently unwrapped the package and picked up the first well read, dog eared, faded red journal on top of the pile. She opened it to the first page and started to read, a sob escaping her lips..... '*Dear Diary, Six months ago I was a young single girl living in a lovely big house with my wonderful parents and beautiful sister, Charlotte.*' Her hands trembled as she quietly closed the book and placed it gently back on top of the pile. 'My books, she whispered, stroking the cover, 'my beautiful books are home again, at last.'

The End

www.ingramcontent.com/pod-product-compliance
Lightning Source LLC
Chambersburg PA
CBHW032047050726
47590CB00001B/169